I0764422

Angel

By the same Author

BOOKS:

THE JOURNEYS WE MAKE
(DCG Publications.)
DEAD ON TARGET: A Further Thornton King Adventure
(DCG Publications.)
JUST IN CASE:- Another Thornton King Adventure
(DCG Publications.)
NO OFFICIAL UMBRELLA: An Autobiography
(DCG Publications.)
DOCTOR WHO & THE SPACE MUSEUM
(W.H.Allen /Virgin Publishing.)
THE DOUBLE DECKERS
(Pan Books.)
HILDEGARDE H AND HER FRIENDS -*Illustrated by Arnold Taraborrelli*
(Abydos Publishing.)
DEAD ON TIME: -The First Thornton King Adventure
(Raider Publishing International.)

PLAYS PUBLISHED:

BEAUTIFUL FOR EVER
(Samuel French, London.)
CHAMPAGNE CHARLIE : A Music Hall Entertainment
(DCG Publications.)
GENERATIONS
(DCG Publications.)
OH BROTHER!
(DCG Publications.)
PETER PAN: A Musical Fantasy
(DCG Publications.)
RED IN THE MORNING
(Samuel French, New York.)
ROSEMARY
(DCG Publications.)
THE 88
DCG Publications.)
THRILLER OF THE YEAR
(Samuel French, London.)
WOMEN AROUND
(DCG Publications.)

Angel

Glyn Idris Jones

DCG
Publications

First Published in Greece 2010

DCG Publications
www.dcgmediagroup.com

ISBN 978-960-98418-6-3

10 9 8 7 6 5 4 3 2 1

Typeset by
DCG Publications

Printed in England by
Lightning Source.

www.glynjones.net

For
Ceri & Dennis

and for Family

Chapter 1

His name is Carlos. He is fourteen years old, going on fifteen; delicately boned and swift, with a small brown face and dark eyes. Even in the heat of the day he wears an old mustard coloured sweater, holed at the elbows, frayed at the cuffs, and unravelling at the waist. The temperature is somewhere up in the nineties and the humidity trying to keep it company but he doesn't seem to notice. Two buttons are missing from the flies of his grubby khaki shorts. The bottom one, undone, hangs by a thread, and the top one broken in half and useless, is hidden anyway by an old raggedy tartan tie knotted about his waist. The soles of his slender bare feet are tough, cracked and pitted with dirt, and the minute translucent tips of broken off thorns. His long black hair curls into the grey speckled nape of his neck. He carries a sturdy catapult made from the forked branch of a silver tree, the tree from which the old Zulu impis, Dingaan's and Tschaka's fearsome regiments, carved their assegais. To the notched end of each fork a piece of stout string is knotted and tied to a rubber band cut from the inner tube of a motor car tyre, then joined by two more pieces of string to the soft folding leather pad that holds his flying pebbles.

The best stones come from the cemetery where ammunition is limitless. The white marble chips and grey granite are the right size and weight, many edged and flint sharp and with his catty the boy is deadly accurate at a fair range and against any target that takes his fancy: that is as long as it isn't likely to hit back or unless there is every chance if necessary of beating a hasty retreat.

He squats astride a marble cross bearing the legend *Asleep In The Arms Of The Lord* and gazes at the dark green branches of a monkey apple tree spread out above him, his toes rubbing dirty smudges down the sides of the polished marble as they grip the column and he waits.

Except for the occasional cooing of a dove the cemetery lies silent beneath its quilt of summer. Perhaps because like the interior of a cathedral it is consecrated ground, holy ground, it seems always to be quiet, even with the intruding sounds of life, the noises of the tangible touchable world outside: the flashes of colour, the flicker of movement passing by outside the stark iron railings, the occasional hoot of a car's horn. It's as though a person were already part of another world just being there, and was only half-conscious of these things filtered, it would seem, as though through a veil, or like a cry echoing from a great distance.

Carlos sighs softly and jellies his buttocks into a more comfortable position against the hard antagonism of the marble. He flicks a fly impatiently from his leg and almost loses his balance, clings desperately to the stone and settles down again, one foot hooked behind the other knee. The fly buzzes back. He watches it for a while but the heat of the day, trapped beneath his sweater, is a soporific that numbs the senses and makes the skin less sensitive to the insect's tickling and he decides to ignore it. He is fast becoming bored with his own company.

Steve and Johnny must be around somewhere. They took themselves off to the other side of the cemetery... God knows what for... and have been gone sometime now, probably messing about down by the crematorium. He raises himself on his hands to look for them but all he can see are the endless rows of graves stretching down the hill to disappear into the gloom beneath a double row of dark conifers. Are they burning anybody today? No, the sky in all directions is clear and blue. No one going up in smoke. In the square, down by the harbour, the campanile stands tall and red, a giant phallus rearing its slender length into the sky. And beyond it, the breakwater, the Indian Ocean, blue and silver in the sun flies shimmering to meet the sky in a haze of heat where the ships on the horizon can be seen and then not seen, like tiny mirages imagined in the distance, part of the sea they ride, part of the sky and the haze into which they disappear.

Carlos felt a sneeze coming on and squinted up into the sun. He sneezed three times, waited for the fourth that did not come, looked again into the sun and deciding the last sneeze wasn't really there, peered around for something else to occupy his interest. He leaned forward so as to see the name written on the stone beneath him and tried to picture what the man who lay there might have looked like. JOHN EDWIN MILLER. The name meant nothing. It was not a name to conjure with, not the kind of name to evoke images of darkness or fairness, tallness or shortness, fatness or thinness. Other than having been an obvious rooinek, a redneck, the derogatory term used by the Boers to describe sunburnt British soldiers, JOHN EDWIN MILLER could have been anything. Maybe if he lifted a pebble off the grave and put it under his pillow at night the ghost of the dead man would visit him to retrieve it and he could then see this John Edwin Miller for himself. Carlos sniggered and spat across the name watching the saliva trickle down the stone before it dried in the heat. He stopped believing those stories years ago, or at least he said he had. So what did John Edwin Miller look like now? PASSED AWAY 18TH NOVEMBER 1949. Hmn, dead a year, more or less. Maybe for some fun they could dig him up one night and take a look. Carlos frowned, shivered, and shook himself a little to stop himself thinking such thoughts. Apart from the sudden scare he had given himself, his arse really was getting numb, and all the manoeuvring in the world wasn't going to make the marble any more comfortable.

He was about to clamber down when a dove flew down and settled on a tombstone close by, eyed him warily for a moment and then, presumably deciding he wasn't worth much attention, billed softly to itself and looked the other way. Slowly, carefully, Carlos took a stone from his shirt pocket and fitted it into his catty, screwed up one eye taking aim, stretched the powerful rubber to its limit and let fly. The leather pad zipped like an angry hornet passed his ear. 'Pow!' said Carlos, 'Bazoom!' and leapt from the headstone. He padded over to the foot of the stone where the bird had fallen. It was not dead, not quite. He picked it up and felt its heart beating so he wrung its neck. Its eyes hooded over and a spot of dark blood oozed from the tongue between its open beak and then from a nostril. He weighed the bird's soft warmth in the palm of his hand, its head lolling over the cup of his thumb and forefinger, and he smiled, looking at it with curiosity as though it were the first thing he had ever killed. He pulled away a few blood damp feathers from the wound, rubbed them off his fingers by means of his trouser leg, and glanced around to see if anyone was in sight. Then he trotted away between the graves to find Steve & Johnny.

The procession wearies its slow way up the hill: a suitably sedate and subdued crocodile of men, women, and a handful of children, some weeping, others grim, most showing some signs of emotion. Maybe it is genuine sorrow of loss or maybe it is the heat that ricochets from their burning skins, that causes their feet, treading the hard hot tarmac of the footpath, hot enough to blister the skin should it be touched and in places melted and running black like lava, feet to swell and ache in seldom worn only for best wear shoes, much too tight, much too new. The heat that their black clothing absorbs and will not release traps it against their bodies so that the sweat streams in uncomfortable rivulets down their backs and the inside of their thighs. The whiteness of the coffin dazzles, and the brass escutcheons of its glittering handles laugh in the sun, mocking the bearers shouldering its dead weight and sharp edges.

They gather around the open grave. A little girl, pretty in her appliquéed white dress and brown legs, slips on the bank of dry crumbling earth and nearly slides in in her eagerness to see the bottom, but is caught in time and cuffed for her carelessness, also for sitting on a wreath and staining her dress. She is about to howl out loud when she remembers the seriousness of the occasion and turns her anguish into a hiccupping sob, much to the gratification of her mother, who immediately returns to her own mourning, like an actress who has stepped out of character for a moment and suddenly remembers she is on stage and supposed to be playing a part. The young priest stands, book in hand, solemn of expression, and the grouped mourners wait.

Of all those who wept on that fine summer's afternoon none could have wept more, or less unashamedly, than Sarah Lerici. She gazed about her at her fellow mourners, some of whom she knew, some of whom she would get to know; at the banks of flowers with their little notes of sentiment edged in black, at the handsome young priest with so serious a face, at the little girl with the sand dirtied pants, at the coffin suspended over the grave, about to be lowered, covered and gone forever. She looked at the earthy mouth soon to swallow it and her body shook so much that a perfect stranger, a small man with a yellow stained moustache, mistook her for a relative or at least a dear friend and was prompted to take her hand and pat it kindly. She cast him a quick look of gratitude and wept into a diminutive lace hanky, already soaking wet. He was not to know but there was no doubt about it, next to a wedding and the final act of *La Boheme*, nothing gave one a better opportunity for a really good cry than a nice funeral and Sarah, in best black from head to toe, thoroughly enjoyed her outings no matter whose funeral it was. After it was all over she would say a few well chosen words of welcome to the new priest just out from home... she peeked furtively from beneath the brim of her shiny, bought for the occasion, brand new hat of lacquered straw with the waxed cherries that were in danger of melting... then he would not feel so much a stranger when he came to visit; such a nice young man, so handsome, and such a beautiful voice. He would have made someone a wonderful husband she felt sure if he hadn't given himself up to God. And the day was so lovely and the mourners so sad that she could not for the life of her prevent the tears that welled up to run down her cheeks, much to the consternation of the little man with the tobacco stained moustache, who was so overcome that he put his arm about her ample shoulders and wept a little himself. The young acolyte, plump as a capon in cassock and surplus, worried about the spots on his neck and swung his thurible with gusto. The mourners mourned and Sarah Lerici wept with abandon.

They were at the far end of the cemetery, behind a clump of azaleas standing side by side in competition to see who could piss the highest and the furthest. The sound of Carlos approaching hurriedly cut short their little game and, in the ensuing panic, Johnny wet his trousers.

'Hey, you guys! Look what I... Ow!'

Half in relief that it was only Carlos and half in annoyance at having been frightened into panicky withdrawal, they turned their attentions to the intruder with a couple of well aimed stones, making him run for it until, at a safe distance, he turned and eyed them up and down, his lip curling in disdain.

'You dirty buggers!' He sneered. 'You're playing with yourselves, I know.'

Steve laughed and made an obscene gesture. 'I won.'

They buttoned their trousers and moved closer to Carlos who remained on his guard in case they were still annoyed but the sight of the dead dove had aroused their curiosity and they stood around staring at it, prodding it, weighing it in their hands. Finally Carlos took it back, thrust a finger into the carcass, hooked it and hauled out the guts, flicked the entrails to the ground and wiped the bloody remains from his fingers up his trouser leg. Johnny, fascinated as always by blood and guts, rolled them in the dust with his toe, then he picked them up and threw them at Steve who ducked and yelled angrily. Johnny laughed and fled to a safe distance as Steve picked up a stone and hurled it at him. It missed him and ricocheted off a headstone. Johnny hopped away and ducked behind another as Steve looked around for more ammunition. Still annoyed, he swore threateningly.

Set in the wall behind the crematorium is a tap, used officially for attaching a hosepipe and watering the Garden of Remembrance. It costs the bereaved a fair sum to have the ashes of their dear departed placed in an urn set in the wall of The Garden of Remembrance. It costs a lot less to have the ashes scattered across the lawn; otherwise they can take them away and do whatever they wish with them.

The lawn is a rich deep green velvet: so green that at first glance it could almost be black; a fitting colour considering its purpose and expensive fertiliser of bone ash. A beautiful lawn, sacred to the memory of the dead and the tears of those who are left to mourn, and the pockets of whichever municipal body and church are concerned with keeping alive the cult of the dead. For it takes a lot of money to die, and to weep, and not everyone can afford it. At the base of the tap is a concrete bed, often overflowing due to its drain being blocked, clogged up with grass cuttings and possibly windblown bone ash, so that the surrounding earth is wet and soggy. Carlos scoops up handfuls of this mud with which he encases the dead bird, pats it down hard, then rinses his hands beneath the tap and wipes them dry on the lawn of the Garden of Remembrance.

Steve, who has momentarily forgotten his grievance against Johnny, builds a fire against one of the headstones, already blackened by previous use and which can act as an excellent windbreak, while Johnny scouts around for more fuel; pine cones and dry wood fallen beneath the conifers. The dead bird, mummified in its clay, is placed in the fire, coals scooped around it, and they settle down to wait. They watch the smoke as it curls away, occasionally tossing another twig onto the fire as the mud hardens, cakes, cracks and turns black. Steve produces the mangled remains of a cigarette from his shirt pocket and lights it with a twig from the fire. He takes a long draw, inhales and opens his mouth wide, looks ruminatively at the butt and then passes it to Carlos. Carlos takes a long draw, looks at it, and passes it to Johnny. Johnny takes a long draw, looks at it, is about to take a second, sees Steve's face and passes it back. And so they sit and watch and wait. Finally Steve tosses the cigarette end away, smoked to almost nothing, before it can burn his fingers. He gazes at the fire for a moment as though lost in thought and then, without warning, suddenly flings himself sideways at an unsuspecting Johnny who, taken by surprise, turns over on his hands and knees but is not quick enough to escape. Steve grabs his ankle to send him sprawling. Johnny turns over, yells and kicks out, backing away on his hands; rolling over onto his stomach again, digs his fingers into the ground to pull himself away, trying desperately to free himself, to get up and run, and yelling all the time.

'No Steve!... Please, Steve!... Steve, listen!... I didn't mean it! Honest!... Oh! Steve!... Honest, man!... It was a joke... A joke, Steve... Steve?'

Then suddenly scared at what Steve might do to him, 'Let me go you fucking big bully!... Go, on fuck off!' He hits out wildly, but Steve lets go only to get a better grip higher up, finally grasping the boy by the wrist and twisting his arm into a back hammer. Then, having him sufficiently under control, he yanks him to his feet. Both are breathing heavily, Johnny wincing.

'Now then...' Steve's knee jerked up and Johnny yelled. He tried crossing his legs in case Steve should have a go at the front as well. It would be just like him.

'Steve, I won't do it again, I promise... promise, Steve, I promise man! I'll do whatever you say, honest... whatever you want me to do, Steve. What's a matter, man? Can't you take a joke? It was only a joke. Hey, Steve! Let me go, man! Come on, don't be like that.' He was half giggling, half crying. 'Steve, you bastard, you're hurting me!'

He cringed, whimpered, giggled, laughed, pleaded. He smarmed, he appealed, but Steve forced him over to where the entrails lay in the dust. Johnny saw where they were heading and tried to break loose but Steve's grip tightened even further and he had to submit.

'Jesus!' He yelled, 'You're hurting me you stupid bugger! You're breaking my arm!'

Never releasing his hold, Steve leaned down sideways to pick up the guts, stuffed them down the squirming boy's shirt and squashed them with a bear hug, and then he turned and pushed Johnny away and kicked him up the bum for good measure.

'That's for earlier on,' he said, as though they didn't already know it, then he returned to sit beside Carlos who hadn't moved except to throw back his head and laugh at the fun. Johnny crouched where he had been left, now almost in tears of rage at the humiliation of that parting kick.

'I'll get you, you skate, you dirty stinking shithouse, you wait.' He was angry and shaken and helpless before the other's strength. He sniffed and wiped his nose with the back of his hand, and he kept his distance.

Steve Laughed. 'Cry-baby. Big cry-baby, why don't you run home to mommy, cry-baby?'

'I'll get you,' Johnny threatened between sobs. He took off his shirt and wiped the mess away as best as he could before slipping the shirt on again.

Steve jeered. 'Tit for Tat,' he said.

'It didn't hit you. It didn't go anywhere near you! Did it hit you?'

'You threw it.'

'It didn't hit you!' As though this was a logical riposte.

'I don't care. You threw it and if you don't shut up you'll get some more.'

'Yeah?'

'Yeah.'

'Try.'

A quick move from Steve and Johnny bolted but not out of swearing range; then as Steve squatted again he crept nearer, still cursing softly, mumbling to himself and casting angry glances in the other's direction. Steve, ignored his presence, gave the underside of his thighs a quick rub with the flat of his hands, scratched between his toes and frowned pointedly at the bird.

Carlos leant forward and hooked it from the fire shaking the burn from his fingers and blowing on them. Johnny and Steve watched closely as with a stick he prodded at the hardened earth. It broke away, pulling off whatever burnt feathers were left, leaving the flesh steaming clean. He tears off a leg and passes it to Steve, licks the juice off his fingers and wipes them up his trouser leg.

Steve pecks at the dainty bone.

'Not much meat on it, is there?'

'What do you expect? A bloody turkey? It's a dove for Chrissakes!'

The flesh is not over tasty, cooked as it is with no seasoning, but they are not eating it because they are hungry. They eat because they have killed it; it is game and game is meant to be eaten, and they are the hunters. Eating it in forbidden territory is all the seasoning it needs.

Chapter 2

The houses, cheek by jowl, are built on a steep hill overlooking the city from the south end. The Lerici properties are small semi-detached on the corner of two streets; their front verandas and doors opening on to a broad level tree-lined avenue while the road that runs steeply downhill at the side of the first house is narrow and stony, and the sunlight dazzles on whitewashed wall of house and yard. It is not the most salubrious of districts. A great many people would reject any thought of living there, where many nationalities and creeds are forced to exist amicably side by side, prejudice to prejudice.

The new government would enforce total segregation and bring in a new universal word - Apartheid.

When Grandpa Lerici settled in this new land he built his house where no house had been built before. He had little more than a bundle of meagre possessions, a razor and a strop, a couple of clean shirts, his best shoes, his rosary, and his parent's heritage; memories of a poverty stricken village, sun baked earth and burning rock above the deep blue of the Mediterranean, and a wife whom he later went home to collect, together with two of the three boys he was eventually to father.

His settling in this new land was not premeditated. Sailing down past Madagascar, with the sea disturbed only by the bows of the rusted old Greek tramp, the seagulls crying in her wake, swooping on the gash tossed over the side, her Portuguese skipper sleeping it off in his never made sweaty bunk; Lerici's thoughts were only of home, of Italy, of prickly pear and mimosa and the heady red wine of the south.

He was not sure just when the gulls disappeared, but suddenly they were no longer there. He lifted his head and sniffed, nostrils flaring suspiciously, his eyes narrowed to slits. The sea was no longer blue, no longer did it sparkle. It lay like mercury; grey, heavy beneath an ominous leaden sky. He knocked the cold ash from his pipe and tapped the pipe against the palm of his hand before slipping it into his pocket. A hot breeze ruffled his hair and caressed the side of his face and neck. He lifted a hand and gently rubbed the stubble on his cheek. The Portuguese skipper appeared on deck, his eyes red rimmed but no longer bleary from sleep and cheap brandy. He was wide-awake. He looked at Grandpa Lerici, his face expressionless, and Lerici looked back. They said nothing; there was no need. They looked away again, Lerici up at the sky, the skipper to move up for'ard. And it seemed only the next minute they were fighting for their lives. For two days and two nights the elements hit them from all sides, the rain and the wind and the sea most furious of all, green mountains of water that crashed down upon them, sweeping three men overboard, tearing at the hatches, threatening to crush them with their weight.

The tub groaned hideously under her torture. How much could she take before she splintered under the hammering? Before she would be happy to give in and die and sink beneath those waves where silence was dark and peaceful and where she could rust and rot until there was no more of her. She was after all, only a puny man made thing; she could take only so much and no more. Grandpa Lerici was certain she had reached her limit after the second night. The storm seemed to be growing worse. By morning there would be no trace but for a few pieces of timber. He clutched a line and hung on grimly as the deck lurched beneath him. 'Holy Mary, Mother of God!' His feet were swept away. He felt his back hit the bulwark and then as she dipped and rolled he slid back and doubled over the hatch, the water drumming down over his back. 'Jesus, sweet Jesus!' He swivelled in a double pirouette, the line twisted about his wrist. He was on his knees clutching the side of the hatch with his free hand. 'Oh, God! Almighty God!' A man's shout was drowned in the howling... The sea tore at him, sucking like the giant hungry mouth of some monster anemone... 'Oh, God! Oh, God!'... the line tightened about his wrist as the water swirled about him... now it was over him... now he was on his belly... there was a roaring in his ears... he tasted blood in his mouth. The ship heaved her bows out of the sea like a whore lifting her bosom and plunged again as though bent on death; rolled like a porpoise without the porpoise's agility. 'Where my foot touches earth... there will I stay. God! Do you hear me? I swear it! Never again will I go to sea! Where my foot touches: there will I stay!'

The Portuguese skipper back in port pleaded in vain. He had virtually to sign on a new crew and when grandpa returned to Italy to fetch his family, he excused it on the grounds that he was only travelling as a passenger and not a seaman. The sea would not claim him.

Now, in the front room of the corner house, a room not often used whose shutters were seldom opened, clean and redolent with the smell of furniture polish, grandma and grandpa, imprisoned in their oval frames, hung with black bows on the anniversaries of their deaths, are ever present; grandma stern and starch stiff as she stares down, reminding her children of the dead hand of discipline; grandpa, in his wing collar and mustachios, kindly of eye and gentle in expression. They gaze down on the mirror polished lino, the hard cold rexine-covered chairs, the brass Bombay ornaments; ashtrays and cobras, and egrets made from horn, giraffes and elephants carved in wood.

The streets have changed very little since their deaths.

Down the hill children play their barefoot games of skip and hop scotch and tag, cowboys and Indians, cops and robbers, where dogs, all skin and bone, range snapping along the gutters: cats perch slit eyed on rooftop and wall, sleep in the sun, wash themselves or explore delicately the little piles of rubbish, rusted cans breeding mosquitoes in the rainy season, the old newspaper wrappings that litter the street, or hunt the cockroaches that crawl up from the gutters and drains. A large tom, moulting, scarred and ear tattered from many a battle, turns over an empty salmon tin with one fastidious paw, sniffs suspiciously, his whiskers twitching, licks the contaminated paw and walks stiffly away, his old dry nose wrinkling.

Squatting at the edge of the pavement, bare legged Africans strum monotonous one string guitars, homemade from lengths of lath and old tin-cans, laugh and chatter in groups and pass comments on passers-by. A young Pondo is styling his friend's hair with a bright shocking pink comb and a tin of Moore's brilliantine. The friend, holding a triangular sliver of mirror, dips his finger into the tin and rubs a little brilliantine on his face to make it shine. He laughs, showing paper white teeth in coral gums. The tip of his tongue amuses him and his friend giggles coyly behind cupped hands.

On the main street, in the dark little shop across the way from the front door, Madame Chang busies her silk bound body with bottles and boxes of sugary sweets, biscuits, purgatives, tinted mineral waters: lime, lemon, orange, ginger beer and cream soda that tastes of the scent of hair oil: aspirins, cough syrup, tins and boxes, packets of pins, reels of cotton and strings of grease-blotched red-skinned sausages that hang suspended over a length of slat next to the fly papers. Beneath the counter, between two day old bread and a litter of aspen limbed still blind kittens, she keeps in an old shoe box crumbling fruit cake to offer those favourite customers who nip in for a slice and a gossip and invariably remember something they meant to get sooner or later, ('I'll nip back and fetch you the money in a minute.')

On the veranda outside the shop, Mr Chang sits impassively surveying the middle distance and gently fanning his face with a small hand carved ivory fan. His bright black button eyes miss nothing. The greengrocer down the road is doing a roaring business: pineapples as big as a child's head, bananas and guavas, avocado pears, mountains of sweet potatoes piled across the pavement and giant watermelons stand cool and green, one or two prize specimens sliced in half to reveal the crystalline red flesh and rows of pips glinting in the sun.

A housewife, watched by a mournful looking donkey that has strayed from God knows where and is straying to where perhaps only God could care, leans across her wooden veranda rails and brushes aside her snot snivelling toe tapping infant as she haggles with an Indian over the price of oranges. His produce is not as expensive as the greengrocer's. Squatting on the pavement, he lovingly handles the fruit in his basket and, betel nut chewing, spits a scarlet stream at a group of red ants foraging in the eye sockets of a dead sparrow. He blows his nose between his thumb and forefinger and carelessly strops them across the front of his shirt, scratches his crotch, and extends three pink-palmed oranges.

'I'm robbing myself, Missus!'

'Not a penny more, you see? And that's too much. Look at the size of those things. You call those oranges? They're more like naartjies, and not even a decent size mandarin at that.'

He pouts and shakes his head sadly, lifts a skinny despairing shoulder and raises his eyes heavenwards, scratching his beard with his free hand. Then after a little silent communion in the direction of the donkey, he nods and hands over the fruit, inwardly cursing. She quizzes it critically, not sure now if she has paid too much, or whether she could have beaten him down further. The child whimpers and puts out a grubby paw. The donkey flicks flies from its ears and nickers showing long yellow deeply grooved teeth.

'You want some nice pumpkin, Missus? I got berry nice pumpkin. Por you I give half price, berry cheap got it.'

A car roars hooting by, scattering dust and animals with impatient gusto. In the distance the trams can be heard clanging up the hill and rattling rocking bucking down again. It is late afternoon and wives in a thousand dim kitchens gather together the threads of the day in preparation for their husband's return from work and the children in from play. In another hour the sun will turn to red and in a few brief minutes of twilight, the day will die.

In the twilight Angelo strolled home, slowly up the steep hill. He was thinking of nothing in particular. Every now and again as though conscious of himself he looked down at his feet moving beneath him. He hardly noticed the scene around him, so familiar and accepted as to be almost unworthy of acknowledgement, certainly not worth thinking about or really looking at. He was almost at his back gate when a high pitched scream from the yard stopped him in his tracks. It was Guido, yelling about something; then suddenly, above the din, his mother's voice.

'Madonna Mia! Guido! Seraphina! What are you doing?'

Angelo pushed open the gate. Mama Lerici, leaning over the veranda railing, was looking down the long narrow yard to where at the end, beneath a grapevine on a high crisscross trellis, Guido and Seraphina had been making mud pies under the mortise machine. Now Guido was sitting there bawling his head off while Seraphina, arms akimbo, hands on hips, stood looking down impassively. Mama heard the gate open and turned her head.

'Angelo!' She yelled, 'Come quickly! Ees a snaig! Ees a snaig 'as bitten your brudder!'

Angelo skipped down the yard and knelt beside his brother who had abruptly ceased his bawling and now sat nursing one hand, his little body trembling spasmodically with an occasional jerky sob. He sniffed and allowed Angelo to examine his injured hand. There was a small blood blister on one finger. Noticing it, Guido forgot his pain and peered at it with interest.

'Ees a snaig, Angelo?'

Twenty odd years before as a young man, Ulrico

Lerici returned to the home of his ancestors and there found himself a shy young bride, bringing her back in pride and possessiveness to the family circle. But Marina, in all the years between, had learnt enough English but had never rid herself of her heavy Italian accent. At first, as the young bride in this strange new land, she had expected to find cannibals, lions, elephants, and all species of wildlife in her back yard; but now, only her horror of snakes, like her accent, remained with her. She knew they were about somewhere, like the devil in the Garden of Eden, only waiting their most opportune moment to strike and, wherever she went, she kept one wary eye open for anything which slithered or looked as though it might turn out to be the constantly expected encounter. As a consequence, her secondary range of vision was always playing tricks and there were constant false alarms. Once she trod on a coil of rope in the dark and stood petrified until suddenly dissolving into hysterics. Her screams brought everyone running and she was carried limp and helpless into the house. And a few poor innocent house lizards sunning themselves had to beat a hasty retreat, possibly minus tail, or come to a sudden and violent end beneath a hurricane of blows delivered by a terrified Mama grabbing at the nearest available weapon – spade, rake, axe, stone. It was no good telling her that, if the creature possessed legs, it couldn't possibly be a snake. It was a reptile and she was taking no chances.

The family tried in vain to convince her that snakes were simply not to be found anywhere near the house, talk her out of her phobia with constant assurances and, when this didn't work, had endeavoured to tease her out of her fear with such things as toy snakes of rubber or articulated wood: but like a small child who fears the dentist, all the talking in the world only increased her dread. As yet she had never really seen an actual live, venomous snake; except in the snake park where the family once took her after much persuasion, hoping that close proximity to them, and the sight of a man actually handling them, might lessen her phobia. Unfortunately it had the exact opposite effect and only intensified her terror so that for weeks afterwards she went nowhere without a broom handle, just in case. She was firmly convinced that not only were they all deadly and instantaneously poisonous but their bodies were slimy like a snail's, and the very idea of one sliding over her foot was enough to bring her out in palpitations and a cold sweat.

'Ees a snaig? Hey, Angelo?' She called again.

'No, mama, it's not a snake.' Angelo gently kissed his brother's grubby brown fingers and smiled. There was a note of patient resignation in his voice. He held up Guido's arm and waggled the snivelling child's injured hand. 'He caught his finger in the mortise.'

Emboldened by the apparent absence of reptiles, Mama wiped her hands on her apron, descended the dozen wooden steps that led from the veranda down to the yard, and marched purposefully toward the little group beneath the grapevine, her broad nostrils quivering, her little eyes fierce with fear and anxiety as Angelo lifted Guido to his feet and the three children set off up the yard to meet their irate mama. Aunt Nina looked out of her kitchen window next door.

'For heaven's sake, Marina! What's all the noise about?'

Mama paused in mid stride to glance up at the window.

'I think it was a snaig 'as bitten Guido.'

Aunt Nina snorted, then sniffed, the sniff accompanied by a little shake of her head. 'One of these fine days, Marina, at last you are actually going to see a snake and then God help us.' And she disappeared into her kitchen.

'Guido, go in da house, look at you what a mess.' With the edge of her apron she roughly wiped away the dribble from beneath his nose. 'You too, Seraphina. And where's your ribbon? Where's your new pink ribbon I give you, huh? Madonna mia, you break a your mama's heart da tings you do!'

She gave Guido an impatient shove towards the steps signalling off a renewed outbreak of howling. Exasperated, she flat handed him on the backside and Guido, suddenly remembering the blood blister, grasped his chubby finger, screwed up his face, shut his eyes tight, stamped both his feet in a flurried fandango of rage and yelled until red in the face. Mama, like someone who inadvertently sets off an alarm and doesn't know how to switch it off, watched this performance for a while before delivering another hasty smack, more sound than hurt, at which Guido promptly sat on his hitable spot and tried to scream even louder. Seraphina stood by watching him, as impassive as ever.

'Guido, Stop a your yellin'!'

'Now what's that child screaming for?'

Aunt Nina poked her nose out of the kitchen window to ask the question and then, as though not really interested in the answer, which wouldn't make a blind bit of difference anyway, immediately withdrew it again. She had made her protest.

Mama decided to try persuasion. 'Guido, I don' stan' 'roun' here all day, I gotta work to do. Your Papa, he's a coming home soon. He's a wanna his dinner. You come on now, Guido, please, you be a good boy for your mama. We gotta nice meat balls for dinner, with spaghetti an' tomatie sauce.'

It has no effect. She gives him a moment's grace to make up his mind then she takes his wrist and tries to lift him from the ground. Still clutching the injured finger he jacks up his knees and swings on her arm, his weight forces her to drop him, but not before she has aimed another ineffectual swipe.

'Hey, Mama! What're you hitting him for? Mama quit hitting him.'

Angelo knows that his mother's wild swings are not calculated to do much damage but he is growing a little tired of the constant wailing. Mama, having dropped Guido, now turns on Angelo and, before the surprised youth has time to evade it, clips him hard across the ear.

'Ow! What was that for?' He yelled, a singing in his ear and his hand cupped over it.

'Not mindin' your own business, that's what for,' she yelled right back. 'I tol' him...' she turned back to point an accusing finger at Guido '...not to play wid dat press wid dat machine. Dat's uncle Pepe's machine. Dat machine shesa dangerous. I tol' him how many times I tol' him? Dere's snaigs in dat corner, in widda grapes. Ha! Guido! Stop a your yellin' or I give a you somtink to yell for!'

Under this new threat, Guido suddenly leapt to his feet and ran up the yard, seating himself, still snivelling, on the bottom step. They followed: an irate Mama, a mute Seraphina, and an irritated Angelo still smarting and buzzing from Mama's hand. He mentally kicked himself for not expecting it. He hadn't been her son for nearly seventeen years without knowing something about her. To add to his annoyance he trod on a sharp stone and hopped about on one foot grimacing with pain. At the steps he held on to a railing and upturned the foot to examine the sole, brushing away the dirt and kneading the bruise with his thumb.

'Now whatsa matter wid your foot?'

'I trod on a stone.'

Mama rolled her eyes heavenwards, slapped an open palm against her forehead and clapped her hands in an attitude of prayer, moving them up and down three or four times until she thought of what to say. 'Well why you no wear a shoes?' Now she accented each word with a forearm gesture and indicated with her upturned open hand his bare foot. 'What you gotta shoes for if you no wear 'em?'

'It's too hot for shoes.'

'So you step on a stone an' you get a sore foot. Ees your own fault. I gotta no sympathy. You get bitten by a snaig one fine day, always bare feet.'

Angelo frowned and muttered impatiently under his breath.

Mama's eyes narrowed almost to slits. 'Donna you look like dat to your mama! An donna you swear.'

'I didn't swear!'

'I tella your father. Just now he's a come home.'

'I didn't swear!'

Aunt Nina poked her head out again.

'For God's sake, Marina! What on earth is all this noise about?' She now sounded really angry. 'The whole neighbourhood will think someone's being murdered.'

As the sophisticated travelled member of the clan who had visited the family home back in the old country and had seen the Pope in the flesh, as it were, aunt Nina believed in decorum at all times, if possible. She disliked noise, she disliked a mess, she disliked family rows. There was a time and a place for everything and the place for a row was definitely not outside the house where neighbours or passers by could overhear and pass derogatory comments with tut-tuts and nodding or shaking heads. She noticed the gate left open by Angelo and two or three black faces, attracted by the hubbub, peeping inquisitively in.

'Angelo... Shut that gate at once!'

They all looked towards the gate and the black faces immediately broke into grins. Aunt Nina was mortified. Angelo went over and shut the gate, swearing softly at the black faces that, instead of showing surprise, only grinned the more before disappearing from view. If they were country boys they probably didn't understand him anyway.

By now, Mama was well and truly spoiling for a fight. She turned and marched back down the yard flaring angrily and waved Nina from her perch. 'Who're you tella my kids what to do? You don' wanna hear no row you shut a your window, no onsa askin' you to listen I'm a talk to my kids. You mine your own business!' She turned away. Then added as an afterthought... 'An' donna you taig da Lord's name in vain!' Mama crossed herself. Aunt Nina raised an eyebrow, made with her lips as if she had just sucked a lemon and shut her window with a bang that dislodged some ancient desiccated putty and seriously endangered the glass panes that quivered under the impact of frame hitting frame.

Mama snorted, 'How you like a dat? I ask you!' and rejoined her brood somewhat mollified by this diversion. Guido, still sniffing and holding his finger, gazed up at her, his dark brown eyes beneath their wet lashes glistening between tear reddened lids, his cheeks stained and one tiny drop of moisture suspended from the end of his nose. Guido was a beautiful child. She turned to look at Angelo, so tall, so slender, so handsome, his eyes, like those of his little brother, large and brown beneath long black lashes: his nose straight with delicate nostrils and his mouth gently curved, slightly exaggerated as though outlined by a sculptor's hand. Is it possible these could be her boys? She shook her head almost in disbelief. She knew she was no beauty, quite plain in fact and her husband wasn't exactly an Adonis. Where could these children have come from? Angelo, watching her, wondered just what could be going through her head and kept his guard. Madonna Mia! She thought, I have a Greek God for my son. I have an angel of my son. Oh, God in Heaven, bless my beautiful boy, protect my boy! Holy Mother of God, pray for my boy.

She gazed at Angelo as she must have done that morning when see saw him for the very first time, lying in her arms, his ugly red face beneath its one damp black curl, puckered and wrinkled. He was not beautiful then but she loved him, oh how she loved him. Her joy overflowed in one breathless unspeakable moment and here, suddenly, in this little back yard beneath the wooden veranda: this yard she knew so well; with its pathetic potted pelargoniums, its trellis, its grapevine... she looked about her... the grey painted corrugated iron outhouse bedroom where uncle Pepe and the two boys slept, Angelo and his cousin Tony. Behind it a lean-to shed and facing it, the outhouse bathroom with it's old temperamental copper gas geyser and the chipped enamel bath: Uncle Pepe's rickety chair stood just outside the bedroom door and, beneath the veranda, there was a wood and wire netting chicken coop, Ulrico's work bench and vice, pieces of timber, loads of rubbish, dustbins. Her glance took it all in, all this familiarity as though she was seeing it afresh, and her throat tightened and her trembling fingers reached out to take her son's hand. Angelo he was named and an angel he looked, so handsome, not at all like his father as a young man though sometimes she saw in him something of the man she loved, the man who was the beginning and would be the end of her tiny world.

'Mama?' Angelo felt a lump in his throat though he did not know why. 'What's the matter?'

'Matter?' She laughed. 'Nuttin' is da matter. Only your liddle brudder got himself in trouble. But you?' The question was left hanging.

Angelo didn't know what to say. Mama pressed the long fingers and gazed at the matt brown skin of his hand, at the little half moons at the base of the nails as though she were gazing at some miracle. All the candles in the world could not flicker their golden light into the eyes of God to reflect the radiance of her gratitude. She looked up and smiled, touching his cheek when he realised she wasn't going to clout him and he stopped pulling back. He smiled in turn; a strangely gentle, half shy smile. He did not understand. Grown-ups, especially those close to you, were strange creatures.

Mama looked down at Seraphina who had not moved but stood still, hands on hips, quizzing them silently. So hard to know what the child thinks. Mama stroked her dark hair and Seraphina wriggled her toes and pushed out her lips before standing on one leg and leaning against the railings, her other foot on her shin. And Guido… ah, little Guido... seated on his step, a grubby cherub without wings, nursing his injured finger. He held it up for her to see.

'Ah, bambino.... Ees a your finger? Ees a your poor li'l finger! Let Mama see.'

She slowly and carefully lowered herself to sit on the step beside him and took his hand in hers, frowning in sympathy at the blood blister, black beneath the skin; touched it gently and clicked soothing noises with her tongue against her teeth. Guido winced and tried to withdraw but Mama, in an ecstasy of compassion, raised the finger to her lips and kissed the hurt. Guido yelled.

'An' now? I kiss your finger better an' you yell?' Aided by using the wooden banister she stood and hoisted Guido up by the wrist, spinning him around to face the veranda and gave him a tap to speed him on his way. 'Go on, up the stairs. You too, Pina, look at you what a mess!'

She stood aside to let Seraphina pass and trooped up behind them, hustling them on their way. Seraphina, head slightly bowed, not looking back, not speaking, clumped up the steps and disappeared through the kitchen door. But Guido, half way up, suddenly ducked beneath his mama's arm. She grabbed at him but he ran down the steps and seated himself once more at the bottom looking hard at Angelo. Angelo smiled but Mama was not amused.

'Guido! You coma here!' She yelled. 'I'm a not tell a you again!'

Guido sat motionless, apparently deaf to all, until after a moment's silence Mama in desperation murmured almost to herself but knowing full well the threat would carry... 'Caster oil!'

Guido turned and looked up quickly to see if she meant it. At the sight of her purposeful entry into the house he leapt to his feet and flew to Angelo for protection, wrapping his arms about the older boy's legs and clinging on tightly. Angelo put his hand over Guido's shoulders as Mama re-emerged from the house waving a medicine bottle and a large unfriendly looking spoon.

'Mama,' he pleaded, 'he's hurt his finger, what do you want the castor oil for?'

'He's bin eatin' da grapes, he's bin eatin' uncle Pepe's grapes. Those are green, those grapes.'

Angelo glanced down the narrow yard toward the grape vine bearing its tight little bunches of tiny pale green grapes all in shadow and shook his head. Was there anyone who could ever remember seeing a ripe grape on that vine? Even with the sun at its highest point that little corner of the yard tucked between the houses and the outside bedroom remained in the shade.

'Mama, what would he want to do that for? Nobody eats uncle Pepe's grapes you know that. They're as hard as rocks and sour as lemons. Nobody eats them. And, besides, he's too small to reach them.'

But Mama wasn't to be out argued. 'He can reach 'em. Dat's how he hurt his finger, climbing on da machine to get da grapes. He eat anythin', that chile. He see somtink, in his mouth it go. Castor oil!'

But Angelo was not in the mood to be out argued either. He put his hand on Guido's head and held it against him, continuing with an air of resigned patience, which would shortly turn to sarcasm and inevitable martyrdom if Mama didn't let up.

'Mama, there were four bunches of grapes, there are still four bunches. If you don't believe me, go look for yourself.' He paused. 'And if I'm wrong, then the snaigs have eaten them.' He deliberately mimicked his mother's accent, which spoilt the effect of his little speech.

Mama's fury boiled over. 'Angelo! Donna you make fun for your mother! I don' wanna no arguments.' She started down the steps.

Chapter 3

The dusty brown 1937 Chevvy coupé sped along the Walmer Road, rattling every time it hit a ridge or a hole in the macadam but it was hard to tell whether the noise came from the car or the tools stowed in the back. The three brothers were squashed uncomfortably against each other in the cabin. They did not talk much and the few remarks that were passed, unless they concerned work, were mostly unimportant.

Bartolo, who was the youngest and the owner of the car, concentrated on the road ahead. There would always be the odd cowboy driver to contend with. Ulrico, being the smallest, there was not an ounce of spare flesh on him, sat in the middle hugging his lunch tin to his chest and keeping his knees away from the gear lever by pressing them against Pepe's legs, while Pepe, the eldest and the only bachelor in the family, gazed out of the open offside window with occasional glances across the way, at the new houses going up on either side of the road. It was going to be a fashionable area in a middle class bungalow kind of way. The land was flat, the soil bad, being a dry grey sand with very little vegetation save drought resistant bush and the tall dark conifers and occasional eucalyptus that lined the highway. But it was out of town, away from the mix up and the hurly burly necessity of knowing people and rubbing shoulders, smelling each other's bodies when too close or in a confined space: mostly folk whose lives held small interest for the brothers, people with whom they had little if anything in common.

Where the Chevvy's rumble, or dicky seat as they called it, had once been there was now a topless metal box that converted the car into a small truck suitable for carting tools, small loads of building materials, kids on picnics, and dogs. Bartolo owned a brindle Great Dane by the name of Tshaka that took up almost as much room as Pepe, a hound that seemed to produce a copious and continuous stream of saliva that descended from its jaws until it dropped off by the force of gravity and its own weight. Fortunately, when travelling, the dog kept its head well over the side enjoying the slipstream so the spittle was blown away by the wind and hit the road rather than mess up the car, except perhaps for a little bit when the dog was changing sides.

But the back, fine though it was for dogs and kids, was not at all suitable for a grown man even when it meant being crushed uncomfortably in the cab. Bartolo and Ulrico always joked that if only Pepe would lose some weight and didn't take up half the cab there would be room to breathe. Pepe smiled indulgently at his brothers' wit and, in his turn, hinted that the old banger had really had its day – 'Look at the rust, man! It's going to fall to pieces any minute and there we will be, sat in the middle of the road.' – so wasn't it high time Bart invested in a new truck?

He and Ulrico, spruced up in their best so as to give a false impression, had visited a couple of showrooms, chiefly out of curiosity. The false impression was obviously successful as beautifully suited franchise owners on seeing them examining a vehicle emerged from their offices to proudly sing their vehicles' praises in hopes of a sale. They gave an exhaustive inventory of all the car's good points including performance, not much of which the brothers understood, neither of them being mechanically minded though they listened with intense concentration, every now and again giving a nod. The salesmen didn't seem to notice no questions were ever asked but more than likely if they'd thought about it would have put this down to the eloquence of their spiel. The mention of *torque* had the brothers confused for a while but they later interpreted it as *talk.* They had heard Bartolo when tinkering with the engine of his Chevvy say, 'There, she's singing sweetly now,' and, if an engine can sing sweetly presumably it can also talk.

The Chevrolet showrooms were naturally the first to visit. If that old banger of Bart's had lasted as long as it had, a new Chevvy would be just the job to replace it. Plymouth was the next car to look at but in this showroom there were nothing but sedans: fine cars but useless for their purpose. They wondered about looking at an English car, Vauxhall for example, but decided against that. Not many people bought English cars or, at least, they never saw that many on the road so they didn't really know much about them. But it had been a fine Saturday's jaunt and they had picked up a couple of shiny brochures advertising the latest models – Pepe loved the glowing metallic colours and the special smell of the heavy paper and Guido would have fun cutting out the illustrations with a pair of blunt scissors – and that's as far as purchasing a new vehicle went. It would be no good either of them thinking of buying one, even if they had the money, as neither of them could drive. They would just have to try chipping away at Bart.

'Okay,' Bartolo surprised them one day by suddenly saying in all seriousness, or what appeared to be all seriousness, 'I'll get a new truck, a proper truck, and we'll split the cost three ways. How does that suit?' Buying a new truck was not mentioned again. Better the discomfort and the cramps, but Pepe would sit in his chair in the yard going over the brochures, every now and again lifting the pages to his nose to sniff the scent.

Pepe, his white hair like a monk's tonsure, a half wreath around his suntanned to an almost mahogany colour bald pate and almost falling over his ears, felt the hot wind in his face through the open window on which his elbow rested, as they drove and he dreamed of faraway places, the places he had seen in his youth, the places he never ceased to dream about: Russia, when St Petersburg was still St Petersburg: America, - he always talked of 'Loose Angeles', probably his favourite city, San Francisco – and South America, the Argentine! Mexico! Ah, Mexico, that was some place, hey? Of all the countries he had visited that, to Pepe, was the most fascinating though he would be hard put to say exactly why. He should have stayed there, he thought. What about the Asia run? Japan, Hong Kong, Ceylon, India. A couple of Indian buses brought him out of his reverie. Horns blaring their conductors, young exhibitionists, swinging out on the safety bars with their shirts flapping against their chests and ballooned away from their backs, their long cocoanut oiled hair blowing in their eyes as they defied the bucking overloaded buses to wrench them from their holds, or the laws of gravity to pull them down. Tshaka let out a series of barks and moved to the back to follow them disappearing.

Bartolo slowed down as the car entered the more built up areas, passed the cemetery and down the hill where the tram lines ran. He slowed down more as they passed Aunt Nina's shop and pulled in slightly toward the kerb. 'You think Nina wants anything taken home?'

Ulrico glanced towards the plate glass window where a brand new smirking wax model stood in an improbable pose sporting a rather heavy two piece wool suit with feathered hat to match, too hot for the climate and too old in style for the model.

'Man, I reckon she's long gone by now.'

'Hmn... yes... looks like it.'

The car gathered speed, skidded slightly on the tram lines like a bitch in heat turning her tail, and they went down the hill in the wake of a lurching crammed to capacity tram. Approaching the turn-off, Bartolo slipped the car into second and slid gently round the corner into the tree-lined avenue. A car coming up the hill slammed on his brakes and screeched to a stop a yard from the fender behind which Pepe sat dreaming. Heads turned sharply. A coloured woman screamed at the sudden squealing of tyres. Pepe hardly noticed. He was in Mexico. Ulrico sniffed and raised a nonchalant eyebrow but his fingers spread and whitened against the metal lunch box.

'You want to be a bit more careful, man,' he said.

Bartolo shrugged and gave an embarrassed grin knowing he was at fault, put his free hand on the horn and tapped it every few seconds to scatter the children and animals barring his way, finally pulling up on the gravel verge outside the house. Mr Chang from his veranda flapped his fan and, lowering his head slightly, smiled in friendly greeting as the three men got out of the car.

'You coming in for some coffee?' Ulrico asked.

Bartolo shook his head. 'No, I'll just nip across the road to old Mrs Chang and get something for Maria. She's expecting me home early tonight.'

Bartolo, when he married had built himself a house out of town, a small wood and iron, neat, almost shed like house. There was no room for another family in the semi-detached and the older siblings, having already brought their wives there, seemed without question to have prior claim although Bartolo still owned a share of the actual property.

'Okay then, see you in the morning.' Ulrico and Pepe waved a desultory farewell and avoiding the front door turned the corner and went down the side of the house, as Bartolo crossed the road to visit Mrs Chang. Ulrico stopped outside the green gate and looked at it as he did every night; nobody knew why because he never said anything, merely shook his head disapprovingly as he ran his hand down the faded green paint, blistered by the sun. He picked at it with a nail and inspected the scarred bleached wood showing through the blisters. A bit more paint flaked off against his palm and then he thumbed down the latch, pushed open the gate, creaking on its rusty hinges, and entered the yard followed by Pepe who made straight for his chair and deposited his cardboard lunch case beneath it. Mama, half way down the steps, yelled at him.

'Pepe! 'Ow many bunches of grapes you got?'

Pepe, who had taken a red polka dot cotton

handkerchief from his pocket with which to wipe the sweat from his forehead and neck, paused and looked up as Mama yelled at him. He looked at the chair into which he was about to lower his bulk. He looked at Angelo and Guido and Seraphina whose head suddenly appeared at the kitchen window, at Ulrico, at Mama and finally at the bottle and spoon in her hands.

'Somebody bin eatin' my grapes?'

"Ow many bunches you got?'

Pepe wiped his neck with the handkerchief, scratched reflectively, ran a finger around his collar and peered around the corner of the bedroom towards his grape vine but it was too far to see without his glasses. They waited. Finally he held up five banana like fingers.

'Five,' he grunted.

'Castor oil!' It was a paean from Mama vindicated.

Seraphina clambered down from the bench on which she had been kneeling to look out of the window and poked her head around the kitchen door. At the sight of Mama descending the steps with the familiar bottle and spoon, she came hurtling out of the house, crashed by her mother who was nearly pushed off balance but still managed to lash out with the spoon, and Guido, leaving the safety of Angelo's embrace, both kids hared for the gate, looping either side of Ulrico who made an ineffectual swipe at them with his lunch tin as they ran through the gate to disappear down the street.

'Hey!' He shouted after them, 'Where you kids think you're going?'

'One of these fine days,' said Angelo following them at a more leisurely pace, 'someone's going to break a leg and Mama's going to come running with the castor oil.' The gate closed behind him.

'Someone bin eatin' my grapes?' Pepe mumbled, asking the world in general, and then not waiting for an answer ambled down the yard to take a look for himself. Ulrico opened the gate and peered down the road. Guido and Seraphina were sitting in the gutter holding hands. At the warning creak of the opening door they leapt to their feet and fled to a safer distance, eyeing Ulrico's head peering around from behind the high wall. Of Angelo there was no sign.

Ulrico frowned, looked up the street and back at the silent children 'You gonna sit there all night?' They shook their heads in unison. 'Then what're you gonna do?' Guido's lower lip trembled but otherwise there was no sign they had even heard him. 'Well, you gotta come in sometime.' With which he went back in and closed the gate. He paused for a second and then opened it again. The children had not moved. He closed it, opened it, listened to the squeak of its ancient hinges: examined the interior surface, shook his head and, turning away, climbed the steps to where Mama stood, kissed her and handed her his lunch tin which she took with her free hand.

'Dosa chil'ren,' she complained, 'dey make a me so mad. Always somtink dey up to. You have a good day, caro, yes? Where's Bartolo? He no bring you home?'

Aunt Nina came out on the veranda carrying in both hands, wrapped in a tea towel for protection, a steaming pudding bowl which she placed on the railing to cool.

'You staying on the veranda, Ulrico?'

'What for he want to stay on da veranda? He joosta come back from work!' Mama pretended indignation.

'All right, all right,' said Nina complacently, 'Only if he's staying on the veranda he can keep an eye on my pudding, can't he?'

'An' whose a gonna take a your pudding, huh? Whosa mad to take a your pudding?'

Aunt Nina pursed her mouth primly, shook her pearl drop earrings, patted her silver hair and eyed Mama up and down. Mama... Mama with her fat shapeless figure, no more fat on her than Nina but Nina was in the trade, she had taken a specialists course in Rome and passed with flying colours. Didn't she have a diploma on her workshop wall to prove it? She knew the efficiency of whalebone even if it did itch when you removed it at night. There was nothing anyone could tell Nina about corsets or how to flatter a figure gone to seed and outsize was her speciality. But Mama never cared one way or the other with her plain, unmade face, her hands red from scrubbing, her straight grey-streaked hair pulled severely into a bun, unflatteringly from her face; her nose too broad and her eyes too small, glittering over their pale blue pouches of fatigue. It's lucky, Nina thought, the children sort of take more after their grandfather, at least as far as looks are concerned. Ulrico wasn't too bad a looker in his youth and you would have thought he could surely have found something better than Marina. Still... Aunt Nina shook her head a little rather like a gourmet surveying a suspicious dish... she might possibly have had a certain attractiveness as a girl and, anyway, men were so unpredictable in matters of love: unpredictable and ignorant; ignorant, mainly ignorant. Look at the way they carry on over calendar girls, pin ups, film stars. Glamour! Put them in a room with a pin up and nine out of ten wouldn't know what to do with themselves. They'd choke themselves in their own embarrassment, talk nonsense, smoke themselves to death or drink too much. Anyway, sex is such a personal matter there is no accounting for taste. It's lucky though the children don't resemble her, though obvious that, if not controlled, Guido was certainly going to take after her in temperament. If only one could know in advance how children were going to turn out. What about her own son, Tony? The drop earrings quivered like glass pieces of a chandelier set twinkling in a sudden tiny gust of wind. She didn't think too much about Tony just as she tried not to think of the man who had been her husband – may God rest his soul he needed it. Anyway, he was a Viljoen, scion of an old fundamentalist Afrikaner family and she should have known better. The marriage on the whole hadn't been a bad one but how could a member of the Dutch Reformed Church ever be reconciled to Roman Catholicism? She sniffed then, with a dismissive shrug and a vague flick of her tea towel at an imaginary fly molesting her pudding, retreated into her kitchen.

'Whosa gonna take your puddin'?' Mama screamed after her.

'The cats!' Nina shrieked back for once losing control of herself, the memory of her husband had this affect on her, 'or the birds, or your children!'

'My chil'ren no steal!' Mama bawled at her unseen adversary, 'an if dey eat a your puddin' dey get castor oil!'

Mama snorted and turned back to Ulrico who having seated himself on the bench at the plain deal table on the veranda seemed content to remain there. She humphed her way across to him. 'Come on inside now,' she ordered and then noticed that Pepe had returned and was standing at the front of the steps gazing up at her in solemn accusation.

'An' now?' She asked, 'you tink maybe I grow up chil'ren joosta eat your grapes? What you grow grapes for? You giva my chil'run da stomach aig. You make poor little Guido hurt his han'. You gotta snaigs in your grapes!'

At a complete loss in the face of this feminine piece of injustice Pepe, who rarely found words anyway, turned sadly away and went into his bedroom taking his lunch case with him. Mama smiled after him. She was fond of Pepe, as was the whole family. True, he never said much, but he listened: he listened to everything and anything they had to say about an unjust unkind world, or anyway gave the appearance of listening; and when one could get him to open his own mouth he told the most fascinating stories. He liked telling them once he had conquered his shyness and was not inadvertently reminded of it during the telling. And the family enjoyed listening to him, seated at the kitchen table after a macaroni cheese or one of mama's nice chicken curries: the recipe brought home by Pepe, given to him by the wife of his Indian friend Patel; an interim period between eating and settling down for the evening, even if that settling down only meant a catnap in front of the stove.

'I can remember once...' that was the beginning, the cue to listen. 'I remember...' Working on the building site or sitting at the kitchen table, Pepe would in the telling, or the dreaming, relive his youth. The prelude to his speaking was invariably triggered in the mind by some incident, as for instance Ulrico would tell one of the children, 'I said don't do that', or 'I told you and I don' tell you again. Next time you get a clip across the ear!' Suddenly Pepe would hear their own father's voice.

'I told you, no!'

'But Papa! I want to go to sea, it is the only thing I want to do.'

'No son of mine will ever go to sea! No son of mine will be a sailor not while I'm alive to stop it.'

'Papa, things have changed since you were at sea. Conditions are not the same...'

'The sea is not the same? Storms are not the same?'

'I didn't mean that. I meant...'

'I don't care what you mean, Giuseppe! I say NO! NO! NO!'

'But, papa, for Christ's sake, why not?'

'I tell you why not. I tell you so you don't blaspheme an' you listen to your father because I know what is best for my chil'ren. I say to God, with my own mouth I tell him, "God," I say "Never again will I set foot on the deck of a ship; never again will I go to sea. Sea is for fishes, land is for man. Let the fishes have the sea I will stay on land." I tell him that. You want me now to go back on my solemn word?'

'What solemn word? You made a covenant for me too?'

'Huh?'

'You included me in the deal?'

'You are my flesh and blood.'

'I am a man.'

'Ah! You are a child! You are a baby. Oh, my boy! Can't you see? I only want to do what is right for you.'

'Can't you let me decide for myself?'

'The sea is no good. What does it do for a man but make him sick? Here I have started a good business. Now we are in the building trade, we make a little money, not too much, too much is no good. We are a family, we love each other, we are happy all together. What for you get this crazy idea?'

'It's what I want.'

'Tsch! Your mother, she don' like it.'

'She doesn't know about it'.

'She don' have to know about it, I say she don' like it. Now I don' wanna hear no more 'bout this crazy notion. You settle down good.'

There was a long silence.

'What would you do if I just packed up and left?'

There was an even longer silence.

'If I went off without telling you?'

'Che minchia!' This was muttered sotto voce. It was not the kind of thing a father said to a son.

'Che cazzo stai dicendo?' This was said out loud. 'I won't hear you talk like that! God may forgive you, I say maybe, but I'm not so sure I will. You go like that you don' come back!'

But Pepe went and Pepe came back, to be welcomed with tears of joy, with arms opened wide: and again, and again. After every trip, be it weeks, months or even years that he was away, grandpa and grandma, brothers and sisters each received their present from an ever generous Pepe and listened agog to his tales. In those days he was not shy in the telling of stories, rather he was eager for they were then not memories but actual. He carried them like a woman carries a child. They were his life, present and accounted for. He knew them as a woman knows the vagaries and the temper of the child whose snotty nose she wipes clean. Later, when images in memory were gazed at, then he would maybe grow shy and look at these pictures in his mind, uncertain whether to bring them out, to parade them in public for fear his public would yawn away their meaning for him. Each time he came home from the sea, grandpa would say to him, 'Giuseppe, you not go back this time, huh?' You stay home now, with us, get married maybe. You see enough of the world, all the world is the same. You are a man now, and we? We get old. You stop with us now, huh?'

But the lure of the sea was always too much to resist. He was to return to it again and again like an addict to his drug, like a man who, having quarrelled with his lover, finds in her absence that he cannot live except in her embrace. If she must hurt then she must hurt, but the hurt is needed. Travelling, always travelling, always eager for new sights, new smells, new experiences. The smell of tar, of ship's paint, of salt; the smell of the sea would stay with him all his life, though now there was only memory, a looking back.

Sometimes now he would go down to the harbour and sit for hours on a capstan at the wharf's edge, watching the ships and dreaming, now and again invited on board by an old friend or acquaintance: and once on deck or seated in a mess, a steaming cup in his hands, he was like a man returning from a long exile. His heart beat faster and the old nostalgia came flooding back in a tide that threatened to overwhelm him with emotion and longing so that he suddenly trembled and the scalding condensed milk sweetened tea slopped over his hands. Hastily he would put down the cup and then, embarrassed, take out his polka dot handkerchief and start to mop up the tea streaming across the metal topped table and dripping onto the deck, but a hand – understanding – would reach out across the table and stop him.

'What we got to eat, Mama?'

From his bedroom Pepe heard Ulrico ask about dinner and Mama answer him.

'Meat balls.'

He popped his head out of the window. 'With tomatie sauce?' he asked.

Mama looked down at him from the height of her veranda allowing a slight pause before she spoke.

'Of course wid tomatie sauce!' This time she really was most indignant. 'What do you tink I put on my meat balls? Grape juice?'

Pepe withdrew his head and slowly, silently, closed the window as though the noise, if he made any, would send Mama jumping off the veranda and down his throat again. But Mama had already turned her interest elsewhere.

'I make you a cuppa tea, Ulrico.'

He nodded, got slowly to his feet and moved towards the kitchen door. Mama patted his cheek in passing and smiled. His beard grew quickly and by this time of the day the stubble showed a dark blue against his tan.

'Like a prickly pear,' she said, stroking it.

He disappeared into the house just as Tony came bounding out from the house next door, rattled down the steps, almost falling over himself in his haste, jumped the last three, ran along the yard and stood beneath Mama's veranda. She eyed him suspiciously.

'Hiya, aunt! Hiya, unk!' he shouted at the unseen Ulrico, 'How many houses you build today?'

'Donna worry you uncle now,' Mama said. 'He's a joost a come home from work. He's a tired so no nonsense please.'

Tony did not move except to intertwine his fingers over the knob and lean his chin on the newel post at the bottom of the steps and try to smile appealingly at his aunt. It didn't work. It never did. She pulled a face.

'What you want to ask?' She asked.

'Where's Angelo.'

'What you want Angelo for? He's a not here?' She looked at Tony and shook her head.

Nina's son, a year younger than his cousin, is short and stocky with a heavy face, broader at the bottom than the top. His black hair curls tightly to his scalp and grows low on his forehead somewhat like a bull's forelock. Whenever he speaks his broad mouth seems to twist into a permanent sneer. His nose is broad and flat and his eyes small. Tony is not a good looking boy. Even his body is ugly, balanced on bending legs and his hands, which might have once looked reasonable, were marred by the nails being practically non existent through continuous nibbling. His mother tried to break him of the habit by rubbing his fingers with red-hot chillies and various other concoctions like bitter aloes, but all to no avail. His skin is pitted with small craters, the legacy of a bad dose of chicken pox as a child, and if ever a child's future was mapped in his face, that child was Tony.

Mama turned her back on him and Tony started up the steps. Hearing the clump of his feet she turned again to face him. He stopped. 'Where you tink you goin'? I tolla you, Angelo he's a not here!'

Tony grinned and tried to push past her again. She

beat him about the head with her wet tea towel. 'You not go in my 'ouse! I tell you, he's a not here! You make me a lair?'

Tony backed away from the tea towel, mainly because the end had whipped dangerously close to an eye. He stood quite still looking at his aunt and then very softly he said, 'Give us a break, aunt. Why're you always getting at me?'

'Because I donna like da tings you do. I donna like what you say. You tella too many lies. You tella too many stories. You make a my Angelo do bad tings. You get into trouble. You go home now. Go on to your mudder. Don' a you worry Angelo, he don' wanna see you. Is nobody wanna see you.'

Tony narrowed his eyes and stood looking at Mama, that faint sneer on his lips. It was not unconscious this time but deliberate. He wanted not to notice the things she said, to give the impression of toughness to this world that seemingly did not want anything to do with him. To say in effect, 'So what?' throwing it away flippantly when 'So what?' in actuality means a great deal. The armour of pride collapses from within: an implosion created by the sudden realisation of hopelessness leaving a vacuum that cannot be filled. The eternal pressure can only be resisted by lies and bravado. Terror creates terror, pain creates pain, and loneliness begets loneliness: scoff at the world that scoffs at you. The truth needs acceptance and for those who cannot accept, the only alternative is oblivion. Mendacity becomes the cornerstone of existence.

But at this moment there is only confusion in Tony's mind and a flurry of vengeful retrospection. Suddenly he springs into life, his body jerks, his head snaps to one side, his arm whips out as he points to a spot just behind and to the left of Mama's leg. 'Look out, aunt! Snake!' He says it very fast so that she does not actually hear the words so much as receive an impression a split second after he has spoken, and his false alarm communicates itself to her, transformed in her into a very real fear. Her eyes dilate in terror and with a shriek she leaps away from the direction of his pointing finger and at the same time he rushes past her. But his headlong charge is brought to an abrupt halt at the kitchen door, where Ulrico, also alarmed by his shout, grabs him by the scruff of the neck and pushes him back on to the veranda, where from the other side Mama, sufficiently recovered but still trembling, cuffs him about the head and then sets to work with her tea towel. Her wild blows descend on both of them indiscriminately and Ulrico is forced to raise one hand in order to protect his own head, holding the squirming Tony with the other.

'Hey!' he bawled, 'What's goin' on here?'

Mama, beside herself with rage, continued to beat her cowering nephew who by this time had joined in the chorus and was yelling at the top of his voice.

In her kitchen, Nina heard the noise and recognised it for what it was but unconcernedly continued with her work. She had dinner to prepare. If her son had got himself into hot water next door it would not be the first time and he could get himself out of it. And Marina needn't think she could come bleating to her either. How many times had she told Tony not to bother those people next door, saying it as though they weren't even family? Not five minutes ago as he ran through the house her exact words were, 'Tony, don't go next door now, you hear me? It will be dinner time soon.'

'He tolla me dere's a snaig! Dat's what he say! A snaig!' She held a hand against her fluttering heart.

Ulrico's fingers tightened about Tony's shirt and with the other hand he tried to wrench the tea towel from Mama or at least stop her from swinging it in all directions. It was not easy.

'What you want to tell your aunt that for?' he shouted above the screaming.

'Uncle, you're hurting me! Oh, Oh! Uncle! Let go!'

'He's a bad boy dat, he's a gangster! He see too many fil-ums. He look at too many comics books. He tell a too many lies.'

Tony, doubled up under Ulrico's iron grip, looked up at Mama and leered, which brought on another attack with the tea towel and the leer turned into a wince as Ulrico's fingers tightened even more but he managed with a sudden twist to wrench himself free, scampered down the steps, practically falling over his feet, losing his balance and almost plummeting headlong down in his effort to get away. As soon as he thought himself far enough away to be out of danger he turned to face Ulrico, angrily defiant; sneering and, from his point of comparative safety, gave with the finger, then turned and fled the length of the yard as the insulted Ulrico advanced halfway down the steps and pointed his own angry finger, wagging it admonishingly. 'Next time I give you a clip across your ear you go crying home to mummy! You hear what I'm saying?'

But as soon as he returned to the veranda, Tony came back. Ulrico was truly irritated. 'Whatsa matter wid youse, man? You got no brains? You don't hear what I'm telling you. What you want?'

'Angelo.' Ulrico was about to speak again when Tony continued quickly, 'And don't shoot me that crap about him not being here. You've handed me that one before.'

'He's a not here!' Mama chipped in, 'He's a not here! How many times I must a tella you? Tch! Dat boy!' She turned to her husband. 'Ulrico I tell you, when I tink of dat boy I feel so sorry for his poor mudder. She my sister-in-law an' sometimes we fight but my heart it goes out to her.' She opened an upturned palm in Tony's direction.

The street door clicked open. They all turned to look at it. It swung back on its rusty hinges to reveal Seraphina.

'Where's Angelo?' Mama asked. Seraphina pointed mutely down the road.

'Where's Guido?' Seraphina lifted one shoulder and looked at the sky.

'Well go fine him. An' call Angelo. Tell him is a time to eat now.'

Seraphina disappeared. Mama turned to the boy still looking up at them from the yard. 'Tony if you wanna your cousin, go fine him. He's wid does dreadful boys again. Why you always go roun' wid does dreadful boys? One day you gonna make so much trouble. You break a your mama's heart da tings you do.'

Tony leant on the banister rail again and tried to look appealing. 'What you got for chow, aunt Marina?'

'Never you mine!' she snapped back.

'Can I eat with you?'

'No, you go an' eata your Mama's puddin'!' She smiled to herself and ushered Ulrico into the house. Tony pulled a wry face and shrugged. He would eat with them anyway. He looked towards the gate for a moment, brooding, and then headed for the street.

Chapter 4

Two bikes stand against a lamppost: another leans against the wall. The ends of towels slung around their necks hang down over their chests or if not too large tucked into their shirt tops, unbuttoned two or three down to take the bulk. Beneath their shirts, they wear only their swimming trunks. They squat at the pavement's edge and pass around the inevitable cigarette one of them has produced. It is not as though there weren't more, or that they could not afford more. After all each of them has parents who smoke and whose cigarette packs are left lying around open and available for the filching. No, the thinking is if more than one is produced, someone could get greedy.

Carlos, having taken his drag and passed the butt along, lay with his back on the pavement and took a pot shot at the streetlamp above him. The others watched. The shot was a good foot or so wide of its mark. Nothing was said but Carlos knew what was being thought. He sat up and searched around for another stone, fitted it, and fired again. With a ping the pebble ricochets off the metal shade, taking with it a flake of white enamel, leaving behind a sixpenny size black spot starred with radiating cracks. Steve sniffed and picked his nose, wondering if he should risk his reputation by taking the catty himself and having a go. He decided against it, a little irritated at himself; looked around and suddenly noticed that while they had been engaged in watching Carlos's marksmanship, Johnny had surreptitiously been getting as much of the cigarette as he could. Steve lashed out with his bare foot, his heel catching Johnny painfully high on the side of his thigh. With a yell, Johnny staggered to his feet, dropped the cigarette butt and limped around in a circle, rubbing his leg, the effect of the kick having almost put it out of action like when it goes to sleep, though there were no pins and needles, just a sort of numbness.

'Shit! What's the big idea? What'd you do that for?' He was no longer moving around but still rubbing his thigh. He looked down to where Steve's heel had connected and knew he was going to develop a bruise.

'One pull you're supposed to have. One pull.'

'One pull is all I had!' He bent down and retrieved the cigarette.

'Come on come on, man, hand it over or you'll just be looking for more than a kick up the arse.'

A myrmidon must know his place. In a gang there can be only one leader. If lesser mortals step out of line, kick them back into it. Meekly Johnny hands over the cigarette. Steve puts it in his mouth and immediately takes it out again, spitting with an expression of disgust. He stands looking at it. The end is yellow and a few wet strands of tobacco hang limply from it.

'Jesus! Look at that! Can't you smoke a fucking cigarette without making Niagara Falls out of it?'

'That wasn't me!' Johnny protested. 'For Chris' sake! You think I don't know how to smoke a cigarette or something?'

Steve was still angry with himself for funking his impulse to show them who was the best shot. 'If you didn't do that, who did?' he demanded. There was only one possible answer of course.

'Carlos.'

For his answer, Carlos swung around and let fly with his catapult. Johnny, who had anticipated this and already retreated a short distance, yelled and had another painful spot to rub where a second bruise would develop. Steve passed the cigarette to Angelo who for fellowship's sake took a hasty draw without inhaling and passed it along. Smoking made him feel sick and that was about the only effect it had. Carlos fitted another stone to his catty and was about to take aim again at the street lamp – he would not be satisfied until the bulb was shattered – when his attention was caught elsewhere.

'Hey, quiet you guys. Watch that cat.'

They watched in anticipation as a long lean black tom poised on the wall, prepared to jump onto the bathroom roof, its tail flicked in angry little swishes from side to side as it kneaded the wall and measured its distance. Carlos took careful aim and fired. There was a short sharp meow as the cat disappeared, knocked off balance a split second before taking off. Carlos leaped in the air laughing. 'You see that? You see that, man? Got him right up the poepal! Hey, find me another stone.' He didn't know what he would shoot at this time unless another cat appeared, but the lamp bulb was momentarily reprieved. Then Tony appeared at the gate. He had seen the cat drop from the wall and bolt down the yard to disappear over the far fence. He looked out and, seeing whom Angelo was with, did not relish the idea of going to call him. One of these days he might call their bluff, but he did not feel too much in the mood right now. He took one step from the gate and called, 'Angelo!'

Angelo glanced up the street but looked away again.

'Angelo!'

'What?'

'Your Ma says you got to come in and eat now.'

'Your Ma says you got to come in and eat now,' mimicked Carlos a little more nursery rhyme in tone in order to provoke Tony. Tony ignored him. Angelo ignored Tony. Tony waited and then yelled again. 'Angelo!'

'I heard you! I heard you!'

'Well are you coming or aren't you?'

'I'll come when I feel like it, okay?' Angelo turned his back and made to lean against the lamp post but his gesture was lost when he knocked over Carlos' bike.

Carlos shouted at him. 'Hey! That's my bike, man! Watch what you're doing, hey!'

With a sharp intake of breath it was now Angelo's turn to limp in a circle. 'Yurra, man! Aina! Fuck it!' He had caught the side of his foot on the sharp spikes of the crank wheel and now, moaning, knelt on one knee to inspect the damage. A good inch of skin had been gouged out and the wound was covered in oil and blood a few drops of which were already dripping on the pavement.

Carlos had picked up his treasured bike and was inspecting it for damage.

Angelo was still inspecting the damage to his foot. 'Shit! Man, will you look at that?' Had he been wearing shoes he would have given the bike a good kick to help relieve the pain.

'Angelo, are you coming?'

'Angelo, are you coming?'

Carlos's repetition seemed to pass over Tony unnoticed. He remained apparently unprovoked but there was an intense desire to bite his fingernails and in the gloom and at the distance Carlos could not see the boy's lip twitch slightly. He only knew that his insult seemed to elicit no response. He suddenly pulled back the leather pad of his catapult and without taking aim let fly at Tony who leapt in the air with a yell of surprise and instinctively stepped back to stand in the doorway lest his retreat be cut off. They saw his mouth move.

'What?' said Carlos, pushing up his chin and opening his eyes very wide. Tony mumbled something more they couldn't hear. They only saw his lips move again and noted the expression on his face.

'What?' Carlos asked again.

'I said what you want to do that for?'

'What you want to do that for?' Carlos sang and then with a change of tone, 'I felt like it. Okay? Any arguments?

You want to make something of it?'

There was a pause while Tony tried to think of an argument to end all arguments but nothing came to mind. He knew that Carlos, as always, was waiting for an excuse to make him fight, and he knew that as small as Carlos was, he did not want to fight him, especially with the others, Steve, Johnny and Angelo, there to witness his possible humiliation. Angelo wouldn't back him up, that was for sure. He wouldn't try and stop it.

Tony's heart was beating just loud enough for him to know that he did not relish the situation. Chicken? Yellow? A streak a mile wide down his back? That's what they would say if he could not think of a way out, a way other than having to fight Carlos that is but still saving face. Of course he could extend the period of bluff, the "come out and fight like a man" bit while the onlookers urged the incipient combatants to stop going around in circles. 'Bash him!' 'Go on, man, do him!' 'Yurra, man! What're you waiting for?' One of these days he thought he really would call Carlos's bluff. He would slam right back. Underneath his sense to live to fight another day he felt that if he did make a stand, Carlos would back down. His show of aggression could be sheer bravado, strutting like a bantam cock in front of his mates.

Play for time. Be saved by the bell: the bell of Aunt Marina's voice for example, calling him, calling Angelo, telling them to come in and eat so that he would have an excuse to turn away, to take one more step towards the safety of the yard. He turned. Behind him he could hear them laugh, one at least making clucking noises. Chicken! Their laughter said it and he did not like it but neither did he like the alternative. One step and he would be through the gate; he hesitated. At that moment the pebble stung him on the calf. He let out another yell and swung around. After a moment he had to rub the spot on his leg where the stone hit him. The boys laughed louder. Angelo was smiling but his eyes were looking far away, over Tony's shoulder and then up the street as though he were part of this ritual but not a part of it. No matter how he felt about him, Tony was after all his cousin.

'Cut that out!' Tony yelled.

'Cut that out!' Carlos responded. 'Come on, man! You wanna make something out of it? Come on. What you waiting for?'

There was another silence as Tony stood glowering and rubbing his leg, knowing that he did not want to make anything out of it but angry with the pain. Instead he weakly admitted, 'That hurt!'

The laughter now was raucous. 'That hurt,' mimicked Steve. 'Oh, cry-baby, oh mommy's little precious, did it hurt diddums then? Come here and we'll kiss it better.'

'Come here and kiss my arse.'

'Boo-hoo! Come here and kiss my arse!' Johnny was overdoing it, sitting on the pavement, holding his sides and drumming his heels on the concrete. Not getting any reaction he desisted and got to his feet. 'I'm going home,' he said, taking hold of his cycle handlebars. 'I've had enough of this shit.'

'Angelo, you coming?' the question was quiet and Angelo's answer equally soft.

'Just now.'

'Okay then.' Tony nodded and disappeared through the gate, just in time to miss another shot from Carlos that hummed past the back of his head. Tony's anger that had lessened slightly erupted with such suddenness it overruled his caution.

'You skinny little bastard! You dirty greasy little Portuguese cunt!'

This was so totally unexpected the four boys stood and starred at Tony, transfixed and unbelieving. When the shock passed the howling began, the baying, the egging on, the cries of the hunters, and then the sparring with words, the ritual working up to a climax. Steve, as the leader would be the first to encourage battle. Suddenly Carlos felt a little less confident, a certain reluctance held him in check. No one had thought for a moment that Tony would have turned back. He saw Steve about to incite him, his whole body tense with the expectation of blood, and so to forestall him he advanced two steps and said with all the menace he could rake up, which at this moment wasn't much. 'What did you call me? You want to barney? Hey?' It was weak and he knew it. He had definitely lost ground.

'Don't just talk to him,' Steve ordered impatiently, 'You heard what he called you. Let him have it!'

But Carlos was not prepared now to advance beyond his two steps and neither was he prepared to be talked into a fight that he never really wanted in the first place, despite appearances, would they shake hands afterwards? Pretend to be palsy-walsy and all made up? No hard feelings on either side and it was a good fight while it lasted, when in fact they hated every second of it, terrified of being really hurt. Carlos saw bleeding noses and bruises. He would taunt, he would jeer, he would provoke, he would challenge, but he would not fight, not unless his dander was really up and all caution thrown to the winds. Fights were something you talked about before they happened and after they were finished but never done with. They were not to be savoured in the moment of trembling legs and pounding heart, gasping breath, flying fists, scuffles, burning ears, tear blinded eyes, sweat and fear. There were those like Steve who relished battle and had no fear but Carlos was definitely not one of them.

'You don't want to mix it with me, oakie. You'll get more than you...!'

He felt himself running out of words. No one seemed to have noticed the protagonists hadn't moved a step towards one another.

'You think I'm scared of you? Look at you, you stupid bugger... who do you think you are?' Tony would have continued but his newfound confidence was built on the quick sands of intuition and quick sands shift. He wondered if he had gone too far and left himself out on a limb with no path of retreat. If only he could get out of it now, Carlos would think twice before challenging him again.

Mama took the food out of the oven and laid it steaming on the table, then she put on the kettles to boil water for washing up. Ulrico washed his hands beneath the cold water tap over the kitchen sink and dried them on a roller towel behind the door, then he took his place at the head of the table and Mama placed the warmed plates in front of him.

'Where those kids?' he asked as though Mama would automatically know their every movement. She lifted her shoulders and made for the veranda.

'I dunno,' she complained, 'I tell dat Tony to go fine Angelo, what's he doin' all desa time?' She leaned over the veranda rail and saw Tony at the gate. 'Tony?' He turned and all but uttered a cry of relief.

'You fine Angelo?' she asked

'Yeah, he's here, just down the road.' His voice was gruff, holding the hint of a snarl, the world should know that he, Tony Viljoen, was not a man to be trifled with.

'You tell him he's a dinner ready?'

'Yeah...' He drawled the word out trying to encase the sound in a wealth of meaning, overtones, undertones, innuendo. What it implied was that he had told Angelo in no uncertain terms to come in for his dinner, and that, had Mama not at that precise moment come out onto the veranda, he would have single-handedly dispersed the gang and dragged Angelo in by the scruff of the neck.

'Well why he's a not come in?' Mama shouted, standing on tip toe and trying to look over the wall and the bathroom roof in the direction she felt Angelo to be. Tony shrugged and swaggered through the gate.

'I'd better go,' Angelo said, and started off.

'We'll come back for you later,' Steve suggested.

Angelo was non committal.

'And tell your cousin,' Carlos added, 'Just wait till next time, that's all.'

Steve was not impressed. He pulled his bike away from the lamppost, mounted it and standing in order to pull up the hill, rode away, the cycle veering hard to either side with each downward pressing of his feet. Johnny took his from the wall and followed and Carlos stuffing his catty in his trunks took up the rear. They shouted to Angelo as they passed, 'See you!' and as they reached the corner and turned into the avenue, sat back in their saddles and took it easy. Guido and Seraphina appeared from around the same corner and Angelo waited for them, ushering them in before following and closing the gate behind him. Inside the yard Tony was waiting for him, puffed up, his bravado protected by the passing bubble of pride and the four corners of his home ground.

'Hey, Angel! You want to tell that friend of yours Carlos to watch out or one of these days someone's going to take him apart, you know?'

'You?' Angelo tried to slip past Tony and up the stairs.

'Well he can't go around just shooting at people like that.' Tony put one foot on the stairs directly in Angelo's path. The boy stopped and looked at his cousin for a moment, then stepped back and very quietly said, 'Well go on then, he's waiting for you. He's still outside.'

The walls of Tony's bubble stretched and weakened but still held, just. 'Don't be like that, Angel,' he said failing to keep the familiar note of pleading from his new voice.

Angelo's face stiffened and his mouth set in a rigid line. 'Don't call me that!'

The anger of most people Tony could pass off sooner or later with an excuse no matter how lame. Angelo's he never could. He was now in a depression, engendered both from reaction to the recent rush of adrenaline and the look of contempt on Angelo's face.

'Well he just wants to watch out, that's all I'm saying.'

'Then what are you waiting for? I told you, he's still out there. Go on... you scared? He's smaller than you are. I would think you could really beat him up if you wanted.'

Like anger, the sneers of most people Tony could pass off as well with an excuse no matter how lame. Angelo's he could not. His depression settled down heavily. 'What do I want to fight him for?' He protested. 'What did I ever do to him?'

'He hit you with his catty, didn't he?'

Tony sniffed. 'Yeah well...' Suddenly he brightened. 'Hey Angel!'

Angelo gripped the banister and his eyes flashed anger. 'How many times must I tell you not to call me that?'

Tony wanted to say something but he didn't know what or how. He wanted to tell this universal favourite that he was Tony's favourite too; that Tony would do anything for him, anything he cared to ask if only Angelo would be on his side just once, only once. Just put out your hand, Angelo, touch my arm, smile at me, look at me without distaste, show me one small gesture of friendship. What have I ever done that you should despise me so much? Is it my fault I am who I am? What do I have to do to buy your affection? Only tell me, Angelo, tell me. Angelo was embarrassed by the look in Tony's eyes, a look he did not recognise, or did not want to recognise. He turned his head and the light from the kitchen caught the soft baby hair of his seeding moustache. Tony's bubble did not burst: it melted, it oozed, it slid wet and soggy and soaking into the earth between them. He would have given anything to be able to say, "I love you, Angel," but that was out of the question. Boys did not use the word love to other boys no matter how they felt. It was not so much something churning in the mind as a positive ache in the belly whilst outwardly he leered, meeting aggression with aggression, defying his cousin to dislike him even more. 'Why... Angel?' He placed an arm over Angelo's shoulder and turned his face up towards him. It was almost as if he was deliberately seeking retaliation. Irritably Angelo shook him off.

'Quit it, Tony!'

'I was only being friendly.'

'Then quit being friendly.' Angelo started up the stairs. Tony followed.

'What you doing after dinner?'

Angelo wondered why he didn't just ignore this importuning, why it always seemed necessary to answer. He could just go straight on in without saying a word. His mother poked her head through the kitchen window.

'Angelo, you comin' in now, your dinner she's a get cold.' And disappeared again. Angelo paused at the top of the stairs and threw his towel over the railing.

'Why do you want to know?' he asked, fully realising Tony's motive.

'Just interested.'

'Well whatever I am doing, you won't be doing it with me. Okay?'

'You going swimming?'

'Ach, man!' Angelo could think of nothing more to say.

Seraphina and Guido who had been waiting for their brother at the top of the stairs suddenly looked interested.

'Can I come swimming? Please, can I come swimming? Please? Please?'

Angelo tousled his sister's hair and laughed. She was a water rat, once in the sea the family had to move heaven and earth to get her out again. Now she was hopping up and down, tugging at his shirt.

'No,' he said, 'I've just come back from swimming. Why do I want to go again? Anyway, it's dark now. Swimming's out.' Then, 'Yes Mama, I'm coming.' as his mother called him from the kitchen.

'About time too,' his father grunted, not looking up from his plate, cutting a meatball in half.

'When can we go then? When?' Seraphina just wasn't going to let go.

'We'll ask mama.'

'Me too, Angelo? Can I come swimming?' Angelo smiled, leaned back against the veranda railing, lifted a leg and gently prodded Guido in the stomach with his bare foot, wriggling his toes. Guido laughed. It tickled. Angelo lifted him in the air by his armpits and shook him, then put him down, turned him about face and patted him on the rump.

'No,' he said, 'didn't you hear what I just said? Go to Mama.'

Guido turned back to look up at his brother. He frowned, tightened his throat, screwed up his face and clenched his fists, preparing to cry. Angelo watched him, interested. Tony started to slowly climb the stairs then stopped, noticing the silence like a conductor's baton raised a moment before the orchestra's opening chord. Guido summoned up all his resources but the tears were not forthcoming. Maybe he had cried too much that afternoon and spent them all. He looked at his injured finger so as to invoke the memory of pain but it didn't work. He stamped his foot in frustration and bruised his heel against the hard board. For a moment he stood in shock, absorbing the impression, then the sudden start of pain opened the floodgates and the up to now reluctant tears rolled down his cheeks as he broke into a full throated roar. Mama came cavalry charging out of the house brandishing a large wooden spoon.

'Whatsa goin' on out here? 'Ow many times I gotta tell you? Now whatsa matter? Is no peace in desa 'ouse?'

The bawling had subsided to be replaced by snivelling accompanied by the occasional hiccup.

'Tony! What you do to Guido?'

Tony gaped in astonishment at his aunt. 'Hey!' He looked around for support, his hands extended in surprise before facing his aunt again, 'What're you putting the heat on me for? Why am I everybody's stool pigeon?'

Angelo winced.

'Madonna Mia! What is the boy talkin' about? Why he no speak a English?'

'I didn't do anything to Guido!'

Guido buried his head in his Mama's apron and snivelled some more. 'They're goin' swimming an' they won't take me with.'

'Who's a goin' swimmin'?' Mama demanded.

'Angelo and Tony,' came the muffled voice.

'No onsa goin' swimmin'.'

Angelo walked around his mother. 'I am,' he said with a smile, lifting his shirt to show his swimming trunks.

'Angelo, no onsa goin' swimmin'! You stay home an' do your homework.'

'Aw, Ma!' He stopped at the door.

'An' donna you argue please Angelo'.

'I haven't got any homework.'

'Why not? Whatsa matter wid your teacher she donna giva you homework? I tell Papa write her a letter.' This was a bluff. If there was one thing Ulrico loathed it was having to put pen to paper even to sign his own name. 'What she good for if she no give you homework?' Mama grumbled on. Angelo frowned and pursed his lips. The tone of Mama's voice indicated that she really was not going to brook any argument. She pushed the now silent Guido towards the door. 'Come on now,' she ordered. Angelo turned away.

'Where you goin' now?'

'To wash my hands and change,' he said. 'I was only teasing. I've been on the beach all afternoon.'

'You no go to school?'

'After school, Mama, after school.'

Mama glared at him and, deciding she had had quite enough for the moment, grabbed both Guido and Seraphina and turned to go back into the kitchen when she noticed Angelo's foot on which the blood had now congealed and dried.

'Aaiee!' She clapped a hand to her cheek. 'Now whats a 'appen to your foot?'

For the briefest moment the idea of telling his mother he had been bitten by a snake crossed Angelo's mind but he thought better of it. She was obviously in a high state of nerves and there had been quite enough hysterics for one evening. If he had told her that she would more than likely have fainted or had a heart attack on the spot.

'It's nothing, mama. I hurt myself on a bicycle, that's all. It looks worse than it is. I'll go clean it up. I've got to wash my feet anyway. I've still got sea sand sticking between my toes.'

Mama clapped her hands together and silently prayed for patience, but before she could raise any objection, Sarah appeared at the inner door and entered the kitchen. At the sound of her voice Mama turned and stared at her, startled.

'Hello, Marina,' Sarah greeted her. 'Ulrico.'

Ulrico grunted. He was mopping up the last of his tomato sauce with a hunk of bread.

'Sarah! 'Ow you come in?'

'Through the front door. How else? You think I climbed through the window?'

From her attitude of prayer, Mama clapped her hands to her temples, her mouth open in horror and marched back into the kitchen.

'I donna like people usa my fron' room!' her accent intensified in her excitement and quickened speech, the words tumbling out too fast to be concerned over niceties of enunciation, 'Who open dat door?' she screamed. 'How many times I gotta tell people? Donna use da fron' room, 'cep' for Sundays, Holy days, feast days, an' birt'days an' datsa all! All dosa feet on my linoleum! Up to milnight I'm a polishin'.'

Sarah looked suitably abashed. Mama was never still in bed later than five thirty in the morning and never after nine o'clock at night but if she said it was 'milnight' then 'milnight' it was. Who was there to say otherwise.

'I'm sorry, Marina.' Sarah apologised, all contrition but still wanted to make an excuse. 'But it's been so hot and my feet are sore...'

'You not da only one wid sore feet. I gotta sore feet. Ultrico gotta sore feet. Angelo gotta sore feet.'

'Angelo?'

'Si, Angelo. Who I have said ow many times to put on his a shoes but no, he know better than his mama an' now he hurt himself on a bicycle.'

Angelo slipped away down the stairs and into the bedroom, followed by Tony.

'Is he hurt bad?'

'Huh!'

Angelo's injury having been dispensed with Sarah returned to the question of the front door.

'... and coming in that way saved me havin' to walk all round the corner and come in the back.'

'Whassa mater wid your own front door?'

'I just thought it would be nice to pay a visit before I go next door. If you want me to go now...'

'Sit!' It is a peremptory order and Sarah sits. So does Mama, but immediately gets up again to go out on the veranda and look for her children, but Guido and Seraphina have disappeared behind the shed at the bottom of the yard. Mama sucks her teeth and shakes her head not quite sure whether she should bother with calling them again. She decides to give it one more try and leans forward to look down the yard over the veranda rail. 'Guido? Guido!' No answer. 'Bambino, you go an' wash a your han's an' face I tell you. You too, Seraphina. You gonna eat now an' then you go to bed.'

'I wanna go swimming,' came a faint voice from behind the shed,

'Me too! Me too!'

'No one's a goin' swimming? Two little peoples comin' in to eat now an' then goin' to bed. Ulrico, go fetch you kids please.'

Ulrico belched, politely holding his hand in front of his mouth, and got up from the table. 'How are you, Sarah?' He asked in passing as Sarah took off her hat and laid it on the chair next to her.

'I'm fine, Ulrico, thank you. Just fine.'

Ulrico surveyed his sister in black. 'Been to a funeral huh?' And before she could answer in never ending detail, 'Marina, is there enough food for Sarah?'

'Of course is enough. Don' I always make a plen'y?'

Ulrico went out and they heard him clatter down the stairs. Mama leant back in her chair and flopped a flat hand down upon the table top. 'Sarah... desa 'ouse... I tell you, it drive me crazy. Is like a mad 'ouse tonight. All my lovely dinner? Goombye! Back in da oven… huh! I take it out again for you in a minute. An' for da kids an' Tony. You lucky you no gotta kids I'm a tell a you.'

'Tony's eating with youse? You spoil him.'

'He likes a my cooking. But he's a no eat wid us,' she contradicted herself.

'What about his mother's cooking? Is no one eating with Nina tonight?'

'You wanna eat here? Youse welcome. Pepe will eat wid his sister, an' Tony will eat wid her.'

'That will make for a wonder of conversation. I would like to listen in to that. Quiet as the grave more than like.'

The mention of a grave brought them back to the

day's events, one of them anyway. 'Ow you keepin' Sarah? It was a nice funeral?'

'O Marina!' Sarah tapped two fingers and a stubby thumb on the tabletop. The fourth and little finger were for some reason kept clear. 'It was the most beautiful funeral you have ever seen.'

Mama jerked her head and flapped a limp wrist. 'You ain't seen mine yet. Tcha! Datsa somtink I'm a telling you!'

'Don't talk like that, Marina, God forbid!' Sarah hastily crossed herself and, just in case she had unwittingly tempted fate or committed a blasphemy, Mama thought she had better do likewise.

Pepe, having removed his jacket and shirt, comes out of the bedroom, his braces dangling, a towel thrown around his neck and a cake of soap in his hand. He goes into the bathroom looking neither to right or left and gently closes the door behind him. The two women can see the bathroom door from where they sit and watch in silence. They hear the bolt thrust home and Sarah returns her attention to the table.

'Dat man, is a time he buy a new vest,' Mama said. 'Is gotta more 'oles dan a honeycomb. Anyway, wid desa kids donna you be surprise, anytink can 'appen. All my nice dinner she's a spoil. Hey Pepe!' She went out on to the veranda. You make sure you put enough pennies in da gas!' She turned back to Sarah. 'Lot of people at da funeral, Sarah?'

'Everybody was there.' Sarah's gesture embraces the entire city. 'She had so many friends, Marina. And the flowers! I tell you. Never in your whole life have you seen such flowers. And the young priest from St Mary's read the service, the new one out from home, Firenze I think.'

'From da North,' Mama said. She wasn't exactly sure where Firenze was, but coming as she did from the heel of Italy and never having travelled except for her journey to Genoa in order to take the boat with her new husband, the situation of Italian towns was a complete mystery to her. For all she knew Palermo could have been in the north and Rome in the south.

'He has a voice as clear as a bell,' Sarah continued, 'So

beautiful, I cried, Marina.' And as though to prove her words she clapped her hands and cried again, shaking her head and rocking gently back and forth in her chair.

Mama frowned and looked under the table at the creaking legs of the bentwood chair, wondering whether she should say anything or would it be too impolite? It was not a new chair and two of its legs at a time by the sound of the creaking were hard put to carry Sarah's weight. But then, her husband, was he not a carpenter? Of course if the chair broke he could easily fix it; maybe just a little glue was all that was needed. Sarah rocked back onto all four legs and Mama, relieved, took her tea towel from her shoulder and flicked it across the table for no apparent reason; maybe just because the tension had broken. She placed her hands on her knees and heaved herself to her feet. It was not so much the weight of her body she lifted but the weight of her tiredness. She had been a small woman in her youth and in parts was still so. Her waist remained slender and her ankles. It was across her hips and belly and the tops of her thighs that the weight had settled giving her an almost ant like appearance. She touched with a fingertip beneath an eye, gently pulling down the skin's tiny wrinkles and soft folds. She pulled at her neck and then angry at the vanity of it, what did it matter what she looked like now? Gave the table another flick with her towel and said, 'What has happen to dat man?'

That man, having made his presence felt by stamping a few times and giving the side of the bedroom a kick, was now advancing slowly and silently on the children who, not too sure where he had got to, were holding on to each other and cowering with delicious fear in a corner waiting for him to pounce. Instead he stopped a little distance away and let out a throaty laugh, followed by, 'Here is the big bad giant come to gobble up naughty children ho ho ho!'

With a simultaneous shriek the two kids leapt to their feet and fled past their father, one on either side and, still screaming, ran up the yard, up the steps, and onto the veranda where they cuddled up to their aunt Sarah who just had time to rescue her hat and place it on her head out of harm's way.

Marina stood gazing over the bathroom roof. She thought of the flat landscape of her homeland; of the family she left behind. Then she thought of Ulrico and her children and the family she had here and her slightly out of focus gaze adjusted itself and concentrated on the steamed-up bathroom window. 'Pepe!' she shouted, 'What for you wanna take a bath now? You gonna eat soon! Nina got a very nice puddin' for youse.' Then she turned and shuffled back into the kitchen.

Sarah, an armful of blissful child on either side, continued as if there had been no interruption. 'And you will never guess, I saw Mrs Bertorelli. She tells me her sister has died. Shame, poor woman.' She took out her handkerchief and wiped Guido's nose.

Mama did not know whether Sarah's poor woman referred to Mrs Bertorelli or the sister. She felt the bottom of the teapot to test the heat. 'I make a youse a nice cup a tea an' then we eat. When is the funeral?' she asked.

'I don't know, Marina, I didn't think it was nice to ask about one funeral while I was at another.'

'You're not goin'?' Mama couldn't hide her surprise.

'I'll keep my eyes and ears open.'

Ulrico reappeared and resumed his seat at the table. Immediately Guido left the comfort of aunt Sarah for his father's lap though in truth he was now getting maybe a little too big for it. Seraphina, not to be outdone, joined them, though she had to be content with standing beside her father, one foot resting on top of the other, her father's arm around her waist.

Sarah unbuttoned and slipped off her special for funeral only shoes and rubbed her aching feet together, left on top of right, right on top of left. Later, before she went to bed, she would soak them in a basin of hot water and Epsom salts; give them a really good soaking. She mellowed in anticipation.

'Oh, yes, I'll be going. Of course I'll be going. Everyone will be there.'

Mama having made the tea, passed her a filled to the brim cup and Sarah, holding it gingerly, spilled some of it nevertheless and used her handkerchief to wipe up the spill.

She sipped her tea, placed her tongue beneath her lower dentures and wiggled them a little. This was followed by a deep sigh.

Mama, busy over her stove, continued the conversation from the kitchen. 'I don' know,' she said, 'all desa people dyin' off lika flies, hmn!'

Sarah wondered whether this was a reproof because of her enjoyment of funerals. Behind her handkerchief she slipped her upper teeth from her mouth and ran her tongue over her palate and the hard empty socket ridges of her gums that were hurting a little then, decorum for the birds, rinsed the set of dentures in her teacup and slipped them back in her mouth. Better. She smiled across the table at the children who were staring at her with eyes like Catherine wheels. Guido slipped from his father's lap and headed for the veranda stairs. Seraphina was quick to follow.

'Where you kids goin' now?'

There was no answer. Guido was already more than halfway down the stairs and Seraphina wasn't far behind. She stopped at the bottom and sat on the tread, watching as Guido ran down the yard and came struggling back lugging behind him a length of red rubber hosepipe with a shiny nozzle. He dropped it outside the bathroom window and trotted over to the bedroom door, lifted Pepe's chair by the arms and staggered back to the bathroom window, dropping the chair with a clump. He peeked up sideways at the veranda pretending unconcern but, deep in conversation, Mama fussing once more over her stove and Sarah enjoying her tea and stretching her toes, no one had followed them out.

Guido took up the hosepipe and climbed onto the chair, then he looked back down the yard and, lifting one hand, silently inserted the shiny nozzle through the slightly open window from which wisps of steam emanated and the sounds of soft splashing could be heard. He looked at his sister who pulled a wry face and shook her head. Guido nodded his vigorously. After some persuasion Seraphina got up and went down the yard to turn on the tap before sprinting back up the yard and standing by the gate. A moment's silence and then a great roar from the bathroom, a spluttering and banging as Pepe under the cold spray struggled from the bath. With a squeal, Guido leapt from the chair, dropping the hose, which sprayed across the yard, its jet now digging a channel in the soft earth near the wall and streaming down the centre where the earth was concrete hard from the pressure of many passing feet. Guido bolted for the street, peeping around the door as Seraphina followed him to safety. Pepe's face appeared at the window, wrapped in a cloud of steam. He slammed the window shut and a moment later they heard the bolt on the door crash back, the door was flung open and there stood Pepe, dripping wet in all his semi-naked hairy belly glory, but for the towel held loosely and rather inadequately in front of him, a trail of wet footmarks behind.

Ulrico, Mama, Aunt Sarah, rushed to peer over one veranda and Nina emerged to look over hers. Tony and Angelo were standing at the bedroom door. Pepe glared about him; they all stared back. Mama put her fingers to her mouth, turned her head away and giggled. Sarah took it up and then Tony and Angelo. Even Ulrico smiled. Only Nina shook her earrings with displeasure and tut-tutted at the disgusting sight. Pepe hastily retreated. The door slammed behind him and the spell was broken, Angelo ran to turn off the water, which had by now created a small lake and many streams down the yard's entire length resembling the Nile delta in miniature.

'Tony?'

Tony looked around the corner of the bedroom. 'Ma?'

'What've you been doing?'

'I haven't done anything! Jeez! Why does everybody blame me for everything?'

'Well come on in now, come on. Sarah?' Nina turned her attentions to her sister who she now noticed standing next door. 'It's time to eat, I've got to get back to the shop tonight. There's a wedding order to finish. What are you always at Marina's for?'

'I'm eating at Aunt Marina's tonight, she invited me.' Tony said it as fast as he could, hoping to take everyone by surprise, which is what it did.

Mama stared at him and was on the point of contradicting his presumption when she thought better of it. After all, why should the boy not eat with them if he was that eager? And there's always more than enough. She giggled again at the memory of the portly Pepe. Nina Viljoen saw the smile and the little movement of the shoulders and, as usual, misinterpreted it. She felt suddenly angry.

'What's the matter with your home?' she snapped at Tony. 'Isn't my food good enough for you? I suppose your Aunt Sarah's eating there too.'

Sarah, who was about to flop back on the porch bench, stood up again.

'No, No, I'm coming.' she took Mama's hand in passing and gave it a little squeeze. 'Thank you for the tea,' she said.

'Your shoes,' Mama said.

'Well come on then, be quick about it,' Nina complained. 'I've left Millie alone in the shop and Elsie's dress has to be finished tonight, unless of course you preferred her to get married in her petticoat.' Nina was going to say "in the nude" but propriety caught up with her and bridled her tongue in the nick of time. Angelo having turned off the tap, returned up the yard.

'You going to be late, Aunt?' he asked. 'I'll walk you home if you like.' His aunt looked at him and pursed her mouth primly, trying not to smile knowingly, then she went inside, saying nothing. Angelo took this to mean she had no objection.

'Tony, go an' fine Guido an' Seraphina for me please, an' you can come eat wid us.'

'Gee! Thanks aunt!'

'Gee! Gee! What's a matter with you boys you can't speak English?' Ulrico growled. 'No wonder you all behave like hooligans.' But Tony was already at the gate and did not hear him.

'You break a your Mama's heart da tings you do.' Mama added for good measure.

'Marina, what is the matter with children these days?' said Sarah who had not moved off the veranda although she had got to the top step still without her shoes.

Tony at the gate, shouted to the children, 'Guido! Seraphina! Your Mama wants you.'

'If we behaved like that when we was young...' Sarah broke off and perplexed they all looked in Tony's direction.

'Well it's time to eat!' he yelled.

'Do you know what happened today in the cemetery?' Sarah asked, with another sigh.

Tony turned to look at the veranda, rapping the side of his fist on the gatepost. 'They're sitting in the gutter,' he said.

'Well they gotta come sometime. They can't sit out there all night. Tell them all's okay. Ain't nobody goin' to say anything so long as they come in now.'

'Your Papa says you gotta come sometime, you can't sit out there all night,' Tony transmitted for the benefit of the vagrants.

'There were some boys sitting on the graves,' Sarah continued, 'walking all over the graves, trampling on the flower beds, turning over the glass bowls…'

Mama shook her head as though there could not possibly be anything worse than the sacrilege already related, but there was.

'Why do they do such things like that? And do you know what else! They were shooting birds with slings! Poor harmless little birds.'

'Slings?'

'Yes, you know, slings!' Sarah mimed shooting with a catapult, not very well, but Mama got the drift.

'No!'

'And they light fires behind headstones,' Sarah was becoming breathless with the drama of it all and her haste in telling, 'and cook on them… and when someone spoke to them about it... they swore!' Mama tut-tutted and looked shocked which indeed she was.

'I ask you! In the middle of a service, Marina, in the middle of a funeral! Have they no respect at all?'

Angelo, who had been standing at the bottom of the steps listening to all this said, 'Do you know who they were?'

His aunt gave him a searching look and said, 'I know.'

Angelo brushed down the trousers he had exchanged for his swimming trunks – he still hadn't washed his feet, Pepe having prevented use of the bathroom, and the salt sticky sand would have to stay or be gradually rubbed off – mounted the steps and went past them into the kitchen. When he had gone, Mama whispered, 'Friends for Angelo?'

Sarah nodded, slowly, deliberately, and with a sidelong glance at Mama calculated to make her heart palpitate with sudden anxiety, but she did not leave it at that. 'I tell you, Marina, if Angelo keeps with those boys there's going to be such trouble. He holds your heart in his hand, that boy.'

'No... Angelo's a good boy, what can I do?'

Sarah shrugged. As a spinster it was not for her to advise on the bringing up of children. 'Well,' she said, reluctantly starting down the stairs and coming back again, 'My shoes. I'd better go I suppose or Nina will start yelling.'

'Come back after dinner,' Mama said, as Angelo appearing at the door, collected Sarah's shoes and handed them to her.

'Thank you, Angelo. You're a good boy,' she said and, slipping them on unbuttoned, hobbled painfully down the stairs.

'We listen to da wireless, talk a little.' Mama shouted after her. Sarah nodded as she went. Ulrico placed a comforting hand over Mama's shoulder and led her into the house. Tony ran back from the gate, up the steps, and paused on the veranda when he saw Guido and Seraphina standing at the gate.

'Come on you two or you won't get nothing. You know what uncle Pepe's like with the tomatie sauce once he gets going.' He waited and encouraged them in with a quick bow like gesture of the arm. 'Come on come on.'

From the kitchen his uncle said, 'Hey, Tony! What's the matter with youse, man? If you want to eat with us come and eat.'

Tony shrugged and went inside. He sat down opposite Angelo in the chair Ulrico pulled out for him. Mama took the plates from the oven and set the tureens in front of Ulrico who unable to wait for the rest of the family, had already helped himself earlier to a couple of meatballs. She passed him a ladle for him to dish up.

'We gonna wait for those two or we gonna say grace?' he asked.

'Say grace,' Mama ordered. Ulrico bowed his head and clasped his hands over the table. Mama, who was too busy to sit down yet, stood by her stove, head bent, hands closed, still gripping her tea towel. Tony smiled at Angelo and Angelo for once smiled back. Mama's food was not spoilt, it smelt delicious. They suddenly realised how hungry they were and the thought of steaming filling food brought peace as Ulrico prepared to have his seconds.

Angelo lowered his head and looked at the oilcloth blue and white squares on the table. Mama lifted her eyes long enough to make sure they were all suitably composed then she said, 'All right now, Ulrico.'

At the gate, torn between their hunger and fear of Mama's wrath, the two children stood irresolute in the dark and gazed at the lighted kitchen window. Pepe came out of the bathroom and went into the bedroom. He did not see them although their shadows, cast by the street lamp, fell long and slender down the yard.

Guido's belly rumbled painfully. His face puckered up and he broke into a howl of desolate anguish. Seraphina put an arm over his shoulder and they waited for Mama to come out and fetch them, all solicitude, all forgiveness, all kindness and love.

Chapter 5

Millie footed the electric motor and concentrated hard as she guided the material through the machine. The needle jigged furiously beneath her dexterous fingers. She lifted her foot from the pedal and stretched out her hand towards a pile of sandwiches that lay in greaseproof wrapping on a bench nearby, rested her elbows on her knees, holding the triangular slices of bread in both hands and nibbled: stopped, looked at the sandwich, opened it inspected the filling. She wrinkled her nose and replaced the bitten sandwich in its packet and after carefully wiping her fingers free of any fish paste with her handkerchief, went back to her work. She could never understand why her mother always went in for fish paste sandwiches; cheap maybe, easy to spread. But then why not turkey paste? Ham paste? She shrugged. In future she would make her own before coming out. Still... she smiled, threading a needle... it was only once in a while when there were too many orders and the pressure of work left no time for meals. She licked the cotton, the hint of fish paste still on her fingers, or was it her tongue? She was aboard a trawler ploughing through swelling seas. Every so often the waves broke over the bows sending streams of white foam down the decks and into the scuppers. She was holding a line, her head thrown back, the breeze blowing her hair away from her face lifted to sky and spray. On the bridge, in the wheelhouse, the first mate in blue woollen jersey and gumboots held the wheel in his strong capable hands, held their safety in his hands as he watched her with his twinkling blue eyes. She knew he was watching her although she did not turn around. Later, below decks, he would take her in his arms and...

'Ow!' She pricked herself with the needle and that brought a momentary end to her dreaming. Mustn't work too late tonight or she would never get up in the morning in time for early Mass and Sister Ursula would have something to say about that for sure. A blob of blood appeared on her finger. She regarded it with interest for a moment before putting the finger in her mouth.

The white church stood solid and square at the top of the hill. It held so much of her childhood, so much... she remembered her confirmation, her first communion. Maybe she should have been a nun. She knew her mother would have liked that: would tell everyone she saw, friend or stranger she might meet on the tram, 'My daughter, the nun.' Visions of stained glass, of ritual and liturgy, strains of sweet music. She was in a daydream again. Now she was walking down the isle in this dress. She touched the white satin in front of her, careful to keep the pricked finger well out of the way. She supposed she really ought to fetch a plaster. What was it like? She wondered. What would he be like? It was… she caught her breath and tucked her lower lip behind her teeth then bent low over her work. After a moment's heavy silence she giggled and looked up, head on one side. Hmn! She saw her left hand, posed it on her straightened arm so as to study it, especially the fourth finger. Diamonds maybe. No, no one she knew could ever afford a diamond. Well what then? Could one have an engagement ring without diamonds? Rubies? She pulled a face. Sapphire. Emerald. Millie sighed and dropping her work, got up and went over to a sink in the corner of the room to fill an old electric kettle which she plugged into a socket on the wall. Then she went out to the lavatory to empty the teapot before returning to look for a plaster in the first aid cupboard.

The bedroom in the yard, like the yard itself, is long and narrow, its corrugated iron walls surfaced on the inside with vertical wooden slats painted a dark green, the depressing colour accentuated rather than relieved by a couple of old advertising calendars illustrated with pictures of girls, one Chinese, the calendar being a gift from Madame Chang and advertising tinned lychees, the other more provocative for a make of tyres.

In a corner furthest from the door, a triangular shelf seven feet off the floor and covered in front with an old blue cotton curtain, faded and torn in places and tacked up with upholstery pins, acts as a makeshift wardrobe. The shelf is piled high with old comics, magazines and dust. There are two windows facing the house across the yard: between them a Victorian tallboy on top of which is a mirror, a hairbrush losing some of its hairs, a comb missing some of its teeth, some metal collar studs back and front kept in an old saucer, one or two broken; a bottle of half used hair oil pungently perfumed, bright yellow in colour and bearing a label garishly printed upon which an Oriental lady surrounded by flowers is performing some strange exotic dance, obviously also a product from Mrs Chang's emporium. There are three narrow iron bedsteads with horsehair mattresses. From the ceiling centre a naked light bulb hangs, not over powerful, by whose dim light Tony on one of the beds is engrossed in a lurid comic. He lies on his side, head propped against his knuckles, his arm fast developing pins and needles unnoticed while he slowly rubs his Achilles tendon between big and second toe of his other foot. He moves only to turn over a page with a flick of the fingers, absorbed in the antics of the blood lusting, be-fanged, be-clawed monsters that howl and grimace their way across the page.

'Aaaaaaaaargh!' screams a shapely blonde with enormous half exposed melon shaped breasts, wide eyed and scantily dressed as the beast's fangs sink into the back of her neck and the blood spurts – Powee!

Outside the door, Pepe is seated in his chair, dozing, his hands over his stomach, fingers interlaced. Guido squats coolie fashion in front of him watching with intent the cigar in Pepe's mouth which, every now and again in his half asleep state, he puffs on, causing the burning tip to glow briefly for a moment like a light seen at sea in the far distance.

In the kitchen Angelo is washing the dishes. Finishing the last one he stacks it on the drainer and shakes his hands over the sink, takes up a tea towel and starts to dry. Mama smiles at his back and taking a covered bowl from the table, goes out on to the veranda to put the leftovers of the meal in the meat safe. On her way back she notices Guido. Her voice sounds tired now as though, having fed her family and her duty done, suddenly there is no longer the need to keep going. She leans a hand on the rail.

'Guido, is a time for bed now, come on.' There is no urgency in her voice, not even a plea. It is a statement of fact. Guido glances up to her and then returns to watching Pepe. For a second the old fire in Mama flickers. 'Guido, please you listen to Mama now, she's a tired! I no wanna tell you again. What you watch uncle like dat for?' There is no response, only a steady gazing straight forward. 'Guido! Already you had one spankin' tonight, you wan' some more?'

There is a cough and a splutter as Pepe suddenly leaps from his chair desperately brushing at his moustache and his shirt front. Without looking back Guido shins up the steps and into the house as Mama yells, 'Guido!' and aims yet another ineffectual swipe at him as he flashes by. Angelo appears at the kitchen door, a plate and a tea towel in his hands with Guido now peeping out from around his legs. Pepe, standing in front of his chair, looks up reproachfully and gingerly touches the corner of his mouth.

'Why don' you tell your uncle wake up? Why don' you tell him his cigar burns him? Hey? Why don't you wake him up and say, "Uncle Pepe your cigar is burning?"'

'Dat chile, he never know when he had enough.'

Mama groused. 'Why you donna tell uncle, Huh? You tink is a funny for people to be hurt? Your Mama she's a very angry.'

Guido pouts, bottom lip quivering, and runs to her for forgiveness trying to wrap his arms about her legs but she impatiently pushes him away and shakes her apron, then wipes it down with the back of her hand.

'No, donna come blubbin' to me please. Donna touch me, I don' wan'a you.' And, as she sees it coming, before he can do anything she waggles a finger at him in warning. 'I joosta tol' you, donna you cry or I give you somtink to cry for!'

Pepe was about to disappear under Nina's veranda when she turned around and saw him. 'Uncle Pepe gonna wring da chicken's neck now. You be careful uncle doesna get a hol' of your neck da tings you do.'

She followed Angelo back into the kitchen and began to put away the crockery. They did not talk. They did not look at each other. Mama yawned and rubbed her hands down her face, massaging the tiredness from her eyes, and yawned again. Ulrico had already disappeared into their bedroom to remove his boots and fall asleep on top of the double bed.

Guido addressed his invisible uncle, 'Uncle, can I watch?'

Pepe was at the chicken coop under the veranda away from Guido's view so Guido moved to the veranda's edge and stood on the bottom rail, remembering not to put his knees through the vertical bars lest they got jammed and swelled up; painful experience having proved a good teacher. He leaned over, trying to see where Pepe had got to. He could see nothing but a foot or two of earth underneath the veranda. He stepped down and lay on his belly, his head over the top step, and looked through the railings.

'Can I watch you, Uncle?' Pepe ignored him. Guido slid down another two steps. 'Can I?'

'No!'

Guido sat up and buttock bounced down another two steps, it was an interesting sensation so he bounced down another two, held the bars and peeped through, his face pressed close. 'Why not?'

'After what you just done to me you ask if you can watch me kill a coocoo? Huh! And take your head out of there! You want to get stuck?'

Guido's head jerked back. He had his knee caught once before but never his head. That idea hadn't occurred to him. He looked at the bars and pushed his hands through to measure the distance between them. It wasn't big enough for his head! Still, better not to take the chance. He bounced down the remaining steps and whined, 'I didn't do anything, uncle.'

'You let my cigar burn me, that's what you did. You think that's clever? My mouth's all sore now... Look.' Guido ran up to his uncle and peered hard at Pepe's mouth as he bent down, the top lip held up by one finger the better to show, but he couldn't see very much beneath the moustache and in the gloom although light was coming both from the houses, the boys' bedroom, and a street lamp.

He made believe he could actually see something. 'I didn't do that.' He lifted an innocent shoulder. 'The cigar did it.'

'You let the cigar do it, that's what the church calls a sin of omission.'

'Shame, poor uncle! Guido's sorry. Is it sore? I will kiss it better.'

Pepe returned to the chicken coop and opened the door. There was a stir and a low nervous clucking from the hens. A particularly nervous bird flapped down from her perch and scuttled away, the others gazed at him myopically. Guido ran over and up to the wire netting pressing himself up against it so that it bent inwards with his weight and circling his fingers through the mesh above his head.

'Supposing I kiss it better for you,' he said, 'can I watch the fowls then? Can I watch you?'

'You want to do penance now, huh? Okay okay, watch if you want.'

But the invitation was superfluous, Guido was already watching. He had no desire to go any closer being nervous of the hens as they were of him. Pepe was moving towards a hen, his hands outstretched, when Guido squinted down at a nest level with his belly and saw an egg nestling there. The clucking grew slightly louder with a hint of warning. Another bird took flight and flapped its unused wings.

'No uncle, not the black and white one.' Pepe stopped in mid-stretch and raised his eyes heavenwards.

'And why not the black and white one?' he asked.

'Cos that one's my favourite.' Guido smiled sweetly at his uncle but to no purpose as Pepe had his back to him.

'They all taste the same!' Pepe hissed, still not looking around.

'But I like that one, it's my favourite! Please, uncle, not that one!'

Pepe sighed and turned to face his nephew. 'All right then, which one?'

'That nasty old red thing... that one.' He pointed to the furthest corner of the run. Pepe turned his head to look and Guido's hand whipped around the door, into the nest and came out with the egg. Pepe turned back just as the egg disappeared behind Guido's back. 'But that one's Seraphina's favourite,' he objected, 'I know that. She told me so.'

'That's all right, she's not here, wring its neck.' Pepe's eyes opened wide in disbelief as he stared at the child .

'What's Seraphina done to you you want to do a thing like that to her?' he asked.

Guido shook his head. 'It's a nasty old fowl, uncle,' he justified himself. 'It's always pecking at mine. Look, mine's got no feathers on its neck at all. Go on, catch that old red thing of Pina's.'

Pepe thought for a moment scratching the side of his head. Guido pulled at the crotch of his trousers, bending his knees slightly in order to ease where they were pinching and waited for his uncle's decision.

'I tell you what we do, this time we kill two white ones and next time we kill yours and Seraphina's both together. That's fair, Huh?'

'Oh, all right then, kill the white ones.' Guido did not hide his disappointment but he did not sulk for long.

Pepe reached out quickly and grabbed two birds. There was a raucous squawking, a frenzied beating of wings and commotion in the hen house. Guido screamed and shuffled backwards his eyes wide in excited terror, one hand like a fast moving metronome, though horizontal, jigging in front of his face. He backed away to an even safer distance and stared fascinated as Pepe came out of the run, took each bird by the neck and violently and expertly twisted both their bodies in the air, snapping their necks. Then he stuffed the carcasses in the rubbish bin and walked back to his chair. Guido was now hopping up and down in agitation, his hand on his crotch, pulling at his little peepee to ease the tension. He ran up to the bin and looked at it, then at Pepe seated once more in the chair and now, by the light from the open bedroom door, looking at his brochure.

'Will they jump out if I open the lid?'

Pepe grunted.

'Will they run around the yard if I let them out?'

Pepe grunted again. Guido ran to his chair, his face very close to the man's, eyes alight, his voice harsh through his breath. 'Are they dead? Why will they jump out and run around the yard if they're dead?'

Guido galloped back to the bin still carefully holding his egg, transferring it from back to front so that Pepe would not see it although Pepe was taking no notice of him whatsoever. He placed a tremulous hand on the lid and held it there flat. He looked at Pepe. All was quiet. He bent down and put his ear against the bin, listening. Not a sound. He lifted the lid a fraction and tried to peep inside but his courage was no wider than one of his fingers and it was an impossibility. The lid lifted an inch but inside there was only blackness and silence and the stench of rotting vegetables. He gave the lid a push and then tried to grab it as it slipped but one hand was not enough. It fell to the yard with a clatter and rolled under the steps. Guido squealed and fled back to Pepe, transferring his egg from front to back. He took hold of Pepe's arm and pulled it.

'Uncle! Its eyes are open and it's making a noise like

this!' Guido crossed he eyes and made a muted gargling noise somewhere in the back of his throat... 'and flapping its wings!'

'Guido, go to bed now, I'm tired.'

But Guido did not go to bed. He ran down the yard and back again yelling, 'Uncle's killed a coocoo, two coocoos, and they look like this!' He rushed into the bedroom and up to Tony still engrossed in his comic, the shapely blonde having been brought back to life as a zombie by the brilliant twisted scientist who wore a surgeon's gown, whose head was shaped like an egg and who wore jam jar bottom glasses that magnified his mad eyes to three times their normal size and who had made and controlled the monster.

'Tony, come and see.' He caught hold of his cousin's arm and pulled. Tony pulled back, hard.

'What's the matter with you?' he snarled.

'Come and see the fowls! Come and see what they're doing! Like this.' He repeated his performance for Tony's benefit.

'Oh shove off!' Tony pushed him away with his foot.

'Don't you want to see?'

'No!'

For a moment Guido stood beside the bed looking at his cousin. He could not see his face, only the top of his head bent low. Tony turned a page. Guido advanced and leaned over to take a look too. 'What's happening?' he asked. There was no response. 'Tony?' Still no response. Tony tightened his mouth. 'Is that woman going to kill that man? Why Tony? What's she want to kill him for?'

'Look will you push off? Stop breathing down my neck!' He grabbed Guido by the wrist and pulled him into a convenient position to push him away, harder this time so that the boy staggered two or three steps back and stood frowning.

'Go on,' Tony ordered, 'On your camel! On your bike!'

Guido pulled a face and went. At Angelo's bed he paused, turned to look at Tony who was once more ignoring him, slipped the egg beneath the bedclothes and went out.

The three boys came racing down the hill, stood up in

their saddles and jerked the handlebars to lift the front wheels over the kerb, and braked to a skidding jarring halt. There was no sign of Angelo.

'Man, what's keeping that guy?' Steve said. The gate being closed he climbed onto the bar and held the top of the wall with both his hands so as to peer over. In the yard all was silent, only Pepe now dozing peacefully in his chair, his brochure having fallen to the ground.

'Can you see him?'

Steve jumped down backwards, caught the bike before it fell, and leaned it against the wall. He shook his head.

'Give him a yell,' Carlos suggested.

'Yeah? You remember what happened last time we gave him a yell? His ma came out with a bloody broomstick.'

Carlos laughed. 'Whistle then,' he said and immediately adopting his own suggestion placed a little finger in each corner of his mouth and gave vent to a short ear-splitting blast.

'Johnny, go get some drinks from Madame Chang,' Steve ordered.

Johnny kicked an empty bottle lying in the gutter, sending it rolling noisily downhill until its mouth hit the side of the kerb and it swerved sharply on its shoulder, coming to an abrupt halt. 'I went last time,' he muttered.

'So what? Go again.'

Angelo appeared at the gate, looked back at the house to see if anyone was about, then slipped out.

'About fucking time too! Where the hell have you been?' Steve demanded irritably and then, without waiting for an answer, jerked his bike away from the wall and flung a leg over the saddle.

'They made me wash up after dinner,' Angelo whispered as though Mama were behind his shoulder and would overhear if he spoke out loud.

Johnny and Carlos mounted their bicycles as Steve said, 'Come on let's get going.'

'You go on, I'll catch you up.'

Carlos shook his head, thinking of all the time they

had wasted waiting for him. 'What they gonna make you do now?' he asked sarcastically.

'No, I'm going to help my aunt carry things up to her shop.'

Angelo said it as matter of factly as he could, he did not want any snide comments, but the boys looked at each other and laughed and there was no mistaking the tone of their laughter. He should never have mentioned her in the first place. He might have known they were never to be trusted. It was Johnny he told. He thought Johnny might understand instead of which Johnny immediately confided in Carlos who in turn told Steve.

'Hey, what d'ya know? Angelo's sweet on that bit of skirt who works in his aunt's shop?'

'Which one's that?'

'You know! We've seen her walking about, skinny thing with plaits.'

'Oh yeah, I remember.'

'Well Angie's sweet on her.'

'Angie's sweet on her. Big joke.'

'Well, that's the last we'll see of you then, isn't it?' Johnny said and Carlos chipped in, 'It's time you had that bint and got done with it, man. Come on, let's go.'

'I'll catch you up!' Angelo shouted as they pulled violently away, bucking their machines off the kerb.

'Get stuffed!' was the reply.

Angelo stood a while watching them until they disappeared down the hill and around the corner. He was annoyed. Why should he care what they said about it? Nothing to do with them anyway. But still he was annoyed. He looked at the empty corner around which the boys had disappeared, trying to sort out the confusion of thought and feeling. A dog trotted across the road, it's back arched with malnutrition. It lifted a leg against the lamp post and urinated, watching Angelo all the time, then it sniffed the post and rubbed its paws on the pavement. 'You're supposed to sniff first,' Angelo said. The dog moved up to him, interested. He looked at it for a moment. It wagged its tail, its eyes now beseeching. He could see the patches of mange down its spine and around its neck. The dog held its head on one side and pricked up its ears, the insides of which were encrusted with tiny red ticks, hard as nails. Angelo made a sudden movement and with a howl of surprise the animal stuck its tail between its legs and fled. 'Silly bastard! I didn't even touch you.' He went back to the gate, opened it and entered the yard, closed the gate behind him and walked over to the bedroom. On the way he passed Guido absorbed with something he had discovered beneath the steps.

'Guido, Mama wants you.' He said it quietly without really looking in Guido's direction or waiting to see whether his brother had heard and was taking any notice. Tony looked up from his comic as his cousin entered the room. He smiled but Angelo ignored him and stopping in front of the tallboy, bent his legs slightly to look into the mirror, took up the comb and ran it through his hair, his flat hand following each movement of the comb.

'You might have helped with the washing up you lazy bastard, seeing as you ate with us.'

Tony stopped smiling and returned to his comic.

'Nobody asked me,' he said.

Angelo, his hair sleekly combed and patted to his satisfaction, threw himself onto his bed and immediately stiffened, raised himself sideways on one arm and slipped the other hand beneath the covers. It came out swiftly with a jerk of reflex action. His heart was thumping at the sudden contact with something unknown. He looked at his hand. The palm was yellow and sticky, fragments of broken eggshell clinging to the skin while from his fingers a glutinous dribble of albumen slobbered back onto the sheet. His lip curled in distaste. He looked swiftly across at Tony who had not moved.

'I suppose you think that's funny, you dirty...'

Tony looked up. It took a moment for him to focus from reading to medium distance, especially in the dim light, and then he saw Angelo's egg covered fingers and laughed. It was the laughter of genuine astonishment but Angelo took it to mean otherwise. More than likely he wanted to take it as otherwise. He was still smarting under the memory of the boys' reaction to his aspirations in the field of young love. Tony was laughing because the practical joke had been a success and Angelo did not like such practical jokes played on him. He leaped off his bed, bounded across the room and threw himself on top of Tony who saw him coming and lifted his knees to ward off the attack, at the same time rolling on his back. But the furious Angelo pushed the knees away towards the wall and holding Tony's body down with the weight of his own, he rubbed the remains of the egg across his cousin's face. Tony yelled and turned his head first this way and then that in a frantic effort to avoid the mauling fingers, trying to hold Angelo off by grabbing his wrists. They rolled to the floor and Angelo, still on top, pummelled Tony who, still playing the game and not realising how angry Angelo was, laughed and squirmed beneath him and the more he squirmed and laughed, enjoying the joke, the angrier Angelo became. He was trembling violently both with exertion and anger held released and his breath was hot in his throat. He tried to rub the last vestiges of egg off his hand in Tony's hair realising his mistake only after the impulse had been satisfied. His hands came away thickly covered now in scented hair oil. Angelo relaxed and Tony, seeing his chance, made a grab for the genitals, a thing a boy might do in a tight spot.

Now Angelo's temper exploded. He lashed out with his fist. Tony, showing sudden alarm, lifted an arm to protect his face. He tried to say something, to tell Angelo he was sorry, that he wasn't responsible, he had had enough, but Angelo's fingers groped their way around his neck and Tony's alarm intensified into panic. He grabbed Angelo's hands and tried to pull them away. There was no sound except heavy breathing and Tony's frightened gasps as Angelo's fingers tightened. He managed to prize the choking fingers apart and screamed once, quickly, before they tightened again. Angelo's beauty fled like a timid deer in panic before the terror of a forest fire. There was no thought, only this wild young animal whose hands seemed to have taken on a life of their own; the zombie killed and reanimated only to hurt, to inflict pain, to mindlessly destroy.

Pepe popped his head around the corner to see what was happening. He had not taken much notice up to now, hearing the laughing and squealing, but his sudden sharp scream from Tony was an urgent signal not to be ignored. He pushed himself out of his chair and rushed into the room, his old legs finding new energy in the emergency. He knew how quickly a boy's playing around begun in jest can end in deadly earnest, in anger and sudden, for no apparent reason, murderous tempers. Taking hold of Angelo beneath the armpits he hauled the now crying boy to his feet and Angelo, still holding fast, dragged the half throttled Tony with him until Pepe tore open his grip and Tony fell back to the floor to lie there whimpering. Pepe gave Angelo a shove in the chest that sent him flying across the room to land on his bed and snapped him back to sanity, and then he knelt beside Tony who now had half risen and was sitting on the floor fingering his tender neck.

'What's goin' on here?' Pepe said. 'Are youse both mad? What you playing at, Angelo? You want to kill your cousin?'

He was thinking of the time he was in the North seas, shanghaied out of the Port of London and freezing to death in the tiny ship ill equipped to sail those icy waters. His fingers were wracked with frostbite so that he wanted to scream in agony, hugging them beneath his armpits, his face contorted with pain. "Rub snow on them," the mate said. For one horrified second Pepe stared at the man. Could he joke about a thing like this? By the time the crew had pulled the maddened Pepe away and explained that it was not a joke but fact, the mate had been in a worse state than Tony at this moment who still couldn't find his voice to say anything.

'What's the matter with you two? You always goin' on at each other? Hey? What's the matter wid youse?' There was no response, 'Why don't you lay off the arguin' and fightin' all the time?'

'He put a raw egg in my bed!' Angelo thrust out his hand towards Pepe, his fingers stretched wide, to show a mess of hair oil and egg. 'Look at the mess it's made.' He jumped off the bed and threw back the covers to reveal the sodden yellow patch.

'I never put it there,' Tony retorted between gasps. The fright had disappeared but he was determined to play it out for all it was worth.

'Well who did then?'

'Hmn! Was Pepe's only reaction when he realised who the culprit was. The boys both turned to look at him but Pepe wasn't going to say anything so Tony crawled to his feet, wiped himself down, and the tears from his eyes with the back of his hand. 'How do I know?' He whined in answer to Angelo's question. 'Blame the right person next time. Guido must have done it. He was in here just now.' He sniffed hard, screwing his mouth sideways to do so.

'That's right,' it was Angelo's turn to sneer, 'Put the blame on Guido.'

'Tch! That boy!' Pepe sucked his teeth. 'He hasn't played enough tricks for one night? Now come on Angelo, shake hands with Tony and say sorry to your cousin.'

'How do I know...?'

'Say sorry or I'll clip you one!' Pepe erupted into a sudden anger that startled them both. They had never seen him like that before. His large knotted hands held a menace that neither was prepared to face up to. Angelo grudgingly held out his hand and mumbled with obvious reluctance, 'Sorry.' Tony hesitated.

'Shake hands,' Pepe ordered.

'Agh! What do I want to shake hands with him for?'

'Tony, you do like I tell you or you get a clip too, now come on.'

Tony nodded his head and sneered, stretched out his hand and briefly touched Angelo's fingertips then grimaced and looked down at the egg transferred from one hand to the other. 'Ooooer!' he said and looked about for a towel but Pepe snatched it up before he could get to it. 'You both go wash in the bathroom now,' he said, 'And don't dirty up the towels.' Angelo turned and stalked away followed by a subdued Tony.

'And no more fightin'!' Pepe yelled after them. He bent down and picked up the comic where it had fallen. It was ripped to pieces.

Angelo pushed open the bathroom door with his shoulder, both hands being egg bound, and it was left to Tony to turn on the tap over the bath. He tried the geyser first to see if Pepe had left any hot water but it ran cold. Tony stepped back and Angelo leaned over the bath and washed his hands. Tony sat on the side and watched until he finished. Angelo did not look at him, merely picked up a towel, wiped his hands, and left. Tony turned off the tap, rubbed his hands on the towel, rubbed the mess off the tap, rubbed his face, neck, and hair and left the towel lying on the floor. He had no taste for cold water. He found Angelo standing in his shirt tails in front of the chest of drawers, pulling on a pair of trunks. 'You going swimming?' He tried to keep his voice as calm and devoid of emotion as possible but the tremble was still there.

Angelo wondered why he had asked such a stupid question. 'What's it look like?' he said, obviously still upset, though not enough to be more than verbally nasty. 'I said I was, didn't I?' He pulled on his shorts over his trunks and picked up the comb to run it through his hair once more. Tony bent down and picked up the torn comic, surveyed it ruefully before looking back at Angelo. 'With the others?'

Angelo nodded, looking at himself in the mirror, then he manoeuvred himself into a position where he could see Tony's reflection. 'You want to come?'

Tony stared into the mirror showing his surprise. He could see the back of Angelo's head and Angelo's reflection in the mirror, and behind it, his own and the look on his face. He turned away to think, wondering what could lie behind this new move. He would have liked very much to go swimming with Angelo, even with a crowd, but not that particular crowd. He had visions of being set upon in the water, of being well and truly dumped. He shook his head.

'Why not?' Angelo queried the gesture. 'Just now you wanted to.'

'Changed my mind.' He sat on his bed, regarding the

torn comic in his hand.

'Why?' Angelo persisted knowing full well there would be no acceptance on Tony's part. He returned to his combing. 'Come with, man, the water will be really warm tonight.'

'You're not asking me because you want me to come.' He tossed the comic on the bed.

Angelo turned to look directly at his cousin and tapped the comb against his palm. Tony avoided his gaze by fiddling with the comic's torn pages and Angelo turned back to the tallboy, threw down the comb and said, 'Okay, don't come. It doesn't matter.' He crossed the room and sat on his own bed, carefully avoiding the remains of the egg, found he only had one sock and returned to the tallboy for its companion before going back to sit on the bed again. He dusted off the soles of his feet with his hand; there were still a few grains of sand between his toes, before putting on his socks, speaking as he did so. 'Only don't say I never ask you.'

'Yeah, all right, so you asked me. You'll hold that over my head long enough. '

Angelo smiled. He pulled the khaki socks up over his knees and carefully folded the tops down, the right height to show off his calf.

'Give us a fag, Angel?'

Angelo, intent on the neatness of his stocking tops grunted, 'No, it's time you bought your own,' he said, 'You're always scrounging, cadging, you're the biggest bum I know, and that's a fact?' He put his knees together to make sure the stocking tops were level and approved his handiwork.

Tony, having picked up and still holding the torn comic, scratched his cheek with the knuckles of his other hand. 'Why don't you like me, Angel? Why don't you like me going around with you?'

'Dogs carry fleas... doesn't mean to say they like it.' He suddenly remembered the mongrel outside, how frightened it was, and the way it stuck its tail between its skinny hind legs as it ran off howling and yelping in terror. He smiled and leaned forward to look beneath the bed for his shoes.

'Very funny,' Tony sneered. 'You're always glad to have me around when someone's got to take the rap for things you do.'

Angelo sat up, his face flushed for a moment from putting his head between his knees. Eyes opened wide in pretend astonishment, he made out to be speechless with wonder. 'What are you talking about? What have I ever done that you've had to take the rap for?'

'I'm always being blamed; you know that, for every lousy thing you do.'

'Crap!' Angelo found one shoe and then went down on his knees beside the bed to look for the other. It had been kicked back against the wall. He stretched under the bed and hooked it out with the shoe in his hand.

'Well you wait, you wait. You're everybody's little angel, aren't you? You can't do a thing wrong, can you? Everybody loves Angelo. The whole world loves Angelo!'

Angelo was putting on his shoes. 'Look, I said I was sorry about hitting you. I'm sorry. I didn't mean to lose my rag. I don't like hurting people.'

Tony guffawed in derision. 'No? Pull the other one.'

'No! I just don't know why you had to be my cousin, that's all.' Having got the shoes on he stood up and polished them on the counterpane.

'Because my father married your father's sister, that's why.'

'Well someone made a balls up then, didn't they?'

'One of these days you're going to be sorry, Angel.' Tony wandered away. 'One day you're going to be in dead trouble and I'm not going to be around. Who're you going to put the blame on then?'

Angelo took a clean handkerchief from the top drawer of the tallboy and had another glance at himself in the mirror. 'You going to drop dead?' he asked.

'No, but you might.'

Angelo laughed and turned around. The laugh stopped, abruptly, as it had begun. He stared at Tony who stood a few feet in front of him, in his hand a black automatic pistol, its muzzle pointed at Angelo's stomach. The torn comic had been dropped on the floor. For a moment Angelo was unable to think, his mind unable to settle on one aspect of this completely new situation in which he found himself. The gun could be real and loaded and if so... or maybe a model... maybe real but unloaded... stolen?... what for?... why?... intentions?... Tony thinking of... what?... why?... surprise... uncertainty. He laughed. 'Hey!' he said, continuing the laugh as he spoke but it was not convincing 'Where did you get that from?' The laughter hid the feeling of anxiety that flickered nebulously in the region of his groin. With this baboon cousin of his one knew only that he was a lout, a nuisance, a cadge and would one day be in a whole lot of trouble. There was absolutely no doubt about that. Despite having grown up in close proximity to each other anything beyond that was pure guesswork. Was there no redeeming feature at all? Surely not. If there was, Angelo wasn't going to bother looking for it.

'Never you mind.' Tony lifted the gun to eye level and squinted down the barrel, pointing it at a spot in the centre of Angelo's forehead, and then he lowered it and tapped the barrel against the palm of his hand. He smiled his crooked smile.

'Did I frighten you, Angel?'

'Is it loaded?'

'Is it loaded?' Tony loaded his voice with sarcasm reserved for addressing idiots. 'Of course it's fucking loaded. What do you think?' The tone of this implied that a gun with an empty chamber was as useless as the questioner's empty head.

Angelo rose to it and was duly irritated. He took a step forward, holding out his hand. 'Let me see.'

But Tony held the gun up and slightly behind him and shook his head. 'Uhuh!'

Angelo felt the irritation rising further. 'What do you think I'm going to do with it?' He all but snarled at Tony, 'Eat it? I only want to take a look.'

Tony whipped the gun into its original position and his knuckle whitened against the trigger. Angelo started visibly.

Tony laughed. 'Safety catch is on,' he said, 'look.' He angled the barrel and flicked the catch with his thumb then flicked it on again. 'Did I scare you, Angel?'

'Put that thing down.' Angelo was now angry and shaken.

'Never seen you so scared before.' Tony played out the scene in great detail, a montage of impressions left by years of gangster films.

'Tony! Put that gun down!'

'Why?'

'Because you great big stupid baboon you're a real thicky! You know that? Why don't you shove it up your arse or look down the barrel and blow your brains out?'

'Don't talk like that, Angelo! Don't say things like that?' Tony lowered the gun and went over to his bed.

'Where did you get it from?' Angelo asked.

'Dettman asked me to keep it for him.'

'I might have known. I might have known. Where did he nick it?'

'Who said he nicked it?'

'His name's Dettman, isn't it? You ever know of him to come across anything honestly? He stole the milk he drank when he was in the cradle!'

Tony stood scowling at the weapon in his hand, and then lifted a corner of his pillow and slipped the gun beneath it. He crossed over to the tallboy and opening one of the drawers began to rummage in it. 'Maybe Uncle Pepe's got a cigar in here,' he said.

'Yeah, you know what happened the last time you tried to smoke one of Uncle Pepe's cigars.'

'I puked my guts out! It won't happen again.'

'Famous last words. Why shouldn't it happen again?' Angelo closed his eyes. It might for a moment obliterate the sight of his cousin going through Pepe's drawer. It could not obliterate the memory of his voice, or the picture of him that remained fixed in his mind's eye, a negative image waiting only for the eyes to open once again, to become a print in full natural colour. Angelo didn't hate his cousin. Hate was not in his nature, but he was embarrassed by him, irritated by him, especially among his peers. Angelo hurried from the room.

Nick's Milk Bar is modern. Nick's Milk Bar is vulgar, loud in every sense. It consists of a long narrow room with a high ceiling from which electric fans and a witch ball rotate continuously. It is all bright lights, mirrors, rexine and chromium plate. Nick's Milk Bar is garish. Nick's Milk Bar is artificially glad. A counter runs down one side of the room, its top interrupted at intervals with milkshake mixers, with glass display cabinets, with containers and placards and typed menu cards. In front of the counter are half a dozen tall swivelling bar stools. The other side is taken up by boxed tables side by side and back to back at which Nick's customers varying in age between early teens and early twenties, sit and sip, suck and nibble and munch their assorted nectars: banana splits, sundaes, strawberry milkshakes, pineapple, orange and raspberry; various ices, cokes and juices. Nick's delicacies appeal to the taste buds not the digestion. In some of his youthful customers the body shows obvious signs of hormonal changes and complaining, from the mouth to the stomach and out again via acne. The condition of the skin is not improved by the garish lights that throw strange hues of blue and pink across their already unhealthy pallor.

Outside the door a group of youths lounge in the manner of youths with a sense of self-importance and too much time on their hands. Slouched, hands in pockets, they chew gum and their talk is really of nothing. Every now and again, one will look inside the café, or up the street, or down it, as though at any moment something, who knows what? Is bound to happen to relieve the monotony of their immediate existence.

In the café itself, the customers at least have the jukebox to fill in the vacant spaces, or to make them shout above its blare, giving their conversation some measure of importance. It sits at the end of the room, its voice dividing the room in two, like some out of space monster, all colour and flashing light; a robot of noise and gaudy design, it's plastic belly showing the mechanics of selection, of discs, and moving chains.

Mama shook Ulrico awake.

'Whassa matter?' he grumbled, still half asleep.

'Come on a veranda,' Mama said, 'We got a visitor.'

'At this time of night?'

'Is a not late,' she parried. 'Come along now, Ulrico. He's a waitin' for you? I put on da kettle.'

Mama waited until Ulrico stretched and yawned to show he was awake. He scratched his chest and rolled his legs off the bed to sit up. 'Make yourself look nice,' she said, smoothing his hair with her hand. 'Comb you hair. Put on you shoes, not slippers.'

'Who've we got?' he asked, 'the Lord Mayor himself?'

'More important. He's a da new young priest come to visit us. You come an' talk to him now.'

Ulrico nodded and yawned again. He wasn't as keen on priests as was his wife and his sister. He would much rather have gone back to sleep or not be woken in the first place. He kicked his shoes into a convenient position and fumbled in putting them on, his fingers kitten weak from sleep. Mama went to the kitchen to put on the kettle. On the veranda she could see the dark head of the young priest and his hand, white on the scrubbed table. She thought she really should have seated him in the front room but it was too late now. Or was it? It was a dithering moment. There was no light on the veranda, the illumination came streaming through the kitchen window and from the street. She went to the door and smiled shyly. 'He's a not long now, father. Joost a comin'.'

Father Joseph turned his handsome head and smiled at her. 'There is no hurry, Mrs Lerici. Perhaps I called at a bad time?'

'No no no!' she insisted. 'Ees early yet. Joost he was tired comin' home from work, you know?' What she couldn't understand was how a young man just out from home spoke such immaculate English. She pondered over this back in the kitchen as she set out three cups and saucers on the table. After wrestling with the problem in vain she could stand it no longer. She went back to the door and said, 'Father, you excuse me askin' you this please, 'ow you talk such a good English?'

He smiled again, again turning that sleek head to face her. His smile was gentle as benefited a man of the cloth. His skin was smooth, pale, no sign of a beard. His eyes were a deep blue, probably because he came from the North. 'Do I? I am so glad.' His English was that of a scholar. Father Joseph had learnt and learnt well, as he did in all matters practical. It was in matters of the human soul, of life and experience that he was still too young to walk without stumbling. Mama, her question unanswered turned back to her stove, deciding not to pursue it. Father Joseph fingered the black homburg on his knees and got up to move to the railing and stood gazing over the rooftops and, in places, the twinkling lights of the city. He wondered how much good he would do in Africa. He could hope, he could pray, he could work hard, but how much actual good. He thrust out his lower lip and swallowed. "Seeing he giveth to all, life and breath, and all things; and hath made of one blood all nations of men for to dwell on all the face of the earth… For in him we live, and move, and have our being."

He turned back again when he heard Ulrico's voice.

He came around the corner at a brisk pace that slowed when he saw the boys lounging outside the café. Too late, they had seen him. He had come briskly around the corner to dislocate the monotony of their evening, his black skin an abrasive against which their prejudice could grind, in which their boredom could discover a brief outlet. Had he sensed their presence he would have chosen another route or at least have crossed the road. Now it was too late, there was nothing for it but to continue his advance, hoping against hope they would ignore him, let him pass. He knew their temper. He saw their heads turn and he inwardly braced himself, preparing to suffer pain if that was how it was meant to be. He was level with them when the first one spoke, no louder than a mutter he could pretend not to hear.

'Hey! Midnight!'

There was a soft all round chuckle and a body suddenly sidestepped to block off his path. He stopped.

'What's the hurry, Kaffir?'

He looked up at the white face in front of him. A voice from behind whispered, 'Haven't you got respect for a white man?' He did not dare look over his shoulder, but gazed straight ahead and tried to pass. The sidestepper sidestepped again. 'Didn't you hear what I said?' he lifted a lazy hand and gave the youth a not very definite shove in the chest. 'What's the matter, skolly?'

The white face smiled. 'You're not scared of us, are you? Huh?'

His mouth was dry. He ran his tongue over his lips. 'Let me go please, baas.' He could feel them all around him now, only waiting. The sidestepper stepped aside and put out a hand in the direction the youth was going. 'But no one is stopping you,' he said with charm and a slight bow, but the black youth did not move: he stood still, uncertain. To stand still was dangerous: to move was dangerous. A foot could trip him. A fist could punch. He turned and looked appealingly at the smiling charming face. It was close enough for him in a moment to register the details, the blonde hair, the blue eyes, the colour of the lips and the tips of the teeth showing through the smile; the creases in the neck. He could see the face but he could not see what lay behind it, there was only the smile and the threat, and behind him, the others watching – all smiling. He moved and immediately the sidestepper was in front of him again.

'Why do you look like that, skolly?'

The black boy, so careful up to now to allow no flicker of expression cross his face, scowled. He scowled at the futility of his position and the sense that there was no escape. His silence he knew would not satisfy them.

'Don't look at me like that, you cheeky bastard!'

His fear taking a definite form, overcoming his caution,

the youth stepped back and in an attempt at appeasement said, 'How am I looking at you, Baas?' Perhaps if he showed his fear, perhaps if he debased himself, if he made out he was much worse than they, if he lay on his back like a dog and pissed himself, if he could buy them off by giving them what they wanted, a proof of their superiority, of their importance. Perhaps...

Sidestepper gave him another shove, this time hard and definite. 'And you don't answer back! Did no one ever tell you that?'

The shove thrust him against the second boy who turned the youth around and grabbed him by the shirt. 'Who're you pushing, kaffir?' He gave a little shake and the shirt, which was old and frayed, tore beneath the collar. 'Hey? What's your name, skolly boy?'

'Gabriel, sir.'

'Gabriel? What kind of a name is that?' He gave another little shake and the tear lengthened. 'That's a white man's name, skolly. That name's in the Bible, didn't you know? Hey? You didn't ought to have a white man's name. Why don't you have a good Bantu name like a good kaffir?'

Gabriel wanted to lift his hands and remove the white boy's from off his shirt, to tell them he was a good Christian, but he did not dare. To lift a finger in self-protection meant instantaneous and certain attack from all sides. His young tormentor pulled violently. The shirt ripped from collar to halfway down the front and Gabriel staggered as, caught off balance, he was given a push into the third boy who, in turn, shoved him hard against a fourth, a boy who looked like a man and thought like a child. Gabriel opened his mouth to plead again, leave me alone, when a set of stony knuckles jarred into his stomach. His muscles tensed automatically and he doubled up, gasping for breath. The man-boy grinned idiotically. Gabriel did not feel the blow that split his lip. He only knew that suddenly he could no longer see very clearly and there was the iron taste of blood in his mouth. They were all pushing him now, one to the other.

'Why don't you fight, skolly?'

'Please...' He found he couldn't speak properly. The words were slurred; they dribbled from between his lips. He ran his tongue over the cut, tasting the sourness of it. A tooth was loose, it jolted in its socket and the sudden spasm of pain brought him back into focus. 'Please, Baas! Let me go, Baas!'

'Fight, skolly!'

'Fight!'

They moved into the attack, first one and then the other. He must not hit back. Whatever happens he must not hit back! He tried to shield his head from the blows and backed against the wall so they could only come at him from one side. He was pulled away and kicked. He felt the ache at the base of his spine and bent his head low beneath his arms. He must not hit back! He must not hit back!

'But, Father,' Ulrico pleaded, 'What does a man do? I've tried...'

He stopped and looked up for a moment as Mama placed a cup of tea in front of their guest. He thanked her and pulled the cup towards him, taking up the teaspoon to stir it while Ulrico went on talking. Mama placed a second cup in front of Ulrico who had hardly paused in his speech.

'The best I know to bring up my kids. Now look what happens. Tonight his Mama tell him not to go out. You close your eyes an' Pouf! He's gone.'

'Wid dose dreadful boys again!' Mama interjected, hovering behind the table. 'I don' know why he go out wid dose dreadful boys. One day he break a his Mama's heart.' She said this as though it were a matter of fact, not mere speculation, as though she had already brought herself to face and accept it.

'Are they really as bad as you make out, Mrs Lerici?'

'Maybe... Maybe not.' She sniffed and thought it over. 'He's a good boy, Angelo,' then qualified it, 'Most times!'

Father Joseph smiled, his gentle man of the cloth smile. 'Perhaps it is only understanding that is needed after all,' and was angry with himself for the unctuous tone that had unwittingly crept into his voice. He told himself a hundred times a day: he would not be unctuous, he would not be pompous, he would not be other worldly; but it was so very difficult to maintain a balance. Too far on the other side the seesaw came down with a bump and one sounded insincere, even flippant.

'You think I don't understand my own kid?' Ulrico's tone was indignant.

'Papa...' Marina smiled, her head on one side gently admonishing him, trying to soothe him. The young priest thought quickly. He did not want to give offence.

'If I don't understand him, who understands him?' Ulrico argued, his tone still aggressive for all Mama's gentle caution. 'I'm his father, he should listen to me, do what I tell him. Isn't that right? Are children not supposed to have respect for their parents?'

Mama intervened sweetly, 'Did I put enough sugar, Father?'

Father Joseph transferred his attention from Ulrico to her and once again that gentle smile flickered across his face. 'Thank you, yes,' he said although he had not as yet tasted his tea.

'More likely he don't understand me.' Ulrico was still going on, his arms folded on top of the table, staring sourly into his cup. He picked up his spoon and stirred. It was hard to be a parent. Father Joseph sipped his over sugared tea and tried to look as though he enjoyed its honeysweet flavour. He was a savoury man by choice. 'Would you like me to talk to him?' he asked. Ulrico looked up.

'He's a not a bad boy in his heart, Father. He joos dosna tink too much.' Mama felt the need to protect her son.

'Has it not occurred to you...?' Father Joseph would have cursed inwardly had he not been the man he was. He heard a note of pomposity creeping into his voice as insidiously as some fifth columnist undermining communications in war. Communication was proving difficult enough as it was without the aberration of preconceived judgement. They might be understanding his words only too well or hardly at all, how does one know? One doesn't know; one can only hazard a guess '...Mrs Lerici,' he continued, 'that he may think *too* much?' Mama looked at Papa who looked at Father Joseph and there was a pause as they endeavoured to digest this; then Ulrico snorted, chuckled, and slowly shook his head. Father Joseph was getting nowhere. He sought for words that would get through, make a good impression, a really good impression that would pave the way for next time, make it that much easier. 'Sometimes...' He jabbed a finger in Ulrico's direction that made him jump slightly. Now they both paid close attention, out of politeness if nothing else. Mama rested her hand on Ulrico's shoulder '...boys of his age, they... they *do* think a great deal, about many many things. I know. I was a boy myself once, as you were, Ulrico' (it was first name terms now) 'and there are many things to baffle them.'

'Baffle.' Mama looked at her husband. 'What is baffle?'

'Puzzle. Puzzle them. They don't have enough experience of life you see. They don't understand the changes that take place, or will take place in their bodies as they grow older.' Father Joseph wondered if he should revert to Italian rather than try and continue in English. 'Would you rather we talked in Italian?' His voice carried a note of urgency in his eagerness to get through to them.

Ulrico shook his head at the suggestion. Mama patted his shoulder, a cursory pat, the kind one gives a dog who has obeyed the order to sit. 'No. Speak in English,' he said. 'We have lived here so long, for me practically all my life, for Marina ever since we got married and all of us have used English for a long time. Only Nina, I think, still speaks some Italian because she went back there to visit one time.

'She saw the Pope you know,' Mama intervened.

'The children they don't speak it at all.'

'Such a pity,' Mama said.

'Well, all I can say is, perhaps you have not been giving him the answers he wants.'

Ulrico frowned and Mama's fingers, sensing his tension, tightened on his shoulder.

The priest knew he wasn't doing very well. 'Perhaps that is why he goes out with, as you call them, such dreadful boys and will one day break his Mama's heart. Perhaps he finds that thinking is painful and when he is with them, well... he doesn't have to think so much. Are any of the other boys Catholic?'

Neither of the Lericis knew the answer to this. If it came down to it they actually knew nothing about any of the boys except for their reputation of being dreadful, as mama put it. Father Joseph braced himself for another sip of tea, feeling the need to wet his mouth. They watched until he had replaced his cup on its saucer then Ulrico broke the silence.

'What are you saying, Father?' Mama nodded. It was a good question.

Father Joseph coughed behind his hand to cover up the pause caused by the emptiness he felt inside him. 'That I should have a little talk with him.' What else could he say?

'All right.' Ulrico leaned back in his chair and shrugged. 'You do that, Father, and you see what happens. He will listen. He will say, "Yes Father," and "No Father," then he will go away and forget all about it. He will go back to the streets and forget every word you said.'

'Perhaps.'

It was ever thus between fathers and sons.

Nick's gawping patrons gathered around the windows to see what was going on outside, those at the back standing on chairs and tables to get a better view over the shoulders of those in front. Nick came barging out from behind his counter, spilling a large ice-cream soda in doing so. 'Get off those tables!' he roared, 'and the chairs! What do you think this place is?' He grabbed at an ankle and its owner teetered precariously, arms wind milling, before coming down to earth. He tugged at a few more in passing as he rushed out on the pavement. 'What the hell is going on out here?' He bellowed, his voice bugle blasting over the yells of the punching, kicking, snarling boys. The punch-up stopped.

'Mind your own fucking business,' the man-boy growled.

Tony stepped around the corner and stood watching. He was wearing a sports jacket for stepping out and his loudest tie, a narrow knotted, broad based affair in salmon pink and green. A cream velvet soft velour fedora was pulled low over his eyes, so low he had to hold his head unnaturally high in order to see the world beyond its brim.

'You want to do any fighting,' Nick said, looking with sympathy at the bleeding trembling Gabriel crouched against the wall, 'You go some other place and do it, but not outside my place, okay?'

Sidestepper laughed and stepped a pace forward, 'You want to join in?'

'You kids...'

'Who're you calling a kid?' man-boy thrust out a chin and glared.

'You kids ought to be sick ashamed of yourselves. Why don't you pick a fight with someone who can hit back?' The third youth piped up. 'He can hit back, can't he? He's got two arms, hasn't he?'

'Oh yes, yes, it's easy for you to talk, white boy. It's easy enough for a white man to hit a black. It's not so easy the other way around and you fucking well know it.'

'Listen to the nigger lover!' Said sidestepper and they all laughed. Nick wanted to slap the grinning insulting face in front of him. He wanted to feel his palm smart and tingle with the strength of it. He wanted to see the boy flinch and the red weal start across his face, the surprise and pain in his eyes, but he controlled his rising anger. He had, after all, to think of his customers. His body could afford a beating: his business couldn't. One inch too far over the line and these louts would call practically every customer out of his joint. Those that did not come out in favour would come out in fear. Gabriel looked up and saw the boys had their backs to him, facing Nick. He caught the white man's eye and Nick nodded. Gabriel slipped away. The boys also saw the nod and turned, but too late, Gabriel broke into a sprint followed by hoots of derisive laughter.

'Next time you kids cause trouble, I'll have the police

on to you.' The derision turned from Gabriel to Nick.

'So go on, man, call the cops! We'll have that kaffir in jail for hitting a white man. There's four of us to prove he started it.' The others concurred. Nick turned on his heels and returned to his café where his patrons, already tired of the goings on outside, had returned to their seats and their own private little worlds.

Tony walked up to the group outside. 'What gives?' he said tersely.

'Hello, Viljoen!' Sidestepper greeted him, 'Man, we were just pushing him around a little, that's all, hey. We didn't hurt him... much.'

They all laughed.

Man-boy said, 'Yeah! No sweat, man.'

'What did he do?'

They stared at Tony as if he were some visitant stranger from a barbaric land ignorant of the whys and wherefores of life as lived on this pavement. "Did he have to do something? He was there, wasn't he?"

'Yeah,' said man-boy, 'getting too bloody cheeky, these kaffirs.' He nodded his head sagely.

Tony looked inside the café. 'Going in?' he asked. They all turned and looked. Nick was once more busy behind his bar.

'That shitty joint?' Man boy laughed loudly, finding no other words to voice his opinion on Nick's Milk Bar.

'Okay,' said Tony, 'See ya!' He flicked the brim of his hat, pushed open the door and entered the jazz and smoke, the smell of strawberry syrup, the hum of muted conversation with the occasional loud laugh, the neon lights, the mirror and chrome. He stood inside the door that swung too behind him and pushed his fedora to the back of his head, gazing around him, slit eyed, menacing. He'd seen it on film so many times. No one took any notice.

Outside, the boys drifted away into the night.

Millie concentrated with a mouth full of pins.

Sometimes she concentrated so much that she forgot the pins were there until a sudden sharp prick made her wince behind pursed lips, then for a while she remembered. She stepped back from the judy and surveyed her handiwork: stepped forward, smoothed the satin, inserted another pin, then stepped back and looked again; head cocked first one side, then the other. She removed the pins from her mouth and sucked air through her teeth. She walked around, seeing the gown from all angles and gave a little, 'Ha!' which meant neither one thing nor the other really; a sort of what does one do next sound. Then she retired further back, seating herself at a workbench in order to see the dress from a reasonable distance and wondered if it was worthwhile having another go at the fish paste sandwiches.

Eventually she grew tired of looking at the gown and not being able to make up her mind and her gaze wandered toward the window with its broken sash cord, its dust covered ledges and faded pink curtain. She gazed at the boxes of cotton reels, the swatches, the odd pieces and patches of material that littered the floor, the empty judies in the corner with their wooden stoppers where their necks should be, standing on poles where their legs should be: narrow waisted, broad hipped, their skins pitted with hundreds of tiny pinholes. She sniffed in the smell of new material, the smell she had grown accustomed to that, like the pins, she had to remind herself of its existence. Idly she pushed her finger into her ear and rubbed an itch then crossed back to the judy and her work: a pin here, a pin there. Her face worked with her hands: a frown here, a smile there: pleased here displeased there. She felt she would like to hum a little song and mentally ran through her repertoire but nothing seemed suitable or came to mind so she decided against it and concentrated harder until the sharp point of a pin momentarily brought her back to earth.

His aunt had not said a word about the size of the parcels to carry. What would she have done if he had not volunteered to walk with her? Angelo felt the weight of whatever it was he carried sapping the strength from his arms. He heaved the brown paper parcels onto his shoulder to ease the ache in his biceps. Nina turned to watch him but said nothing; looked away again. They walked at her pace which meant slow. By the time they reached the shop he would be carrying the parcels on his head like a native woman carrying putu, mealie meal porridge in a pot, or water in a five gallon paraffin tin, chin held high, back straight, very good for the posture, pulled the tummy in. As long as he took care and didn't drop them he could carry them standing on his hands and balancing them on his toes for all she cared. It was nice to have him by her side, walking the dark streets, the small oasis of light inhabited by black figures that turned to watch them go by. From light patch to light patch, in silence except for an occasional grunt from Angelo, they walked up the hill to the shop. Now his calves were beginning to ache; his breath coming short and sharp.

'Can't we stop for a rest, Aunt? My legs are really hurting.'

'It's not so far now, you know that. You can almost see the shop from here.'

'Yes, but the rest of the way is the steepest bit.'

'Give me one of the parcels.' She selected the smallest and kept on walking. He stood watching her back for a few moments and then decided he had best follow. He dreamt of Millie as he walked. What would he say to her? What would she say to him? Words do not come easy. Words are difficult to find. They run the wrong way off the tongue, retreating into the dark recesses of the mind, burrowing deeper into corners from where they refuse to be coaxed, receding further and further until they are lost, never to be found. And without the key of words, the lips remain sealed, the treasure chest cannot be opened, its contents can only be guessed at.

'How's it coming along Millie?' Nina swept aside the wooden bead curtains dividing the workroom from the shop and marched up to the judy. So intent had Millie been in what she was doing, she had not heard the opening of the front door, and it wasn't until Nina spoke that she realised she was no longer alone. She jumped with a little squeal and her lips fastened hard on the pins through which she eventually mumbled, 'It's nearly done, Mrs...' And then she saw Angelo and three pins pricked her tongue all at once so that she grabbed them in a handful and those she could not grab she spat out.

'Hello!' Angelo said, softly so as not to scare her away. Millie smiled faintly and, although in the light it was difficult to tell, Angelo thought she blushed. He could not really be certain. Maybe it was the memory of spitting out the pins but Millie knew she was blushing and the knowledge only made matters worse. She could feel her ears burning and pulled at one lobe between her finger and thumb as though to admonish it for giving her away.

'Good, that's fine,' said Nina, inspecting the dress. 'Then we'll get it finished in time.'

'Mrs Cochrane telephoned again to ask when it would be ready.' Millie spoke quietly but very fast. 'She seemed terribly anxious.' She picked up another box of pins and, holding them in one hand, went back to her work without looking at Angelo, although she knew he was watching her closely and the blush, which had momentarily receded, reappeared, a deep rose beneath the brown of her skin. She could not concentrate so intensely on her work, finding it difficult to pin with one hand, and the awkwardness showed. Angelo stepped up behind her. 'Here,' he said, 'let me hold those for you.' She looked up and, seeing his outstretched hand, dropped the pin box on to the palm. To put the box carefully there and risk touching his hand was to court disaster. The first mate, he of her romantic dreaming, in blue woollen jersey and gum boots tried to intrude from behind the wheel, but Millie's dreamboat was fast heading towards the rocks and the mate didn't stand a chance against the close proximity of flesh and blood opposition, especially flesh as handsome as the youth who now stood holding a box of pins and gazing intently at the pinning and the pinner. Nina appraised the work with an experienced eye. 'Well…' she tugged at a hem…. 'Put a tuck in here. If we get it finished soon, Angelo can run it up to them tonight, hmn? Then there will be plenty of time for alterations.'

'Yeah, I don't mind.'

'Well don't trip over yourself in rushing forward.' Nina looked at him over the shoulders of the judy and Millie but Angelo was studying Millie's neck. Nina smiled. 'And Millie can go up with you for a fitting.' Angelo glanced at his aunt and noticed the smile. 'How do you think it looks?' Nina asked.

'All right.' Angelo looked over Millie's shoulder, the judy's shoulder and over his aunt's head. He did not want to be committed to an opinion. What did he know about a woman's clothes? Dressmaking was not the subject a man should be interested in unless the dress was already fitted.

'Is that all you can say?'

Angelo stopped gazing at the ceiling and focused on his aunt's face. At least he tried to give the impression of looking at her, his gaze had in fact reverted to the back of Millie's head, bent forward towards the wedding gown in which she was taking an unusually close interest, almost as though she were hypnotised by it.

'Well...' he said slowly, 'it depends on who is going to be in it, doesn't it?'

Nina snorted and tossed her head so that her earrings bobbed violently. 'Every bride, no matter how plain she may be at other times, looks beautiful on her wedding day, Angelo that is a known fact.'

Millie looked up, saw Mrs Viljoen's smile, blushed, and looked away again, smoothing with her hand the dazzling white satin.

Angelo, having grown tired of holding the box of pins, retired to sit on a bench, first ascertaining there were no loose pins or needles lying around to do any damage. He played with a used cotton reel, rolling it about the bench, found another and tapped the two together rhythmically. 'I don't know so much,' he said, 'not some of the ones I've seen. Don't know what their husbands saw in them in the first place.'

'Anyway,' Nina gave the judy an affectionate pat, 'in one of my gowns they would.' And then suddenly she remembered her duty as an employer. 'Have you eaten, Millie?'

'Yes, thank you.'

'What did you have?'

'Some sandwiches, and some fruit.'

'You don't eat enough. Growing girls need plenty of food.'

'What about boys?' Angelo said, wanting to be part of any conversation.

'Yes, growing boys too of course. Time to think of your figure, Millie, when you're old enough to worry yourself to death about it.' She picked up one of the parcels Angelo had brought in and went towards the front of the shop just as the telephone rang. She dropped the parcel and went into the shop to answer it. Angelo looked at the parcel, then at the arch through which his aunt had disappeared and thought to himself, "Now she was going into the shop with the parcel when the telephone rang so why did she drop it? Surely she could have dropped it in there and saved herself the trouble of having to come back for it?" He stared at the abandoned parcel and decided that women are curious creatures, then dismissed it with a shrug and turned back to Millie who had left the gown and was now seated at the bench, intent on a piece of hand stitching. He watched her for a while saying nothing, his hands clasped about his knees. In the front room he could hear his aunt's voice and then the ting of the bell as she replaced the receiver. He glanced over his shoulder. Through the beaded curtain he could see the model in her woollen outfit, standing in the window, illuminated by the street light, and a second later the shadow of his aunt moving across the room and then the hand drawing aside the curtain. She stood there admiring the wedding gown from that distance. 'Yes…' she positively purred with satisfaction, 'That is without any doubt a beautiful dress.'

Millie looked up from her work, dropping her hands in her lap. 'Yes,' she agreed, 'It is, very beautiful. You really are the very best dressmaker in town, Mrs Viljoen.'

'No one to touch you,' Angelo confirmed.

Nina looked at him sharply to see whether or not he was serious but his face gave away nothing so she assumed the compliment was intended. 'And what do you know of dressmaking, may I ask?' She pinched his cheek affectionately, gazing at him and smiling. He withdrew slightly and his face was solemn. Nina laughed. The boy was the image of his handsome grandfather. The looks had obviously jumped a generation. Where, in Ulrico and Marina's house, the patriarch's portrait shared honours with his wife; in her house he shared them with that great patriot, Garibaldi himself, his portrait over the fireplace between a pair of large Staffordshire poodles. She turned back to her assistant. 'Millie,' she went on, 'You really must eat more, child. Look at you! You're all skin and bone.'

The skin between Millie's eyebrows wrinkled a little but she returned to her stitching without a word. If they had been alone she would have giggled but, with the presence of Angelo, the criticism was too much to laugh away.

'She looks all right to me,' Angelo said approvingly.

'And no one asked for your opinion, thank you.' Nina slapped the cheek she had recently pinched and the sound of her palm against his face, soft in itself, echoed loudly in the small silent room so that they all started and then laughed. 'It was that course in Rome that did it,' Nina said.

Millie looked at Angelo and Angelo looked at Millie with a *what is she talking about now* face. They smiled at each other. Angelo felt his heart quicken.

'Oh!' Angelo exclaimed, realising what his aunt meant and wondering suddenly if the thudding beneath his shirt could be heard across the room. 'Oh, no! you were good before that, aunt.'

'Ah!' his aunt wagged a wise finger. 'But the diploma makes all the difference don't you see?' She breathed the words as though she were waving a wand and uttering some incantation. The words of the diploma were a rune that automatically implied superior ability and status.

'It gives you class, aunt,' said Angelo leaping off the bench that was growing painfully hard. 'It's a very good-looking diploma.' He dusted off the seat of his pants and stood looking at the framed print. It was a little on the florid side to say the least but it was Italian which would explain it.

'Impressive is the word, Angelo, impressive.' Nina laid a hand on the parcel she had left behind. 'That was a good idea of mine, taking in Rome and the course in one go. Good for my soul and good for the business. It's just a pity it wasn't a Holy Year. You should go to Rome, Millie, I wish I could have taken you. You wouldn't stay skinny for long there I can tell you, not with all that delicious pasta you get to eat there. The Italians know how to eat.'

'I'd like to go…' Millie said, 'one day.'

'I'll take you there… one day.'

Nina looked at her nephew and sniffed. 'What on?' she asked. 'The smell of an oil rag?'

'On a ship of course.' He replied. The telephone rang. Angelo immediately looked at the parcel beneath his aunt's hand and wondered whether she would leave it a second time. Did she need an excuse to come back and keep a watchful eye on them? It was her shop, she could come and go as she pleased and if it pleased her to play the chaperone... but maybe she did not want them to think that.

'Shall I answer it?' Millie asked, half rising.

'No, no, I'll go. I want to do some book work anyway.' The telephone rang monotonously. 'It will be Mrs Cochrane I suppose,' Nina groused. 'That woman! The way she carries on you'd think I'd allow her daughter to walk down the aisle in her birthday suit.'

'If you don't answer it,' Angelo interrupted her, 'it'll ring off.'

Nina picked up the parcel and headed for the archway, pulled the bead curtain aside and turned to look over her shoulder. 'Well I won't dress any of her others when the time comes,' she threatened. 'She's got four more and they're more trouble then they're worth.' The telephone continued to ring. 'Angelo, don't you stop Millie from working now. We've got to get that dress finished tonight.'

She disappeared through the curtains and the wooden

beads rattled as she let them go. The ringing stopped as she lifted the phone and barked into the mouthpiece.

'Or maybe we'll fly,' Angelo said, turning back to look at Millie. 'People are using aeroplanes more and more these days. There's jet planes coming along now. No propellers. Soon you will be able to go anywhere in the world, fast. Not like a ship that takes weeks.' He had moved over to Millie's bench and was standing in front of her. She looked up with a questioning frown. 'To Rome,' he explained. 'Oh!' she said, and laughed. Angelo pretended to study the wedding gown. 'It's a pretty dress,' he praised her, 'You're very clever.'

Millie was pleased with his praise but felt she should be modest. Praise was not something that often came her way. She certainly never received any at home where her mother was always too busy bringing up her children to look at them except with barking orders. "Don't do this! Don't do that!" And such criticism. Certainly not at the convent where abnegation and the strict rules were irksome to a dreamer. The nuns felt she was always flighty and irresponsible. For all their other worldliness they were practical women and had they been devoid of a sense of humour, which fortunately they were not, they would have positively disliked her. She felt they did dislike her but then she was going through that period when the slightest reproof and the ever-ready tears would flow. They could still flow, but not quite so readily.

'Oh, I only helped to make it,' she explained away her cleverness. 'Your aunt does the pattern, that's the clever part, and the cutting which is terribly important.'

'Go on,' Angelo teased, 'what would she do without you?'

'Find someone else.'

'Not nearly as good as you though.' He leaned across the bench, resting his elbows on it, shoulders hunched. Millie lifted up the material and took a pair of scissors with which to cut the thread. Normally she would have bitten through it. He stretched out and touched her hand. She nearly dropped the scissors in her sudden anxiety. 'You have pretty hands,' he said.

She snipped the thread and laid the material and the scissors back on the bench. 'Shall I make you some tea?' She asked, pushing back her chair and her voice suddenly no more than a whisper.

'No, thanks, I've just had dinner.' He got off his elbows and sat on the edge of the bench. Disappointed, Millie went back to her stitching. 'How are your family?' She didn't know them very well, only from visits to the shop but she felt it was polite to ask.

'Fine, thank you. How's yours?' He glanced towards the shop but his aunt was obviously still talking on the phone.

Millie shrugged. 'They're all right.' Her fingers moved quickly, in – out – in – out. There was a long silence. Angelo sought desperately for words, something to say to break it. He began to panic slightly. Movies? No, he hadn't been to any worth talking about and even if he had, who wanted to hear movie stories second-hand? School? Urgh! In the silence, as her fingers guided the needle, the first mate put in a brief appearance, but one giant wave and a strain of organ music put paid to him once and for all. Millie glanced up quickly to see Angelo's pensive face half in profile. She saw the brief brown length of leg between his shorts and his stocking tops and reached for the scissors with hands that trembled ever so slightly. Angelo moved, turning to pass the scissors to her. She too would have liked to ease the strain of the silence that lay between them but there seemed nothing she could say. After all, she hardly knew anything about this boy. She only knew her feelings towards him and even they could be nebulous at times. Suddenly Angelo laughed. Ah, good! She sighed with relief that the tension was over.

'You would have laughed tonight though if you had been there, seen it.' Angelo chuckled. Millie waited, threading another needle. 'Uncle Pepe, you know my uncle Pepe, well he was fast asleep in his chair, see? The one that sits outside the bedroom.' Millie wanted to say she hadn't ever really noticed the bedroom, let alone seeing inside, or uncle Pepe's chair, but she let Angelo continue in case her interruption brought on another attack of silence. 'But he still had his cigar in his mouth and it just about set fire to his moustache, you know?' Millie's eyes opened wide in terror and anticipation of the horrors to come although it couldn't be all that bad if Angelo found it so amusing. But then the oldest joke in the world is the sight of a man slipping on a banana skin, even if he breaks his neck in the process. 'So he woke up yelling and screaming and Guido, you know my little brother, Guido?'... Millie nodded... 'He was sitting there watching all the time without saying a word, and uncle Pepe said to him, "Why you don't wake uncle up, hey? Why you don't tell uncle his cigar burns him?"'

'He's very sweet.' Millie said. Angelo looked at her. 'Who? Uncle Pepe?'

'Yes.' She laughed, thinking of him. She had seen him on visits to the house next door with Nina. 'And Guido. I like your family.' There was a pause. Millie was smiling to herself, thinking of the Lericis, seeing the house. Angelo watched her and his heart now really quickened its pace. 'Do you like me?' he almost blurted it out. It almost seemed to him that he had shouted it. He had not intended the question. It was out before he could close the gates. His face was serious. Millie glanced up and the silence fell once more between them, there was only a boy and a girl looking at each other, and then Nina's voice from the other room.

'Angelo?'

'Yes, Aunt?'

'Leave Millie to get on with her work.'

'I'm not doing anything.'

Conspirators, they giggled at each other. 'Anyway,' Angelo continued, 'Uncle Pepe gave Guido a good ticking off. Told him that's what the church calls a sin of omission. Hey! I might be going swimming later tonight; do you want to come with?'

'Oh, no!' Millie shuddered.

'Why not? The water's warm.'

She shook her head. 'My mother would never allow it.'

'All right then, I'll walk you home after we've been to

Mrs Cochrane's.' Millie shook her head again.

'Oh, yes, I forgot. Your mother. She's very strict, isn't she? But someone's going to have to see you safely home and it might as well be me. I'll wait in the street until I see you're inside.'

'No, she's not really so strict.' Millie was surprised to hear her voice raised and she wondered why she should try to defend her mother. 'I mean my mother, she's not really that strict. I think she's... afraid.'

'What's she afraid of?' Angelo laughed through his question though he certainly guessed what her mother was afraid of. Millie said nothing. She was thinking of her mother, of the things her mother said: hateful things, hurtful things, transferring her own inadequacies and fears to her children, to the boys particularly. They displayed symptoms of her insecurity. They wore glasses; they suffered from hay fever, and one with asthma, the youngest, grossly overfed, eating his way to some sort of security. Of what? Of what was her mother so afraid? If Angelo didn't know, she couldn't tell him, she just couldn't! 'The thing all mothers with daughters are afraid of,' she said finally. She felt the need to say something to this boy that would bring them closer together in an intimacy of thought, understanding, that she longed for without knowing how much. She wanted to show more of herself to him, to make him understand the years of their not knowing each other, of their separate existences.

'Oh!' said Angelo, her words reinforcing his thoughts, and he was suddenly angry without knowing why. Millie saw his anger and wished her words undone, realising the harm they had caused. Angelo walked away. 'People have dirty minds,' he mumbled. He crossed over to the window and drawing aside the pink curtain, gazed out into the blackness. There was nothing for him to see out there, only a wooden fence, but he did not want to face Millie and what she had just said. He tried to figure out why he was angry but it didn't seem to make sense, at least nothing fell into place, his thoughts were random, disappearing as fast as they appeared, jumbled, confused. He wanted to hold her. He wanted to kiss her. Of course he wanted to kiss her. He dreamed of it. He imagined her lips, how they would taste, what he would feel. In his thoughts he had kissed her a thousand times. But no further! He had never thought further than that first kiss. When it came to that!... came to that... he always imagined some other girl, someone like Rita, or someone who never really came into focus, a nebulous imaging. Or he imagined some part of the anatomy of a girl; the legs, the breasts, even the... But now he thought of Millie in the light of her mother's fear and he struggled to put the thought from him. This was not how he imagined them to be. But was it not a logical conclusion? Is this not what it would, must eventually come to? Yes, but not yet. 'You know...' He tapped the pane with a bent finger, then turned to look at her again. It was easier with the lapse of thought time and now that she had returned to her work and wouldn't look at him '...When I was a kid...'

Millie pictured a little boy rather like Guido, which was what Angelo must have looked like, and while he spoke she saw him doing all the things he described.

'I often used to come up here and play.' He looked around the room and started to wander from bench to bench, touching something here, there, pulling out a box, rummaging. 'It used to fascinate me, all this stuff lying around, materials, thread, hooks and eyes, bias binding, silk, and all that.' He mentioned each item as he touched or saw it. 'My aunt named everything for me and she used to give me all the used cotton reels to make things with. I used to like them new though she wouldn't let me touch those. Said my hands were grubby and I would only dirty the cotton.' He picked a reel out of a box, a shiny pale green, tossed it in the air and replaced it. 'All these bright colours. I like mauve. It's a real coolie colour though, isn't it?'

She moved back to the judy, listening to him rattle on, and now she stepped back satisfied. 'There,' she said. They stood for a while, side by side, looking at the gown. 'The bridesmaid's dresses have already been delivered,' she said. 'They're in powder blue, very pretty, and the veil is over there, ready to go.' She pointed to a large brown paper package lying on the table and her hand brushed Angelo lightly in passing. He made no move towards her for all her nearness, remembering what she had said about her mother's fear and feeling that if he moved now, she would resent it. 'Why don't you try it on?' He suggested.

'Oh, no!'

'Why not?'

'Well for one thing it's very bad luck. There's an awful lot of superstition connected with weddings. Do you know? If you take a piece of wedding cake and put it under your pillow at night you dream of your future bridegroom. Well in your case,' she added hastily, 'bride of course.' But Angelo was not listening. His lips were dry and a feeling of cold spread from his groin upward into his belly. He wanted to swallow and gulped. He wanted to press his hand against his stomach to relieve the ache that had settled there. 'You would look very nice in it,' he whispered. 'Beautiful. I'd like to see you in it.' She shook her head, smiling secretly, and turned to look at him. He leaned forward, awkwardly. It seemed as though he would never reach her. The room disappeared. She disappeared. Everything disappeared. There was only the feeling and a reaching out and then his lips touched hers, like a butterfly, unsure whether or not to alight. She drew back her head and very softly said, 'Angelo.'

'What?' His voice was hoarse, harsh, sounding strange.

'Don't.'

'Why not?'

She did not answer; just stood there, looking at him.

'Millie...?' Silence. He could not only feel but hear the beating of his heart. 'Why not?' Silence. 'Don't you want me to?' she shook her head, slowly, but he leaned forward again and this time the butterfly settled. She did not pull away but her lips remained tight and immoveable, not answering and when he pulled back not knowing her reasons, she glanced sideways towards the shop, 'Your aunt,' she whispered.

Angelo looked at the floor and scratched his forehead. He nodded, more to himself than to her, though it showed he understood. 'Well,' his voice had returned to normal, 'Now that the dress is nearly finished we can deliver it and I can walk you part of the way home.' She nodded and smiled. Never again would she see the mate behind his wheel in his woollen blue jersey and gumboots. He was banished forever.

Chapter 6

Tony marched up to the counter and flat handed its shiny surface. 'Hiya, Mack!'

Nick paused in polishing a glass, glanced up for a second with his mouth twisted in an imitation of Tony's leer. 'Since when was my name, Mack, Mack?' he asked, returning to his glass.

'Now don't be like that, man.' Tony's voice was insultingly familiar.

Nick forgot to keep his mind on the job and a clean triangle of glass came away between his thumb and forefinger. He threw the broken remains into an old biscuit tin beneath the counter and advanced down the counter towards Tony. 'What do you want?' He was virtually at exploding point and in no mood for any more adolescent nonsense.

Tony pretended surprise. 'Hey!' he said, 'aren't you pleased to see me? I'm spending money in here, man!'

Nick looked at him and wrinkled his nose. 'Yeah?' He paused for effect. 'Whose? Or have you robbed a bank?'

Tony's eyes for once narrowed on their own accord. 'Don't talk like that, man.' His tone was surly now.

For the most part Nick was an extremely patient man. He had to be. He had a loudmouthed wife, five children between squalling and bawling age, a bond to pay off on his house, and a horde of youngsters let loose every night on his hands and capable of turning his establishment into a zoo. He wiped down the counter briskly in case his patience should be lost. 'Come on come on, I haven't got all night to stand around.' He flicked a damp cloth in Tony's direction being unable to resist a small sign of protest.

Tony stepped back, blinking, and drew the gun from his pocket. He leaned across the counter and snarled at Nick, 'Don't talk like that, man. Be nice to your customers.' He tapped the counter with his free hand.

Nick leaned forward in a copy of the boy's pose and said in a gentle voice, 'Look sonny, be a good little boy and put away your toy, huh? I've had enough trouble tonight with that mob of brainless gorillas outside. Friends of yours, no doubt, and I don't want any more, see?' He reached out and patted Tony's cheek and the boy jerked back and scowled. Then he put away the gun. 'Now what's it to be? Sir! Nice big milkshake? With a big straw? What flavour does big spender fancy?'

'Chocolate.'

Tony sneered and, as Nick moved away to make up the concoction, he turned to survey the café and its denizens, leaning back, both elbows on the counter. One or two people noticed him and nodded distantly, condescendingly he inclined his head in their direction before looking elsewhere. He crossed one leg in front of the other and pushed his hat to the back of his head. Nick returned with the shake in a long heavy glass and tapped Tony on the shoulder. Tony disengaged his limbs from the cinematic pose he had learnt from Saturday afternoons at the bioscope, picked up the glass, and sauntered away.

'Hey, Sonny?' Nick called after him. 'Haven't you forgotten something?' Tony swaggered back and flung a coin on the counter. It rolled on its edge and Nick caught it just in time. Tony leered and swaggered away again. Nick shook his head and smiled at Tony's back. If the intended insult had not been so obvious he would most probably have let loose his reined in anger but, as it was, Tony's act dissipated it entirely. He rang up the amount on the cash register and surveyed his domain with a sudden kindly eye. They weren't really so bad, just one or two troublemakers, and they were only kids after all. Pity some kids had to be so destructive he thought. He went back to polishing his glasses as Tony wandered across to a table already occupied. The inhabitants did not look up at his approach and he stood irresolute before deciding to make a bid for entry. 'Hi!' he said.

A boy did look up and nodded before returning to the conversation which was being carried out sotto voce. Tony placed his glass on the table and balanced one cheek on the edge of a bench. They turned to look at him, saying nothing, then the boy next to whom he sat, turned to the girl next to him and said, 'Shift up will you?' She obliged. Tony looked across the table at the girl sitting opposite. She had not yet learned the art of subtle makeup. Somehow she gave the impression she never would. Her already thick lips, constantly moistened by the tip of her tongue, were thickened even more with a smear of vermilion that clashed wildly with her orange hair fuzzed about her head like an untrimmed bush. The lipstick was smeared across her front teeth and her eyelashes dripped droplets of mascara. A boil on her neck, covered with a plaster, set off the unfairness of it all and in the artificial lights the result was bizarre. Tony however, who's taste resided solely in his mouth, was not objecting. He tried to infuse his crooked smile with charm,

'Mind if I plant myself?' he said. A rhetorical question as he had already done it.

She raised her eyebrows very quickly, what was left of them after the tweezers had done their work, and turned away before she answered. 'Sure, as long as you don't take root,' and then lowered her head to suck on her straw.

Tony scowled at his chocolate milkshake as though it had done him a permanent and unforgivable injury.

'What we gonna do now?' Johnny asked, his question not directed to anyone in particular.

Silence.

'I got to go,' Angelo murmured.

Silence.

'What for?' Steve asked.

Silence.

'It's getting late,' Angelo replied.

Silence.

'Let's go down to Nick's,' Johnny suggested brightly.

Silence.

'What for?' Steve asked.

'Something to do for fuck's sake! All right?' He lifted his shoulders and rolled his eyes heavenwards. No one answered him. He looked from one to the other and then away. 'Jeeeez!' He said.

Carlos leaned against a lamppost and stared at the distance.

Tony was getting nowhere. He caught the snatches of conversation which might have been interesting had he been in on it from the beginning. As it was they continued to ignore him, including the girl with the orange hair. He slid his foot out from under the table, and touched her ankle with the point of his toe. She turned lazily in his direction and withdrew the ankle, shook her orange head without saying a word, then went back to her three friends. Tony sighed and went back to sucking on his straw.

'You want to go to Nick's?' Steve asked.

Carlos shrugged with one shoulder.

'You want to go to Nick's?'

Angelo shrugged. He was thinking of Millie.

'Johnny?'

'What?'

'Do you want to go to Nick's?'

'What's everyone else want?'

'Shit!' Steve said.

Tony looked around the café then twisted in his seat in order to see behind him. He felt the hard outline of the gun against his thigh and winked at a girl in the next booth who studiously ignored him. If he had had cash to spare he would have made a selection at the juke box. He resigned himself to listening to other people's music, took a sip at his milkshake and stirred the melting ice cream with the end of the straw growing soggy.

'Well what're we going to do?' Johnny howled with a sudden change of mood. 'We can't hang around here all night doing fuck all!'

Carlos shifted his position slightly. 'Why not?' he asked. There seemed nothing against it.

'I'd better be moving anyway,' Angelo said.

'Why?'

'Because it's getting late.' A note of irritation crept into his voice.

'So?'

'And I'm not supposed to be out.'

'Agh!'

'Oh, let's go down to Nick's dammit!' Johnny wailed.

'What for?'

'For something to do, for Christ's sake!'

Carlos spat. 'Yah!' he said. 'That is such a creepy joint.'

'We might find a couple of loose bints,' Johnny suggested. 'Some of the dames in there are really hot for it, you know?'

'You wouldn't know what to do with one if she shoved her twat in your face.' Carlos eased back his shoulders and stretched.

'Okay!' said Johnny even more brightly, 'Let's go down to Rita's place.'

'What for?'

'For something to do, that's what for!'

'You want to go to Rita's?' Steve asked.

Carlos shrugged.

'You want to go to Rita's?'
Angelo shrugged.

The boys stood around, leaned on the juke box, their gum chewing jaws making time with the music: fingers clicking, fingers tapping, toes tapping, heads jerking. They closed their eyes to the cigarette smoke that curled up from beneath their nostrils, breathing through their mouths. Staring down at the table top, Tony toyed idly with the straw in the empty but for the froth glass in front of him, every so often looking up morosely at the girl opposite but the conversation absorbed her solely and she continued to ignore him. A couple had paired off and now sat holding hands beneath the table making sheep's eyes at each other. He saw the movement as she put her hand on his thigh, high up towards his crotch. Soon they would get up, leave before the others, refusing the invitations to move on elsewhere. They would find a dark corner somewhere and neck until the girl felt things were maybe getting too dangerous and say a hurried goodnight, leaving the boy not knowing quite what to do with himself until he sought out his old companions and with a heavy dose of lover's balls and complaining bitterly about his treatment. Tony nodded to a passer-by then looked across the table, leaned back in his seat and called, 'Hey!' there was no response. 'Hey, Blondie!'

She disengaged herself momentarily from the conversation and withered him with a glare. 'In case you hadn't noticed,' she said, 'My hair is not blonde. It's titian!'

Tony stretched across the table and touched her arm as she turned away again. She withdrew the arm as though a viper with bared fangs had slithered over it. 'What?' she snapped.

'You want something? Milkshake or something?'

'No!' Then remembering she was a lady, 'Thank you!'

'Okay okay, please yourself, I was only asking. No harm in asking is there?' He pulled a wry face and snorted to himself then he placed the straw in his mouth and sucked violently and noisily on the froth. The froth at the bottom of the glass gurgled loudly. Tony blew bubbles. They all turned to look at him and Tony looked over his straw but when he saw their faces, he looked down again.

'What gives with this guy?' a boy asked.

Orangehead took it upon herself to reply. 'You'd think some people were brought up in a pigsty the way they behave!' Tony answered her with a loud belch. She flashed him an angry look, patted her bushy hair, sniffed quickly and said, 'Excuse me! I'm going to the washroom.' She picked up her plastic handbag and wobbled off on unimaginable heels.

'Well are we going or aren't we?'

There was no answer to Johnny's question. 'If her old lady's out,' he wheedled, 'at least we can get a drop of vino there. Her old man boozes on muscatel.'

'What does her old lady drink?' Carlos asked, not really interested.

'Cooking sherry. She doesn't cook with it, she just drinks it.'

Steve looked from one to the other.

'How about it? She's easy meat, Steve, anybody's.' Johnny tempted him.

'What are you telling me for? You're the one suggested going there.'

'I tell you,' Carlos picked dry snot from his nose and looked reflectively at his finger before flicking it away in Johnny's direction, 'he wouldn't know what to do with it anyway.'

'You don't have to know with her,' Steve laughed. 'She does it all for you.'

Angelo coughed. 'I think I ought to be going home.' He said.

'Don't be a fucking drip!' Steve thought of Rita. Why not? If he got drunk enough he could get on the job, bag though she was to look at and somehow she didn't seem to be all that hygienic, as if he could talk 'We'll go to Rita's place.' He made up their minds for them. 'Johnny can spin discs.'

'Yeah,' Johnny interrupted, 'That's where all her lolly

goes, on discs.'

'And Carlos can get pissed on her old man's vino.'

'And Stevie boy can have his shag!' Carlos said.

Johnny was now eager to move. 'Yeah, come on, Angelo.' He waggled Angelo's arm and looked at him pleadingly. 'You and me can spin some discs, Huh?'

'Maybe she's out,' Angelo tried to object, but no one took any notice of his objection. Carlos licked his lower lip in anticipation of the sweet muscatel and Steve developed a far away look. If he didn't feel like it when he got there, and he knew he would feel like it, he stirred already just thinking about it, Carlos would oblige with a public exhibition. Rita would like that.

Rita was fifteen with the body, not of a mature woman, but somehow it seemed, or at least gave the appearance, of being a woman past maturity. Somehow it would seem as though she had never known innocence, not innocence of the mind which can exist long after the body has followed its natural appetites and curiosity. This innocence she had never known. A precocious child, her mind had grasped the body's needs before the body was aware of their existence. She seduced her first boy at the age of twelve by arousing his adolescent sexuality, playing suggestively with a leg of an upturned three legged stool in a class room during lunch break, accompanying the performance with suitable poses and a lascivious commentary that had him heated and flushed in a matter of seconds, then diverting his aroused lust despite his adoration and sexual peccadilloes at the time for his best friend, into her own channels. The boy's instincts dictated that aroused, he should escape to the lavatory to masturbate in silent privacy, disturbed only by the fantasies of his unformed sex, but she had him cornered in the stationary room amongst the smell of chalk, pencils, pens, erasers, ink, and new exercise books before he really knew what was happening to him. The memory of that smell would arouse him for years to come. She ravished him with the rapaciousness of the female spider that in the end will destroy the male who gives her satisfaction. He hated it. He hated the feel of her flesh, her wet lips, her watery saliva. He hated her predatory hands. He was ashamed and outraged, nevertheless he couldn't prevent his erection and he climaxed.

He had been unfaithful. He felt he could never face his best friend again. The school bell rang but he ignored its summons. When all was quiet and everyone had gone back to their classrooms so that, where it had been a moment before a screaming yelling battlefield, an unnatural hush had now settled on the playground, he slipped off home and told his mother he was ill. She felt his forehead which was hot and feverish and ordered him to bed immediately. He insisted on bathing first, which convinced her he really was ill even to the point of needing an urgent call to the doctor. The memory of this episode haunted him for days though the smell of the stationery cupboard could still cause a stirring. He lived in constant fear of being found out, of pregnancies, of venereal disease. At every opportunity he looked for signs. The slightest itch of the scrotum and he went ice cold with fear. He did not dare touch his eyes for fear of going blind within forty-eight hours, or was it twenty-four? He could not remember clearly, but the danger was there, he had read his mother's encyclopaedia of sexual knowledge and that is what it said, or so he remembered it. He steered clear of Rita lest she grab him again but he watched her closely from a distance, especially the belly that remained as it had always been. Gradually the fear receded and by the time he had overcome it and approached her as a man of the world she had already seduced a number of his schoolfellows upon whom she could call at any time for their favours. He was rebuffed, and retired to his solitary fantasies only now they were filled with the smell of chalk and new exercise books. Sessions in the cinema, sessions in the shooting range, sessions in the stationary room, sessions after school, morning, afternoon and evening: how many adolescents dreamed of this fledgling nymphomaniac before she would, in her mother's footsteps, graduate to the dockside and the easy pickings of those who had been at sea for weeks and had come ashore with a full pocket.

Steve mounted his cycle and stood both feet on the

pavement either side the bar. 'Climb on, Angel.'

He patted the seat of the saddle. Angelo climbed on and Steve shoved off, wobbling at first with the extra weight, the front wheel turning sharply to either side to maintain balance until, as they gathered speed, the cycle straightened on course. Angelo felt nothing, thought nothing. He watched Steve's lurching back as the boy forced down the peddles, clutched the pommel, his feet dangling either side a few inches above the road.

Orangehead whispered in her girl friend's ear and the two of them giggled. Tony eyed them suspiciously, maybe the joke was on him. He wished he could hear what was being said but Orangehead's mouth was hidden behind her cupped hand and so close to the listening ear no one could overhear. Maybe it was just women's talk they didn't want any of the boys to know about. Maybe they were discussing one of the others. Tony looked down the table. The two that were holding hands now gazed cross-eyed at each other, their foreheads and noses touching. Maybe that was what the others were giggling about? The second boy with a strong face and the most piercing blue eyes was someone no girl would giggle at except in frustration or jealousy.

No, Tony couldn't help suspecting they were laughing at him and there was nothing he could do about it. If he challenged them they would tell him to mind his own business in no uncertain terms. He pushed out his lower lip with his tongue, rolled the tongue from one side of the mouth to the other and tried to stare the two girls into taking notice of him but it didn't work. He squeezed a pimple on his chin and put his hand in his pocket to take out his handkerchief instead of which his fingers found the gun. Tony smiled and pulled it out, leaned back in his seat and toyed with it until he had everyone's attention. The giggling stopped and there was silence. Tony raised an eyebrow and glanced slowly round the table. They were all looking at him now. He stood up, making as though to go, and slipped the gun back into his pocket.

The handsome boy leaned across the table and said,

'Hey! Wait a minute, man. What've you got there?'

Tony did not like this boy. He did not like him because he seemed to have everything. Tony did not have everything and everything Tony wanted was to be the same as Angelo. If this boy had been Tony's cousin, as Angelo was, if he had grown up with him that would be different. This boy was a stranger and Tony resented him passionately. 'What's it look like?' He growled sidling, knees bent, out from between the table and bench.

The handsome one was too eager and showed it. 'Hey!' His snapping fingers called Tony back. 'What is it? A Luger?'

Tony smiled. Handsome one had made a mistake. Handsome one had shown his ignorance. He laughed scornfully, one side of his upper lip raised in a sneer. 'You crazy or something?' Listen to that girls, Tony Viljoen was asking handsome one if he was crazy, that's a turn up for the books. 'Don't you know the difference between one gun and another? A Luger! Ha!' Tony showed the company with what contempt he greeted the handsome one's ignorance. The boy did not like it. He flushed and glanced quickly around the table to gauge reaction. All faces were on Tony, waiting for him to produce the gun once more. Handsome one let it pass but would not forget. There would be time to deal with this pipsqueak. Boy, if there was one thing he hated it was a greaseball like that.

The one with the orange head stretched out a lazy brokenwristed hand which she waved vaguely in Tony's direction. 'What you doing carrying a gun around for anyway?' she asked 'Is it loaded?'

Tony wrinkled his mouth and raised a supercilious eyebrow. 'Of course it's loaded. Not much good without ammo, is it?'

The boys were growing tired of his act but their curiosity still got the better of them and they were reluctant to send him packing. They were eager to see the gun again, to handle it, feel it lying there in the palm of their hand, feel their fingers curled about the butt, pretend to fire it, show their knowledge of its mechanics. A boy at the next table leaned over to see what was going on and then stood up and leaned back on the bench: another followed suit and then a third. Tony was now the centre of attention with three tables, more than he bargained for. He was suddenly apprehensive. He shouldn't really be opening his big mouth. What would Dettman say who had trusted him with the weapon? He didn't know where Dettman had got the gun, hadn't thought to ask, and Dettman more than likely wouldn't have told him anyway. He thought of Angelo's reaction to it but there was no backing down now without incurring the immediate dislike of everyone present. He glanced across at Nick but Nick was serving a group of three and not taking any notice.

'Anyway,' Orangehead persisted, 'I don't see what you want to carry a gun around for.' She flapped her loose fingers. 'It's not as though you're going to do anything with it.' She gazed up at him with wide eyes, inviting confidence.

Tony's look in reply implied that she would be very surprised if she were to know what he intended doing with it. 'It makes me feel good,' was all he said. 'Well, guess I'd better be shoving off.'

Handsome one shifted forward in his seat. 'Aw, hang on, will you? I just want to take a look-see, that's all.' Tony reseated himself and looked across at the counter. Nick had noticed the little group and was eyeing them suspiciously. 'Nick's watching,' Tony said conspiratorially, 'Laugh.' It was an order and they complied. Tony was pleased. He had found his passport to popularity but was wise enough to know that once their curiosity was satisfied, that passport would no longer be valid. 'Who's got a drag?' he demanded. The boys fished hurriedly in their pockets and simultaneously he was offered the choice of three packs. He looked from one to the other, taking his time, then made his selection. He rolled the cigarette between thumb and forefinger and then between his lips, wetting the end; lit it from a proffered match, took a pull and exhaled a cloud of smoke, throwing back his head and blowing it toward the ceiling. Paradise gained. It was not often that Tony Viljoen was the hub of the wheel. 'Molto gracious!' he said politely, looking across the table at Orangehead. 'You want a milkshake or something?' He asked.

'Yes please.' She smiled politely.

Handsome one was getting irritated. 'Look, skip her milk shake, dago,' he said. 'If she wants one let her go get it herself.'

'Well thank you very much!' Orangehead was piqued.

'She can wait,' the boy continued acidly. He stretched a hand across the tabletop, palm upwards and curled his fingers towards himself. 'Show us the gun!' It was an imperative demand, either Tony show the gun or his magic spell would be broken; his moment of glory was fast fading. He stretched out a leg to ease the pressure of his thigh against the pocket, slipped in his hand and came out with the weapon. Slowly and deliberately he pointed it at Orangehead. The rest of the crowd laughed. Two boys were now standing in front of the table, hiding the proceedings from Nick. Orangehead giggled weakly, then winced and fidgeted nervously. She raised her hands in mock surrender.

'Don't do that,' she squawked.

'Why not?' He put on his grimmest, most dangerous expression, and then laughed.

'It's dangerous, that's why not. You shouldn't play with guns anyway... Please!... don't! There could be an accident.'

'There's nothing to be scared of. I can handle it.' He spoke as one totally familiar with firearms.

'Yes there is,' she contradicted him. Her voice was no longer a squawk but still trembled slightly showing her nervousness, there was a pleading in it that delighted Tony. 'Please put it down.' She tried hard to make it sound natural, not begging, 'It's loaded, you said it was.'

Tony laughed louder. 'What you so scared of, man, the safety catch is on, it can't fire.' He lowered the muzzle down the side of the table holding the gun diagonally to the floor. 'Look.' His finger tightened on the trigger.

For a split second there seemed to be a complete silence in Nick's café, a moment between records, a moment between conversation, a moment when everything is still, suspended before some momentous event in small lives, then the silence was broken by a shattering roar. The gun clattered swivelling to the floor. The milk bar reeked of gunsmoke. Tony grimaced in fright more than in pain and clutched the edge of the table. The boys yelped and jumped about. The girls screamed. Orangehead put her hands to the side of her head and shrieked in long punctuated hysterical howls. Nick's fingers jerked spasmodically against the glass in his hand and the blood spurted from his gashed thumb. The number on the jukebox broke into violent drumming to add to the cacophony. Pandemonium!

Chapter 7

Father Joseph picked up his hat and brushed the brim with his cuff. He was about to thank Mama for the tea, to say how pleased he was to have met them and that he would certainly see them again soon, Sunday no doubt, at Mass, but mama's ears had been alerted by something elsewhere. She got up, went over to the veranda rail and watched Guido and Seraphina lugging a heavy filled watering can up the yard. 'Guido! What you doin' now?'

Father Joseph came out to look. The two children stopped and peered up at Mama. They could not see her face, only her silhouette against the kitchen light.

'He's watering his condensed milk,' Seraphina explained.

Ulrico got to his feet to join the pair on the veranda. 'What?' he yelled.

'Uncle Pepe told him...' Seraphina was being very patient and explaining most carefully, choosing her words slowly, 'Uncle Pepe told him, that if he planted a tin of condensed milk, a cow would grow. He dug a hole and he planted it there.' She pointed in the direction of the dark area beneath the veranda. 'And so now we are going to water it.'

Mama threw up her hands in despair. Ulrico smiled and Father Joseph laughed, shaking his head. 'Oh, there is an example of faith,' he said, 'To believe without question.' But then he paused to think about it and wished he had not said that. They were, after all, believing a myth, a story an adult had told them as a joke. There would be no promise of fulfilment in their childish dream. Their faith was misguided. He hoped the two adults did not see this.

But mama was too angry to see anything. 'What does uncle Pepe tella chile somtink lika dat for? Pepe!' she yelled for her brother in law but if he heard he was not going to answer. 'Guido? Where you get dat tin of condensed milk? From Mama's kitchen, No? Huh? Guido?' But Guido had dragged his watering can under the veranda and was too busy pouring to take much notice.

Mama had bent right forward and looked down on the child's bent back as he started to empty the watering can. She started down the stairs.

Guido braced his knees against the can and some of the overflowing water trickled back and coldly over his bare feet. He giggled and wriggled his toes.

Then he saw it. It came from under the house, sliding towards him, its black tongue flicking in the light cast from the bedroom window, its little black button eyes unmoving. Guido screamed and dropped the can. The snake stopped its advance. Guido ran jumping to Mama who had made it to the yard, lifting each leg as high as he could as though he was treading on red-hot coals, screaming at the top of his voice and grabbed at her skirts as if he would clamber up her body. She lifted him behind her to the safety of the steps and stood between Seraphina and the monster now slithering across the yard. Her face was set and her eyes gleaming. The snake had reached the bathroom wall and was feeling its way along when the edge of the spade came down across its back, a short distance from its head. With an alarming hiss it coiled and writhed, its tail about the spade's handle, but mama held it there. The snake's body touched her hand, she held it there, pushing deeper and deeper, leaning her whole weight against it. Then she stood back, gave it a wallop for good measure, and she laughed and her laughter went on for a long time.

Ulrico had come running down the steps and he came up behind Mama, placing his hand on her shoulders. She turned to look at him, still leaning with one hand on her spade, with the other she wiped away a wisp of hair that had fallen across her face, and the laughter gave way to a smile of relief. Her heart was pounding, her breathing hard, her body still trembling.

Father Joseph came down too, and Guido and Seraphina cautiously approached. They stood there, looking down at the dead creature, still twitching at Mama's feet: Mama, a female St George who had at last slain her dragon. Pepe came out of the bedroom and Seraphina, for once excited, ran up to him, grabbing his hand, chanting and skipping, 'Mama killed a snake! Mama killed a snake!' Pepe joined the little crowd to admire. Sarah came out of the house next door and leaned over the veranda rail.

'Mama killed a snake! Mama killed a snake!' Seraphina ran down to stand beneath her and ran back again as Guido took up the chant. 'She hit it with a spade,' he cried, running down the yard to tell his aunt. 'She chopped it up! Come and look!'

Sarah smiled. 'So you finally saw your snake, Marina.'

'And she killed it!' Ulrico said with obvious pride and squeezed his wife's shoulder.

Mama, having recovered from her effort, and the adulation, now turned on her children though there was not so much anger in her voice as before. 'Guido, how many times Mama tell you, Huh? How many times she tella you? Dere's snaigs over here. Dere's snaigs in dat grapevine. Dere's snaigs all over!' Mama vindicated was making sure that the world knew it was full of snakes. 'I'm a not tell you again. I give a you good 'hidin' you play under there!' Guido looked dutifully solemn but Seraphina had been turning the snake over with a stick. 'Look, where she broke its back.' Guido knelt beside it and stretched out a hand which he hastily withdrew as Mama screamed. 'Guido! Donna touch!' Guido looked up, giggled from the fright she had given him and wiggled his fingers before burying them out of harm's way beneath his armpits. 'It's pretty,' he said.

Sarah, who had come down to take a closer look agreed, 'It's got diamonds down its back.'

Nina, who had arrived home in time for the great event but had not come down to see, shouted from the veranda, 'What kind of snake is it?'

'Night Adder,' Ulrico shouted back.

'How do you know?' Sarah asked.

'We find them on the building sites sometimes, you know, under the rubble, bricks and stuff.'

'Is it poisonous?'

'Poisonous?' Mama yelled, wondering what on earth her sister in law could be thinking of. 'Of course it's a poisonous! All a snakes are poisonous!' Mama was an authority on reptiles, especially now with a real dead specimen in her very own back yard on which to vent her accumulated knowledge. She shovelled the dead creature onto her spade and marched up the yard with it, everyone following. The triumphant armies marching into Rome with the loot of ravaged countries they had conquered, could not have felt more proud then Mama carrying her trophy with Guido and Seraphina providing the trumpets, 'Mama killed a sna-ake! Mama killed a sna-ake!' They paused before Marina threw the snake on the compost heap behind the workshop.

'He was a beautiful snake.' Father Joseph said, admiring the brown and silver velvet looking skin, the belly a pale almost luminous blue. 'But then, as we all know, so was the devil in the Garden of Eden.'

Guido felt a note of disapproval in the priest's voice. 'Mama killed him,' he asserted, his voice brooking no argument.

Father Joseph laid a hand on the boy's head. 'Yes yes,' he said with a sigh. 'There is no room for snakes in a back yard, not even beautiful ones with diamonds down their backs.'

Sarah said, 'You can bury him tomorrow, Guido. You

can give him a nice funeral.'

'I'll dig him a grave,' Seraphina volunteered.

'Will we make him a cross?' Guido wanted to know. Pepe nodded. 'I'll make one for you,' he said.

'Wait a minute! Wait a minute!' It was the voice of authority. Mama gazed round at the assembly. 'You know what Angelo he tell me 'bout when you kill a snaig?' They waited. 'You gotta burn it!' She put her hands on her hips and looked around to see the reaction. They all stared at her waiting for an explanation. 'Because...' she raised a finger... 'if you don' a do dat, he's a mate she come a lookin' for 'im, an' bite us all in our beds!' There was a general chorus of 'No!' Only Guido and Seraphina gazed at Mama wide eyed in terror at the thought of a writhing snake beneath the covers. 'Yes!' Mama yelled. 'You gotta burn 'im, an' da smell is enough to fright away he's a mate so he no come near you. I tell you now. Pepe...' She waved an imperious hand... 'You burn 'im for me. An' you don' talk nonsense to my chil'ren again if you please.' Then she marched back up the yard ushering her children in front of her. Pepe looked at Ulrico who shrugged. He knew that Mama would never sleep until she smelt burning snake flesh. 'Burn him,' he said. Pepe went into the workshop to fetch a can of paraffin. Father Joseph looked down at the adder, its black button eyes unmoving, its tongue black at the fork, turning grey towards the root, lying far out in death. 'It is strange,' he murmured, 'how so beautiful a creature can be capable of so much harm, and so much sorrow, through no fault of its own.'

'In the wrong place in the wrong time,' Ulrico added.

Pepe returned with the paraffin which he proceeded to pour over the corpse, then he soaked a piece of newspaper in the stuff, set alight to it, and dropped it over the paraffin soaked earth. There was a whoosh of deep orange flame and a cloud of black smoke, then the pungent odour of burning snake flesh filled their nostrils and the still of the night.

Chapter 8

Strains of Sinatra, blue strains in a brown atmosphere. The house is many shades of brown. Its walls are brown, its woodwork – doors and windows – are varnish brown, the furniture is brown, the people who live in the house are brown, a pale insipid brown, except for Rita, mostly a dark brown from the many hours spent lolling on the beach, white as blancmange where her bikini covers her.

The boys are in luck. Rita's mum is out, no one knows where exactly but it really doesn't matter. Probably nursing a brandy and ginger ale with a block of ice, a brown drink for a brown lady: her legs crossed, one over the other, holding the glass in her nicotine stained fingers, pulling incessantly on a cork tip cigarette, scarlet stained from her lipstick. Stubbing it out with quick short heavy-handed jabs into an overflowing ashtray on a glass topped table in the lounge of a seedy hotel, across the table a new found acquaintance at whose quips she giggles, pretending coyness at smut, the life and soul of the party, good time girl, great fun. She doesn't really fancy him. He has a beer belly and heavy unshaven jowls and it looks like he sweats a lot and isn't too fussy about washing but so long as he's footing the bill who is she to be particular? It's been a long time since she could be particular. The thought makes her want to down her drink in one quick gulp.

Dad, in dinner jacket and black bow tie, has gone to a meeting of his lodge, carrying a small solid leather case holding his saddle and regalia, medals and books, his only possessions of value, a post office sorter with not much to say, making just enough to keep their heads above water. He does not know his wife well. He's not sure he ever knew her really and the longer they are together under the same roof, still sharing the same bedroom, the same double bed, the more of a stranger she becomes. He can look at the wedding photographs taken all those years ago, he thought he knew her then, and he wonders who the person is who has taken her place. He does not know his daughter at all. She is a complete stranger to him. He is a little brown man who once had secret farfetched dreams. Carlos has discovered what has taken their place: sweet muscatel, two bottles of syrupy red and one white; sick making in its sweetness. The cooking sherry, half a bottle of pale pink, more like a rosé in appearance, is vinegary so after one sip and an 'argh!' it is left on the shelf.

Carlos rocks back on his chair, maintaining a balance by tapping out the rhythms of the song flat handed on the table in front of him. The kitchen is small and filthy. A cockroach, a black bull of a roach, scuttles out from beneath the grease-dripping sink and waves his antennae at the world before scuttling back and disappearing down a damp rot hole in the wooden floor. Another roach, smaller than the first and brown, scuttles out to take his place and makes a dash for the other side of the room. Johnny's foot comes down hard and fast. There is a crackling of roach and the guts squash white on the brown floor, and then merge with the brownness, rubbed between leather and wood.

Johnny looked at the mess on his sole. 'Jesus!' he exclaims. 'There must be fifty million cockroaches in this place!' He stares with distaste at the dish littered sink, the pot encrusted with half dried porridge, soaking off. He picks up a wooden spoon and scrapes off a layer, plays with it for a while, wondering whether or not to jokingly flick a lump of porridge in someone's direction. He decides against it and drops the spoon back in the pot. A bottle half filled with milk gone bad stands on the drainer. He picks it up. The white curd separated at the top and beneath it the pale green watery whey. It's not sour milk, not maas. Maas you can drink. Maas is not milk gone bad but gone sour. Although he's not too fond of it himself his mother's a great one for drinking maas. This bottle is milk gone bad. He sniffs at it and hurriedly bangs the bottle down on the drainer, tossing the smell from his nostrils with a quick flick of his head. 'Doesn't anybody ever clean up in this place?' The question isn't directed at anyone in particular. Nobody would answer it anyway.

Angelo leans across the table, hands cradling his elbows, listening to the music and thinking of Millie.

Steve had changed the record. *This is a lovely way to spend an evening, can't think of anything else I'd rather do.* Carlos stops his tapping; the number is too slow, too blue for the jazz drummer he imagines himself to be. He takes up the bottle of wine and throws back his head, his lips tight about the mouth of the bottle: a private love affair.

Angelo watched the movement of his Adam's apple as he swallowed; up, down, up, down. Carlos lowered the bottle and wiped his mouth with the back of his hand, then went back to rocking on his chair. Angelo pushed his own away from the table, stood up and went through into the passage, darker brown with no illumination except the pale glow from the street lamp outside the front door, filtered through coloured glass, dark red and blue squares.

'Hey, Angel!' Johnny shouted after him, 'Where you going?'

Angelo didn't answer. He pushed open the door to the front room. 'Hey, Steve.'

A muffled voice came from the rexine couch, 'Go away! Can't you see I'm busy?'

'It's time we were pushing off, man.'

'It's time you were pushing off.'

Angelo realised it was pointless. He looked around

the room, the curtains were brown, the woodwork stained. There were three monochrome pre-Raphaelite prints in sepia and two in blue and yellow of Arabs and camels in the desert at sunset. On the mantelpiece above the elaborate but small, cold, and empty cast iron Victorian fireplace, the mirrored overmantel reaching nearly to the ceiling, a head held high proud plaster Rin-tin-tin stood majestically on a rocky outcrop, the back of his head reflected in the mirror behind him. Facing this ornamental dog with one ear missing stood a young lady in a long pink dress, her body arched back, holding down her beribboned picture hat against the breeze with one hand and in the other hand, a leash, at the end of which two borzois strained, seemingly trying to get at the proud Rin-tin-tin standing at the other end of the mantelpiece, his one eared head turned towards the room. Behind their reflections Angelo could see the room and the reflection of the couple on the rexine couch. He closed the door behind him and went silently back down the passage, back to Sinatra and Johnny and Carlos. Johnny was standing by an ancient refrigerator, its once white enamel turning yellow and chipped around the edges of the door. He was still cockroach hunting. Carlos was toying with the second bottle of muscatel. They looked up as Angelo entered.

'How they doing in there?' Johnny asked. 'Has he got it up yet?'

Angelo shrugged and went back to the chair. 'Who cares?'

Carlos was beginning to look decidedly uneasy.

'Hey, let's leave them to it!' Johnny said. 'Let's go down to Nicks.' There was no reply. 'Come on.' He moaned, 'I'm so bored.'

Carlos turned to him. 'You were the one suggested coming here in the first place,' he murmured, his speech already slurred. Johnny moved up behind Angelo's chair and leaning forward, buttocks thrust backwards, put his straight arms over Angelo's shoulders and laid his cheek against the other's. 'Come on, Angie,' he said coaxingly, his arms folding over Angelo's chest, 'Let's you and me leave this lot and go down to Nick's.' Angelo did not move. 'Come on, Angie'…

'Hey, you two,' Carlos called out, 'don't you look sweet.'

Johnny placed his lips against Angelo's ear and whispered. Angelo laughed, moving his head away and shaking the tickle from his ear. He looked at Johnny's smiling face and placed the back of his fingers against the mouth. Johnny pushed his lips against them and raised his eyebrows but Angelo shook his head. Johnny sighed and wandered over to the passage door, stopped there, thinking better of it, came back to the table and started idly to sort through the records. 'Boy, I'm browned off!' he said, echoing the sentiments and the atmosphere of the whole house.

Chapter 9

Millie said her prayers, crossed herself, and hopped onto the bed. She wished her mother didn't make her wear these very heavy flannel nighties. They were strictly for small kids. She looked at the tiny pink roses on the material and her downward glance fell between her small breasts. She looked at her fingers, at her toes, smiling to herself, then she jumped off the bed and padded across to the dressing table, sitting in front of it and gazing at herself in the mirror. She peered from all angles, turning her head first one way then the other, trying to catch her profile. It would have been easier had her dressing table been equipped with side mirrors, as it was she developed a cramp in her neck. She went back to the bed, undoing as she walked the clasp on the chain she wore about her neck, on which hung a tiny gold crucifix. She dropped it on to the bamboo table and leapt back on the bed. It was a large bed with hollows into which she could snuggle. She snuggled and gazed at the ceiling. If only she had a photograph.

'Millie?'

'Yes, mom?'

'Put that light out now.'

'Yes, mom.'

She giggled and pulled up her knees to slip her feet beneath the covers, turned on her side to reach the bedside lamp, clicked off the light, rubbed her nose in the pillow, heaved a sigh and closed her eyes. Angelo...

...Tony was suddenly awake, gazing at the ceiling and wondering what the taste in his mouth could be. For a second or two his mind was a blank then he lifted himself onto his elbow to see where he was. The bed was white and surrounded by a fence of white metal framed screens of creased dark blue cotton. Next to the bed was a white locker on which a lamp gleamed, a bottle of water with a tumbler inverted over the neck, and an ashtray stood next to it. He opened the locker door, leaning out of bed in order to reach it. It was empty. Beneath the blankets one leg was protected by a wire cage. He lifted the covers and peeped underneath. He was dressed in striped flannel pyjamas, not his own, and the foot under the cage was encased in brand new shiny white plaster of Paris. Tony leaned out of bed again and pulled aside one of the screens. The ward stretched away in a dim double row of beds and sleeping patients. At the far end, in front of a pair of double doors, the night sister in her blue cape was sitting at a desk, scribbling by the light of an anglepoise lamp. A man in a white coat came through the doors and stood whispering to her. Outside the door there was a shadow of another man. The sister looked up and they both glanced in the direction of Tony's bed, then the man went back and opened one of the doors. The shadow came through; a man in a khaki uniform who, with the doctor, came walking up the aisle between the beds towards Tony. Tony lay back on his bed and closed his eyes. His heart was thumping behind his ribs and his belly was icy with fear.

'Next time you come,' Rita murmured, 'Come on your own.' Her fingers stroked the velvet skin of his stomach exploring the little hollow above his thigh, inching towards his pubic hair.

'Okay,' Steve replied, 'When?'

Her fingers moved up over his chest, paused on the slightly raised nipple, then burrowed into his armpit. 'Whenever you like!'

'Yeah?' He laughed softly. 'And your old man on my tail?'

'My old man walks about in a dwaal. He doesn't know what time of day it is. He wouldn't know his arse from his elbow. He'd probably think you were a plumber come to clear a drain, something like that maybe.'

She pursed her lips and the hand slid back down his chest, down his belly. 'Whistle outside my window.'

'What about now?' He suggested.

'What about it?'

'Now.' He moved her hand so that it touched his prick but she moved it away again.

'You're doing all right, aren't you?' she said.

'Let's go to the bedroom.'

She shook her head.

'Why not?'

'She might come back.' She inclined her head towards the street outside.

'We'll get the boys to keep a lookout, come on.' He half rose from the couch.

'No!'

Steve flopped back again and stroked persuasively. 'There's nothing to worry about. They can warn us as soon as they see somebody coming. They can see right down to the end of the street. Come on. Hmn?' There was a silence as she looked at him. He raised his chin in little jerks of encouragement while she thought about it. His eyes pleaded, saying only one thing. She shrugged assent. Steve smiled.

Angelo opened the door and stood there. 'Hey, Steve!'

'Christ! What is it now? What's the matter with you man? Steve got off the couch and hitched up his trousers, tucking in his shirt.

'I'm pushing off.'

'That's a fucking great idea,' Steve growled. 'I don't

know why you came in the first place. Why don't you just relax and enjoy yourself like the rest of us.' He grabbed Rita by the arm, pulled her towards him, and held her close by the waist. She looked at Angelo for approval, holding her hand over Steve's crotch, giggling and pressing herself against him. Angelo's face registered nothing. The giggling stopped.

Johnny's cut.'

'What?'

'He's cut,' Angelo repeated, remembering how Johnny in the kitchen looked. 'Slewed! Blind as a bat!' He looked at Rita. 'He drank most of a bottle of your dad's wine.'

'So what!' Steve tried to return to his hugging but Rita held him back for a moment with both hands against his chest and looked at Angelo who continued quietly, his voice flat, uninterested. 'Carlos is cut too. He finished it off and they drank another besides.'

Steve swung around, glaring at Angelo, his fists clenched. He was not sure whether Angelo was deliberately putting a spoke in his wheel or whether the situation demanded attention.

Angelo's face remained impassive as though he were really not a part of all this, which somehow he felt he wasn't. He couldn't figure out what the hell he was doing there. Why had he agreed to come in the first place? Why had he not left? What was happening here held no interest for him really. At this moment he actively disliked all four people in this house. He wanted out, and yet he did not move, only talked.

'Well what the bloody hell's it got to do with me?' Steve swore angrily. 'I'm not their keeper! If they want to act like baboons let them go do it someplace else.' He calmed down a little after this outburst and smiled engagingly. 'Go put on another record, Angel.' He winked at Angelo and inclined his head toward the door, then he turned back to Rita and tried to nibble her ear but she pulled her head away, not looking at him. He turned back again. Angelo had not moved.

'They drank a whole bottle?' Her voice was quiet, hardly more than a whisper.

Angelo who, after giving her the information, had

kept his gaze on Steve, looked at her as if for the first time and she sensed his dislike. He raised two fingers. It could have been a gesture. It could have been information.

Steve was laughing in apprehension at the ground he had lost and, it seemed, was unlikely to recover. 'Hey!' he said through his laughter, 'What is this? The brush off?' His mauling was clumsy now, made clumsier by her struggle to remain out of his grasp.

'Two!' She shouted at Angelo, trying to push Steve away.

'That's what I said. If you don't believe me, go take a look for yourself. I think they're both going to puke their guts up.'

She started for the door.

'Hey, Rita!' In three strides, Steve had caught her, just as she was disappearing into the passage, and held her by the arm. She tried to prize apart his fingers. Like her mother she bruised easily, the slightest knock or pressure and she was black and blue, but the possible bruising was not what worried her at the moment. It was the thought of her homecoming parents, particularly her mother. Father she thought she could handle, it was only a matter of selecting the right words, but once her mother started it was a stand up fight and she was likely to come off the worst, lacking experience. But Steve held on to her. He was really worried now with the worry of incipient frustration. Things were not going to turn out the way he wanted whereas only a minute ago...

'Hey, Rita! What does it matter for Chrissakes? Forget it will you?' It was not going to be, he could see that, but he was too far gone to stop trying.

She spun on him, wrenching free her arm, her eyes blazing. Angelo stood motionless behind them, watching it all. 'Forget it?' she screamed at him. She shook back a lock of hair from her face and pulled a bra strap back into place. It immediately slipped again. From the kitchen came the sound of singing, or what passed as singing, in accompaniment to the record now playing. 'Now you listen to me... you get out of here now and take your drunk friends with you... right this very minute... go on!' She wiped her nose between her thumb and forefinger and stared angrily.

Steve tried to placate her, soft voiced, smiling. 'Aw, cool it, honey. What're you getting so het-up about?' The Hollywood act didn't go down well. It only incensed her further. 'We'll get you another bottle of vino for your old man.'

'To-night?' She spat it out like a roof top cat, stiff legged, back arched, top lip curled away from her gums and fangs showing.

'What do you mean tonight?' Steve whined, and then fighting back, 'Where the hell do you expect me to find a bottle of vino this time of night? All the bottle stores will be closed. And anyway, I don't have the money.' They stood glaring at each other. The desire had died in Steve but his back was up. He felt a strong urge to slap her, to slap her really hard, possibly again and again.

'And what happens when my dad gets back and finds two whole bottles of wine gone? Hey?'

Steve suddenly responded to the real anxiety in her voice and his desire started to make a comeback. His voice softened. 'Look, don't worry about that now? Come back to Stevie, come on,' he pleaded, trying to pull her through the doorway and back into the room.

'Oh, get lost!' She gave him a shove that sent him flying off balance so that he fell against the back of a chair, twisted over on to his stomach and, as the chair toppled over with his weight, landed head down, bum in the air, jack-knifed like a puppet that's flopped forward when its strings are loosened. Angelo laughed, stifling the sound of it so that Steve wouldn't hear, and immediately was solemn faced again as Steve pushed himself up and turned in time to see Rita storm out of the room and head down the passage.

The singing stopped. They heard her screaming at Carlos and Johnny and then the sound of laughter from the two boys as they evaded her. Angelo moved over to the mantelpiece, turning his back on Steve, and laid a hand on the lady in the picture hat. Steve came up behind him and Angelo looked at him in the mirror. His expression was not pretty.

'Now what the hell did you want to tell her that for?' Steve fumed. 'I was just getting nicely settled, man.'

Angelo lifted a shoulder. 'It's late,' he said simply.

'Well why don't you beat it then?' Steve asked addressing their reflections. 'What's keeping you? Go on, on your camel!'

Angelo moved away from the mirror and seated himself on an arm of the couch. 'Her old man will be coming back soon, what about Johnny and Carlos? They got to get home.' He drummed on the rexine with his fingers and then tried to pick out with fingernails a protruding upholstery tack that could cause some shallow but nasty damage.

'They can get home on their own, all right? That's their lookout, isn't it?' Steve walked about the room, not looking at Angelo and Angelo not looking at him. After a moment Steve hit the wall with the side of his clenched fist, his other hand tight around his cock. He almost wanted to bring himself off then and there. 'Shit!' he hissed.

Angelo, who had been studying his shoes, looked up, got off the couch and walked to the door, just as Rita entered the passage pushing before her a virtually incapable Johnny with his arm over a more capable, because he could hold his drink just a little better, Carlos. Angelo backed up so that they could enter the room. Johnny clung to the door for a second; holding them up but another thrust from Rita shot Johnny practically into his arms. He went down on one knee, all but pulling a giggling Carlos after him, but with Angelo taking the other arm they hauled him to his wobbly feet. Johnny smiled seraphically, his eyes shut tight. Rita took up Steve's jacket that had been flung over a chair and tossed it to him. He caught it one handed and swung it so that nothing fell from the pockets. 'Now get your friends out of here,' she commanded and there was obviously no point in arguing with her though he tried.

'Aw, lay off, Rita, will ya? They're okay.'

'You reckon so? It doesn't look like that to me, you know?'

She was looking at Johnny who now lay sprawled in

the chair that Angelo had righted, his legs stretched out in front, head back, eyes closed, still smiling happily. 'Get them out of here!' she screamed, 'And don't ever bring them back!'

'Come on, Carlos.' Angelo took Carlos by the arm but he pulled his arm away with a jerk and a snarl. 'Take your hands off me!' It seemed an impasse had been reached. Steve stood stock still, obviously unwilling to do anything. He still clung to his faint hopes of bringing it off. Angelo too was really loath to interfere. He could go home on his own but, if these two refused to move, what then? He was worried they would cause trouble for Rita.

Johnny opened his eyes, lurched out of the chair and staggered across to Rita, throwing his arms around her neck. She stepped back only to be brought to an abrupt halt by the sharp wooden edge of the mantelpiece. The plaster ornaments rocked on their bases. Rin-tin-tin was in dire danger of losing his whole head if not more. 'Hey!' Johnny laughed, passing from their trembling to his own reflection behind them. He opened his eyes very wide. 'Hey! Lookee see there what I see! Who dat?' Rita tried to disentangle his arms. 'What's a matter, Rita? You mad at us? Don't be mad.' She held him by the wrists and pushed him away in disgust. 'Steve!' she was pleading now looking to him for action as she headed for the door.

Johnny lurched back again like a rubber ball flung against a wall and staggered after her. 'What've we done, Rita? Huh? Huh, Rita? Tell me what we've done.'

Steve had had enough, all hope now definitely gone. He flung his jacket over his shoulder, deciding at last to make a move, crossed over and pulled Johnny back with his free hand. Johnny swivelled on rolling heels and threw his arms over Steve's shoulders. 'Lay off, Johnny!' Steve ordered but Johnny just smiled foolishly. 'Wha's matter, Stevie? Tha's my ole pal, Stevie, hey, Steve? Give us a kiss, Stevie.' He giggled and his head dropped on Steve's chest. Steve pushed him away and he collapsed once more into the chair, laughing to himself. 'You're pissed!' Steve stated the obvious, not making an excuse for Johnny, merely pointing out to him the reason for his behaviour and not knowing really how he was supposed to handle the situation.

'Don't push the kid around,' Carlos growled truculently, feeling kindly disposed towards his fellow inebriate.

'He's drunk as a fucking skunk!' Steve yelled.

'Okay okay! So he's drunk! But don't push him around!' Carlos yelled right back, fight happy, the alcohol now doing the talking.

Steve's instinct was to lash out at the mutineer but he was too disappointed in the night's proceedings to want to worry overmuch about anything now. What angered him most was that he had deliberately talked himself into wanting her and it was easier he found to talk oneself into something then to talk oneself out of it. If push came to shove he didn't even like the cow. He didn't even find her attractive if it came to that. It was just there to be had, any old port in a storm as the saying goes. He might as well have gone off and married his hand. And now, would he be able to laugh the whole thing off? When they discussed the evening's events tomorrow, and the subject was sure to be mentioned with much ribaldry, would he be able to make his excuses convincing enough when taxed with his lack of determination? They all knew her reputation. So half the boys who said they had been with her did so out of bravado or because they had to boast of some experience, and experience with Rita was the least likely to be put to the question, but the reputation existed nevertheless. He was angry not so much with Angelo for breaking it up, with the boys for their part in maintaining the discord, opening wider the wound he had tried so desperately to heal, but with himself; and that kind of anger is the most difficult to forgive. He was now in the passage ready to leave. Rita stood with folded arms waiting for their departure.

Johnny scrambled out of his chair, stood in the doorway and said to Rita, 'What you got to eat, man? I'm fucking starving.' He turned as though to head back to the kitchen but she barred his way.

'Yeah, so am I,' Carlos said.

Johnny staggered his way out into the passage.

'Steve!' Rita cried, 'Stop him!'

They followed the floating Johnny who, by this time, had weaved his way to the fridge, yanked open the door, and was virtually swinging on the none to safe handle.

'Hey, Rita!' He yelled, 'What you keeping in your fridge, man?' He lifted a piece of grease proof paper and peeped beneath it. 'Polony! Polony! I love polony!' He moved over to the table with his prize and lifted a piece of old pink processed meat, hardening and curling slightly around the edge, dotted with diamonds of white fat, held it high above his head, dropped it slowly into his mouth; caught it between his teeth and pulled out the ribbon of red skin which he waved in the air before letting it drop to the floor. Then he moved back to the fridge to join Carlos who had arrived and was rooting away happily and noisily. He came out with a tomato, bit into it, and the pippy juice dribbled down his chin. Carlos thrust out his jaw, elbow held high, to avoid spilling it on his shirt and, to get away from Rita's clutches, they headed for the far side of the table, rounding on either side, meeting in the middle.

'Polony for tomato!' Johnny yelled. 'Fair exchange's no robbery!'

Carlos rammed the half tomato into Johnny's laughing face and Johnny rammed a slice of polony into Carlos's.

'Polony!' he cried joyfully, 'Elephant's maidenhead!'

They were laughing, chewing, spluttering, laughing, and hardly able to stay on their feet.

Hard case as she was, Rita surveyed the scene and was close to tears, mainly of frustration in her inability to handle the recalcitrant marauders who seemed now to be totally out of hand. She followed them around the table which left the other side open and the way to the fridge. She watched helplessly as they returned to their foraging.

'Let's get the food!' Johnny ordered. 'Boarding parties! Grappling irons out!' he tried to climb on a chair to shout out his orders but the chair wobbled and he fell off.

'Steve,' Rita pleaded, 'Get them out of here, please!'

Steve and Angelo grabbed the two boys and tried to pull them away from the fridge but Carlos caught hold of

Johnny and Johnny caught hold of the handle and the fridge lurched forward on its two front legs and a bottle of milk toppled and spewed over the floor.

'Whatsa matter with you guys?' Steve demanded. 'If you can't take your booze...'

'Who can't take his booze?'

'Can't rake my booze?'

'Who says we can't take our booze?'

'I do! Now come on come on, for fuck's sake let's get out of here!'

Johnny flinched at the fury in Steve's voice and his tone was immediately repentant. 'It's because I've been drinking on an empty stomach, Stevie, tha's all,' he whined. 'Gimme another piece of that polony. I love polony.' He rubbed his hands down his face and shook his head, blinked hard a few times and tried to focus. The room was tilting crazily and beginning to spin giddily. He closed his eyes but that only made it worse. His head was hot and he felt the floor undulating beneath his feet. He floated and listened to his own heavy breathing. They had disappeared, Steve, Rita, Carlos, Angelo, it seemed they had all disappeared, there was only this crazy floating world and his own breathing. Where had they gone to then? He was at home in bed. He heard his mother's voice calling him, 'Johnny? Johnny!' he opened his mouth trying to draw great big dollops of air into his lungs but the world would not stop moving. It was flying through space, spinning, spinning... He was going to be sick. He was going to puke up his ring. He groaned and opened his eyes. They were watching him closely.

'You okay, Johnny?' Angelo asked, worried by the boy's ashen face. Johnny nodded.

'Come on,' Steve said, 'Let's go.'

'You okay, Johnny?' An anxious Carlos took his arm and peered closely into his face.

'Sure!' Johnny shouted. 'Sure sure sure sure! I'm okay! I'm, okay! I'm, okay! Come on, let's go, let's go, let's go.' He put an arm over Carlos's shoulder and the two of them followed Steve into the passage. Carlos yelled over his shoulder, 'Night

Rita! Thanks for the party!' It was at this moment that without warning Johnny opened his mouth and everyone leapt out of the way as the floodgates opened to send a shower of spew splattering against the wall, over the floor, down his front, over his shoes.

'Oh my God!' Rita cried, all but wringing her hands

'Sorry, Rita, sorry.' A second shower followed. 'Sorry, hey.' He doubled over in agony. His stomach was empty now, there was no more to bring up, but his muscles kept going into spasm as they contracted. He started to groan.

Rita was now almost hysterical. 'What am I going to do?' she wailed. 'Who's going to clean up this mess before my parents get home? Oh, God! Smell it! Smell it! Oh, God!'

'He's not going to help, I can tell you that,' Steve said.

For a moment Rita stood looking at her unwanted guests and then turned and went silently back to the kitchen.

Carlos blew her a kiss and made a lewd gesture then they made for the front door.

For her they were already non-existent. She had to set about urgently cleaning up the mess in the passage. The floor, linoleum covered, was easy though she had no idea how she was going to set about the wall. As for the missing vino... She was already working on a scenario in her mind. She heard a noise in the kitchen and went to investigate; thinking maybe it was a cat. Instead she found the back door open. A native must have climbed over the fence and broken in. He didn't come around the front because he heard her moving about, so he just took the two bottles of wine and fled when he heard her coming... She suddenly noticed Angelo had not left with the others but was standing watching her.

'You want some help?' he asked. 'I'll give you a hand, clean up.'

Outside in the street the boys called for him. Rita shook her head denying his offer of help. 'I can manage thank you.' He did not move. 'Too bad it's so late,' she said. 'You could have stayed, or come back.' Angelo shook his head, turned, and walked away down the passage.

As he appeared at the front door, Johnny and Carlos

broke into wolf whistles. Rita came charging out. 'Shut up, you skollies! You hooligans!' She hissed loudly. 'You want to get me in more trouble?' There was a chorus of shushes, Johnny and Carlos facing each other, each with a finger to his mouth and making all the noise as she slammed the door and her shadow disappeared. Carlos started to break into song but broke off, an anxious look on his face as he leaned against the veranda rail.

'Oooh!' he groaned, 'I think I want to be sick now.'

Steve climbed onto his bike that, with the others, had been left locked against the veranda railings.

'Puke then, see who cares,' he said. 'Puke your fucking ring up.'

'It's not funny, man, I feel terrible.'

Steve astride the saddle, both feet on the pavement, took out a cigarette and lit it. 'Well go on then, puke and get it over with. Man, I told you not to look so deep in the bottle.' He pulled on his cigarette and blew a cloud of smoke into the still night air. Carlos was quiet now, waiting in apprehension for the nausea he knew was going to hit him. He could feel his stomach heave but maintained enough control to stop it from out and out rebellion. He dreaded being sick. It was too painful, too humiliating. Last time he drank too much and was sick he swore he would never do it again so why had he? The others waited with him, knowing how he felt but making sure they stood well clear, wondering if they could cope when it eventually arrived. But Carlos wanted sympathy from all of them, Steve as well as the other two. He wanted Steve to show some understanding. 'It wasn't the vino, Stevie, it was the polo...' In talking he lost control. He lurched over the gutter, clung to the lamppost and bending forward, vomited noisily, choking and spluttering as the sudden up rush filled his mouth, his nose, blinded him, choked him. His guts heaved and he clung with trembling fingers to the cold iron of the post.

Steve looked at the sky, then ruminatively at his cigarette, rolling it between his fingers and blowing on the lighted end so that it glowed a fiery red. 'You guys ought to learn how to hold your liquor.' There was a temporary lull from Carlos. 'You busted me up nicely with Rita just as I was getting going.'

His only answer was another bout of retching noises from Johnny, the smell of Carlos's vomit having reached his nose. There was nothing to come out and his throat closed tight. He gasped and struggled for breath, the muscles of his stomach a hard ball of spasm.

'Aw, Crap!' Carlos said, seemingly having recovered somewhat from his own bout of nausea, 'We did you a big favour. Aren't you finished yet, Johnny?' Johnny groaned loudly.

Angelo put an arm over his shoulder. 'You'll be right, Johnny. Just try and relax, huh?' He ran his fingers affectionately through the boy's hair and thought how silky it was. There was a sudden false alarm. Johnny bent forward hastily but, apart from the contraction of his stomach, nothing happened. Angelo rubbed his back and Johnny stood up straight again. 'Here,' Angelo said, 'Give us your hankie.' Johnny fumbled in his pocket and came out with a grimy handkerchief. Angelo wiped his trembling lips, shook his head and laughed sympathetically, then stuffed the handkerchief back in Johnny's pocket. 'What you been using that for? Is that your spunk rag?'

'Rub my stomach, Angel,' the boy said. 'It's sore as hell.' He sniffed in self-pity and Angelo complied, rubbing in gentle circular motions. Gradually Johnny relaxed, feeling better. 'Jeez,' he said, 'Why can't I be a horse?'

'What do you want to be a horse for?'

'Horses can't be sick. That's what a jockey told me once. They can't be sick, he said, they're not made that way. If they was to be sick they'd die. They rupture themselves or something. I think I'm going to die. I'd like to be a jockey. I've never been on a horse. Watched them exercise down the Walmer Road.'

'Who said a horse can't be sick?' Carlos asked.

'I told you, that jockey I spoke to, he told me that.'

'Well he doesn't know what he's talking about then.'

'Why not? He should know if anyone does. A jockey

should know. Isn't that right, Angelo, hey?'

'Bullshit! What do jockeys know about horses? All they do is ride them and they don't do that any good either. You put a jockey on a horse that's not galloping, you put him on at a trot or a canter and he'd fall off, I'm telling you. Jockeys are hopeless.'

'Well that's what he said, horses can't be sick, he said, they're not made to be sick.'

'They can be sick.' Carlos was pretty definite about this. 'The trouble is, if they are, it kills them.'

'That's what I just said, you prick! What did I just say?' He turned to Steve and Angelo for confirmation.

Angelo shrugged. 'I think we ought to get moving,' he said.

Johnny turned a tearstained face in his direction as Carlos, ignoring this, continued. 'So you ought to be glad you're not a horse.' Johnny pondered over this, looking to Angelo for confirmation as to whether or not horses died if they were sick but, as Angelo didn't know one way or the other, he said nothing.

'I'll tell you something else interesting about horses,' Carlos said, climbing on to the veranda rails and settling himself down comfortably. 'When a stallion get a cockstand, if you're not careful he gets too excited, you know? And he can push it up the wrong hole.' Johnny gazed at Carlos in astonishment. 'No, yurra, it's a fact, man,' Carlos insisted. 'And you know what happens then hey?' Carlos clicked his fingers and jerked his forefinger towards Johnny's face to emphasis his tagline, 'Dead! In twenty-four hours she's dead as a bloody doornail, boy! I'm telling you.' Johnny waited for an explanation but as it didn't seem to be forthcoming he asked for it. 'Well,' Carlos replied, 'He ruptures her you see. He tears the inside wall of her what's it, and that's her lot. Can't be fixed.'

'Go on!' Johnny said after a suitable pause for digestion.

'Okay, don't believe me, but next time you see that jockey pal of yours, you ask him. Horses are randy buggers you know. That's why they tie a little leather thing on them.'

'What leather thing?'

'It's a sort of thong they tie on the end of their pricks.'

'What for?'

'Stops them tossing themselves off.'

'What? You're pulling my leg. Horses don't toss themselves off.'

'Shows you how much you know about horses. Haven't you seen them do it?'

'No. How do they do it?'

'They beat their pricks against their bellies, man, like this.' He illustrated with a gesture of his arm and closed fist. 'So they tie those things on them to stop them doing it.'

'Poor bastards. Fancy doing a thing like that!' Johnny was most indignant.

'Well,' said the voice of authority, 'You got to be careful with pedigree racehorses you know. Can't have them going around doing themselves damage. I mean they cost a lot of money those things, thousands of quid!'

'Yeah, but that's unnatural!' Johnny protested. 'It's cruel!'

'No more cruel than castrating them, is it? Better I'd say. At least they take the leather thing off when they do mate. They get some chance to do it, don't they?'

'Well no wonder they get too excited,' Johnny reasoned, 'When they spend most of their lives tied up with a leather thing. Shhh!' He shook his head in stern disapproval.

'Yeah,' Said Steve, suddenly joining in the conversation, 'But that's like us, isn't it? When you come to think of it? Only we don't have a leather thing tied to us. We're just told, 'Lay off' just like that. So what happens?'

They all waited to hear what happens but Steve exited as abruptly as he had entered. He did not feel like elaborating the point. The fact was he did not know how to elaborate it. The word frustration had never entered his vocabulary and its machinations were more than he would understand. He felt only that it existed, that it worked in various ways, but he could not lay his finger on any one thing and say, 'this is the result of frustration,' or qualify his feelings and say, 'this is the result of frustration.' Without the word there was no thought, only feeling undefined, only nerves sharpened to the point of anguish, only a lashing out; anger, spite, vindictiveness and the desire to inflict pain. Only resentment: only boredom. But these were not conscious efforts of thought. They were merely feelings, emotions whose well springs remained hidden, motives behind motives, brought out in physical action, in sweat and speech, in kicking, punching, running, thieving, swearing, smoking, in denial, in perversity.

Steve looked at the darkened house and wondered what she was doing in there; still cleaning up no doubt though the light wasn't on in the passage. Maybe she was playing fuckfinger as he had got her so hot, so worked up. At the thought of it he felt himself stirring again then he flicked his cigarette away in a looping arc. It hit the pavement, splintering into a shower of tiny glowing sparks, dying in the fraction of a second. 'Let's get going,' he said, one foot now on a pedal ready to push off. Angelo and Carlos made a move and then,

'No, hang on a sec.' Carlos requested. 'It's coming on again.'

'Well put your finger down your throat and I hope it fucking chokes you.'

Carlos turned and snapped, 'Aw, fuck you, man! What's eating you?'

Steve all but fell off his bike in his angry haste to answer. The machine clattered to the pavement, its front wheel spinning slowly in the air, as he stumbled towards them. 'I should knock the living daylights out of you, shithead!' he exploded. 'There I was, just ready to get going, and you lot had to come in and make a balls up of it for me! That dame really goes for me, you know that?'

'Too bad,' Carlos sneered, 'You and one million other guys!'

They stood facing each other, their antagonism broken only by the sudden sound of Johnny retching again. He crouched over the gutter rocking back and forth with Angelo beside him, holding his stomach in an effort to relieve the spasms that buckled his body. He was crying now, when he could, his eye blinded by hot tears, his nose and throat raw and burning, his stomach aching with cramp as the muscles contracted and refused to let go; unable to breathe, struggling not to panic, his cheeks feeling as though they would burst with the up rush of blood that turned his face a dull maroon. Never again. Never again.

Carlos took over the other side. 'Easy now,' he whispered in encouragement, 'Just take it easy, Johnny. Take it easy, man.'

They kept their hands where they thought it would help but both averted their faces. Angelo felt his own gorge rising at the stench and the sound of it and wondered how long he could hold out. But the taste of vomit in Johnny's mouth only made the spasms worse. He felt it would never end, this agony would never end. Steve, still furious, moved away to pick up his bike. He had had enough. He was going home. What did he care what they did with themselves? Ruined his chances, spoilt his evening, why hadn't he just gone to the flicks on his own? He would think twice tomorrow about going out with this little lot. Fucking kids!

Chapter 10

Sergeant Nel wished he had a moment when he could enjoy a nice quiet cup of tea. The rush hour still had another hour or more to run. Hour? He glanced up at the charge office clock. Another two and a half was more like it, and then from about two to five there would be comparative peace before it all started again. He looked around the room and scratched the side of his nose with the blunt end of his pencil, then he settled down to complete the form on the counter in front of him.

Being a policeman would not have been Nel's first choice of a lifetime occupation but when you came from a large poor white family, even with the jobs available only to whites, the choice was limited. There were jobs on the railways, in the postal service, but Nel wanted to feel he had more to give than just holding down a job, he had felt he could be of use to the community, and so he chose to be a policeman despite the fact that South African policeman on the whole had the reputation of being as thick as two planks.

The telephone rang. It seemed to sergeant Nel that it always rang incessantly whenever he was at his busiest with constables coming in from their beat to make out charges, cars rolling in, marias from shebeen raids and shanty town. The two went hand in hand he supposed but it made life extremely difficult, trying to divide the attention. He let the phone ring while he finished what he was doing then lifted the receiver. 'Central Police Station.' Sergeant Nel was approaching retiring age, a gentle man with an engaging smile and a shyness that seemed strange in one so experienced in the degradation of human nature, in one who had seen a life time of police work, the horror and depravity of which human beings are capable. He detested violence and yet he had deliberately involved himself in it. His life was circumscribed by violence of one sort or another. Surrounded by the sordidness of a police station and by his less sensitive, more callous comrades, he seemed to be a misfit, until one realised that he actually liked people. He did not pity them: he liked them; and where he could, he helped them, gently, firmly, generously, without ostentation, without fuss. For thirty five years he had watched the flotsam of his small corner of the world washed by the tide of life up to the counter of his charge office, and there were many with cause to be grateful that Sergeant Nel was on duty when they arrived: the sick, the squalid, the weak, the brutal, the moronic, the misguided, the lost, the lonely, the perverted and the evil; drunkards, maniacs, petty offenders, thieves, vagabonds, and killers, he had seen them all at one time or another. There was not an S.A.P form he had not made out and, at the end of it all he remained almost childlike in his simplicity and his compassion. Perhaps it was the staunchness of his Dutch Reform Faith or perhaps it was his roly-poly pink wife and his children, now grown up and presenting him with grandchildren that held him like a lifeline to his honesty and his first principles. He listened to the voice at the other end of the phone, glancing around the office as he did so.

The room is divided into three sections, the counter running its full width dividing it in half and a wooden and asbestos partition dividing its public half again; one side for Europeans, the other for non-Europeans. Even in crime there is segregation. The whole place from floor to ceiling is painted a sombre green. Green seems to be a favourite colour for paint. On the working side of the counter a number of heavy plain tables are littered with papers except for one, slightly smaller, surrounded by files and upon which stands a radio and microphone. In the centre of this section there is a large black safe on a concrete base. When a prisoner's valuables are taken from him, they are listed and packaged and he signs a receipt for them. They are stowed in the safe carefully labelled. The prisoner is taken to the cells divested of anything with which he could do himself an injury; tie, belt, shoelaces. The back wall is lined with shelves divided into partitions, each holding a numbered form, on front of each partition a gummed label to say what it holds. Beneath the shelves stand a row of cupboards one of which houses the .38 revolvers and ammunition. The force at one time used .45's but a forty-five feels like it weighs a ton, makes a nasty mess and they changed over to .38's: smaller, neater, less weight and easier to handle. The sten guns and rifles are kept locked in the armoury and are only issued in states of emergency. Each man when he goes on duty is issued with a revolver for which he signs, noting the serial number, and six rounds of ammunition. When he returns, he hands in his revolver, the number is checked, and the six rounds are accounted for and put back in the cupboard before he is signed off. If he returns with less than his six rounds he has to have an exceptionally good reason for doing so and makes out a statement on the prescribed form. Sometimes, through horseplay or carelessness, a round is lost in the station itself and immediately a search is instituted; in the off-duty room, in the yard, in the cars, under tables, through papers, in pockets until, with a general sigh of relief, the missing bullet is found.

A large sign beneath the wall clock reads, NO SMOKING, but this does not seem to apply to those on duty until a superior officer puts in an appearance. Then, like guilty schoolboys indulging their vice in the bog who hear a master approach and whisper 'cave,' the cigarettes are hastily stubbed out and an attempt made to wave the smoke out through windows.

Behind the counter in the Non-European section, Constable Meyer is giving himself a manicure. Constable Meyer is a young man meticulous about his person. He likes perfumed bath salts and *Eau de Cologne* and his girl-friend uses *Californian Poppy*. They are a sweet smelling couple. He is forever washing his hands or running a comb through his curly blonde hair or, as now, cleaning his nails. He keeps a duster in his drawer with which to polish his shoes, and a stiff brush with which to keep his uniform free of fluff, and worse. Even in he height of summer he likes to wear blue, blue being so much neater and smarter than khaki. His fingers are long and slender, the immaculate nails are filed to a sharp point. His nose, like his nails, is sharp. Unlike Sergeant Nel's nose which is a button. His chin is also sharp, and his eyes are a pale grey, the pupils of which when contracted are like two glossy black pinheads, almost hypnotic in their intensity. He does tend to be rather dark around the jowls.

Opposite Meyer, on the other side of the counter, Native Constable Kumalo is busy taking a fellow African's fingerprints, holding the prisoner's hand in both his own and pressing the thumb down on the ink pad, transferring it from there to the appropriate form, pressing it down and rolling it from one side to the other to obtain a complete print. But the man was picked up in a shebeen, is drunk, and afraid. He does not know what the white man's law will do to him. They have been through his pockets and taken everything from him. There it all sits on the counter, what there is of it, a few small coins, a couple of padlock keys, some beadwork given him by his girl, a box of matches. They wouldn't let him go through his pockets himself, no... they had to do it. He screwed up his eyes and half shrugged, thinking about it; staring at his belongings in wonder as though, now they were taken from him, they were no longer a part of him; he would never see them again. If he put out his hand he could still touch them were they lay, his pass, his small penknife with the celluloid handle, his handkerchief with knots in the corners because he used it as a hat when the sun was hot, his ointment tin of snuff, its metal shiny with use and scouring beneath a garden tap.

He sniffed and craned forward to see what this black policeman was doing with his thumb. Putting it down on paper? No! Hurriedly he jerked the thumb away. Stupefied, Kumalo stared for long seconds at the black smudge on his beautiful form. He frowned heavily and pushed out his lips, looked up at Meyer who had paused in his filing and stood, hands poised in front of his chest, the file still held against the nail. Kumalo reversed the position of his lips, pulling them in against his teeth, pulled his chin into his neck and raised both eyebrows, giving a look of amazement. He glared at his prisoner and waggled an admonishing finger at him. 'Hey!' He barked, a warning not to do it again.

Without a word, Meyer passed Kumalo a clean form taken from beneath the counter and, removing the spoiled one, crumpled it up and tossed it into a wastepaper bin. Kumalo held the re-inked thumb above the virgin form and looked at his prisoner. The man was trembling.

'Hey!' Kumalo kicked him on the shin with his heavy policeman's boot. 'Stand still you black bastard or I'll give you a taste of this!' He picked up and put down his knobkerrie which he had previously laid on the counter and, deciding he had frightened his man enough to be allowed to get on with the job, pressed the thumb down on the paper. Again it was jerked away and Kumalo howled with rage. Meyer put down his file exactly at right angles to the edge of the counter, leaned across and, his face expressionless, backhanded the prisoner viciously across the face. The man staggered back and stared in terror at the policeman before him.

Sergeant Nel turned away as he replaced the receiver on its cradle but when he heard a dull thump and the man groan, he turned back again. The office which had emptied for a few brief relieving minutes was filling up again, not only with people and policemen, but piling up with evidence which would all have to be stacked behind the counter until ready for delivery to the law courts. There were two more Africans on a housebreaking charge, a coloured man on a liquor charge, two drunks, a white boy arrested for trying to steal a cycle, an

African woman, her sleeping child tied to her back, waiting for news of her husband who had been missing since the previous night, two prostitutes picked up for fighting in the street, the one with scratch marks left bleeding down her cheek against which she held a handkerchief stained red. Her eye was turning black from the edge of a handbag delivered at full force. It was going to be a real shiner, that one. At the back, a woman was screaming at two native constables who were trying to hush her up. She was a shebeen queen, brought in many times before for brewing and selling illegal liquor.

Then there was the evidence: two bottles of cheap red wine and a bottle of full strength cane spirit, (the coloured man was on the blacklist, he should not have tried to buy it) two forty-gallon drums of shimyaan, home made beer, most of it emptied but enough left to stink the place out. The cycle, a racy model in scarlet with disc brakes and three speed, stood propped up against the counter while it's would be owner sat weeping on a bench. Nel glanced at him, he could not have been more than twelve, then he looked over to the coloured section. Kumalo's prisoner had disappeared from view. Nel saw him lying doubled up against the partition, groaning and clutching his ribs. It was pretty obvious what had happened. Other prisoners were staring at the fallen man in fascinated horror.

Nel took a deep breath and coughed. 'Meyer.'

'Ja?' Meyer was smiling primly. As soon as things calmed down a little he would go outside and wash his hand, contaminated by the black skin.

'Where's Smith?'

Meyer glanced at the charge office clock. 'He's gone to inspect the cells.'

'Kumalo!'

'Sir?' Kumalo snapped to attention, the toecaps of his polished boots shining like glass. It was a matter of pride to Kumalo that his boots were shinier than Constable Meyer's. The men were constantly ribbing him about them, forever trying to catch him unawares and step on their shining surface, but Kumalo had become an adept at nimbly evading all attempts. Only once, engrossed in a legal document, had he been caught out, the result being a tiny scratch on the gleaming toecap. Five minutes later the constable who had broken through his defences found him busily filling up a form. 'What you doing, Kumalo?' he asked.

'Making out a charge,' Kumalo said.

'Oh? Against who?'

'Against you.'

'Me?'

Kumalo nodded, frowned over his writing.

'What's the charge?' the constable asked.

'Wilful damage to property,' Kumalo answered.

'You be careful my fine black friend that you're not out on a charge of wilfully wasting government stationary. Go on; get the hell out of here!'

'Meyer,' Nel turned to the constable, 'Give Kumalo the mortuary keys.'

'Kumalo, take those to the cells, find Constable Smith and tell him there's an ambulance on its way and he's to open the mortuary.'

'What is it?' Meyer asked.

'Suicide.'

Nel went back to his stool. He did not want to talk to Meyer and the work was piling up but, even though he did not want to talk, he could not help thinking of the little man who had come in a few nights earlier looking for his wife. 'She's run away you see,' he told Nel. 'I think I know the man she's gone off with. Yes, I could see it coming, but I want her back. I must have her back.' He gazed at Nel with sad brown eyes, pleading for a miracle that would bring back his errant wife. 'I'll forgive her,' he went on, 'Yes, I'll forgive her. I won't make trouble for her. If only she will come back.' There was a silence. Nel gulped. What could he say to this pathetic little man that wouldn't sound trite? He tried to sympathise but the man did not want sympathy. He wanted a practical method of getting back his wife and the method was not available. 'Are you sure there is nothing you can do?'

'Look,' Sergeant Nel had said. 'I tell you what I'll do...

you tell me where you think your wife is and I will send a man around to talk with her, see if he can't persuade her to come back to you, huh? How does that sound?' He nodded his head, smiling encouragement, but the little man blinked, 'I do believe I know who she gone off with,' he whined, 'but where they have gone to is anybody's guess.' Sergeant Nel sighed and leaned back on his stool.

'I know,' the little man said it for him, 'There's nothing you can do to bring back a runaway wife. Well...' His head wobbled on his skinny neck, not just up and down but all ways at once, 'She's run away before you know, I don't know why, and she's come back too.'

The little man paused to think and then he said, 'Can I stay here the night? Please? I won't be any trouble; you can lock me in a cell. I don't want to go home. We never had any children you see, I think that's why she keeps running away, we never had any children and there's...' a tear rolled down his cheek and he blinked again, owlishly, wiped it away with the back of his hand. 'There's nobody there.' He stared at Nel with longing, with the dumb pleading ache of the lonely. Nel shook his cropped iron grey head and pinched his button nose. 'I'm sorry,' he excused himself, 'I'm very sorry, but the cells are full. You don't want to spend the night with drunks and criminals now do you?'

'Oh, that wouldn't matter at all!' The little man smiled eagerly. 'I just don't... want to... spend it on my own, in an empty house. You understand.'

'No. I'm sorry. It can't be done.'

The little man nodded his head and turned on his heel to slouch out of the station. Nel watched him go. Once he had reached the street and mingled with passers-by he was lost, just another tired soul in a large city.

But it seemed the little man was convinced that this time his wife would not return. He went home, took an overdose of aspirin, all there was available to him, and went to bed. He lay there in the dark, staring at the ceiling like a small boy seeing figures in the dancing shadows, and the tears rolled down his cheeks and down his scrawny neck beneath his ear, turning cold on the pillow.

Suddenly the enormity of what he had done filled him with terror. He sat bolt upright in bed. It took courage to die. He had never in his whole life done one courageous thing. He was almost too timid to cross the road except in company, dithering about the kerbside until he saw someone else cross and darting after them. He fell out of bed and pausing only to slip on his dressing gown and slippers, rushed out of the house, screaming at the top of his voice. He slipped on the gravel path, tearing his pyjamas and grazing his knees, but was up again and at the gate, yelling blue murder, bringing out the neighbours and, in time, the ambulance arrived.

In the hospital he was fairly happy, at least he had company, but the long sleepless night passed and the long sleepless day. Every time a nurse passed his bed he would call after her. 'Nurse? Any news?' to which the answer was always no. Finally, the strain was too much. She was never coming back, he could see that. He slipped out of bed and padded down the corridor. At the same time his wife was turning her key in the latch and letting herself into the house.

Now he was coming back to the station to sleep, but not in a cell: this time it would be in a mortuary fridge on a narrow steel tray with a label tied to his toe. It didn't matter any more whether she came back or not.

'He threw himself down three flights of stairs, down the well, bounced off the sides on the way down.'

Sergeant Nel could hear the young house surgeon's voice; flat, uninterested. Death from multiple injuries, they would not actually know what exactly until after the post mortem.

'God,' Nel thought, 'how I hate the night shift!'

A van drew up in the yard and disgorged half a dozen Africans rounded up after a drunken brawl. The first to fall out had a gash in the head that bled constantly spattering blood in all directions. He held his hand against it but the blood oozed from between his fingers and dribbled down his forearm. The rest followed, all of them injured either by fist, knobkerrie or knife. Nel, who had gone over to the window to watch them alight, thought to himself, 'Why don't they take them to the hospital first? Why bring them here?' He returned to his stool, looking up at the clock before sitting down. Would it never be six o'clock? Would it never be the day to retire? He did not think he could take much more of this.

Kumalo stomped crunching down the yard and stopped outside the first cell. He peeped through a spy hole. This was an African cell, the largest of three on that side of the yard. In the full light that was never switched off, Kumalo saw twenty or more bodies huddled together on the floor, wrapped in flimsy grey blankets. One boy was pushed right up against the slop bucket; obviously his first time in jail. As the inhabitants of the cell were more or less asleep, Kumalo concluded that Smith had not bothered to go in, merely spied through the hole and passed on. Kumalo too passed on. Just as well. To have gone in on his own apart from being highly dangerous would be to break regulations. Cells were always inspected in pairs, and if they were entered for any reason, one of the pair should remain outside to lock the door and keep watch through the spy hole. The next cell was for Indians. This one was empty. The coolies must have been behaving themselves recently. The third cell was for coloureds. Kumalo peeped through the hole.

A coloured boy, naked but for his grimy shirt thrown over his shoulders was bucked down in front of Smith who was strapping his bare buttocks with the leather thong on the end of a wooden truncheon. The native constable with him, who should have been outside, was busily searching the cell, taking absolutely no notice of the whipping. Kumalo knocked. Smith paused in his beating and nodded to his companion who crossed over to the door.

'Who's there?' he demanded.

Kumalo shouted out his name, number and rank and the other opened the door. Kumalo knew the door was unlocked, against regulations, but he had not wanted to pull it open for fear of offending Smith who looked at him now standing in the doorway.

'What do you want?' the man growled. Kumalo glanced

at the boy who had not uttered a sound beneath Smith's attack. The boy looked up, thankful for the temporary respite, but Smith lifted a foot and kicked him savagely, yelling, 'Put your bloody head down!' and then quietly, looking away, 'No one gave you permission to look up.' The boy who had been knocked to his knees by the force of the kick, picked himself up, slowly and painfully, and resumed his former position, his head hanging low, hands over his ears. There was no need for Kumalo to ask what the boy had done. The dry musty odour of dagga, cannabis, filled the cell. The native constable with Smith, one Tefu by name, held out his hand in the palm of which lay a single match cut into four and with these pieces, a tiny sliver of striking paper.

'But we haven't found the dagga yet!' Tefu explained.

'I told you!' Smith bellowed, 'It's up his arse!'

'Ugh-Ugh!' Tefu shook his head and waved his hands in denial of this.

'Get it!' Smith ordered.

Tefu stared at him in horror. 'Who me? How! Baas!' he shook his hands in a flurry of agitation. 'Come on,' Smith said, pointing his truncheon to the boy's bare back, 'get on with it. You didn't join the police force to keep your fingers clean, get it!'

'It's not there Baas!' Tefu pleaded.

'Look, you silly Kaffir, where else can it be? We've searched this cell from top to bottom, we've stripped him naked, we've looked in his hair, in his ears, in his mouth, in his crotch and under his foreskin, between his toes and up his fucking nostrils. How many holes do you think he's got? There's only one place it can be, now come on!'

Tefu shook his head despairingly and uttered little groans of dismay. Smith gave up. He turned the boy, stood him upright facing him and, holding his neck with one hand, whipped him across his face with the thong, not too hard so as there wouldn't be any mark, just enough to sting. The boy winced and tried to avert his face but whichever way he turned it, that was the direction of the blow. 'Come on, you!' Smith shook him. 'Where is it?' There was no answer. He let go of the boy's neck and pointed to the bucket in the corner. The boy turned to look. 'Shit!' Smith commanded. The boy backed up, not daring to turn his back on Smith for fear of kicks. He squatted on the rim of the bucket and winced again as his bruises, under the weight of his body, flattened against the hard rim. 'Okay,' Smith said. 'We're waiting.' They waited. The boy gazed at them in silent terror. 'Come on, Come on,' Smith's voice was quiet but he waggled the leather thong menacingly.

'Please Baas!' it was the first time the boy had opened his mouth. 'Please, my Baas...'

'I'm not your Baas!'

'Please, Baas... there is no dagga there.'

'What do you think I smell in here? Where is it then?'

'I finish it, Baas.'

Smith stepped towards him.

'No, my Baas, it's the square truth, so help me God, Baas!'

'Listen to me you little bastard,' Smith pointed his truncheon, 'You sit there until you produce dagga, is that understood?'

'But Baas!'

'Do you hear me?' Smith yelled. 'I want to see it or you'll wish you had never been born!'

'Please, my Baas, please don't be so angry, my Baas, please Baas!'

'Angry!' Smith walked towards him and the boy got up and moved away to crouch back against the wall. 'Do you know the trouble you could get me into for this? Do you?'

The boy pressed himself against the wall, forgetting the pain of his buttocks in his terror. He whimpered and shook his head, the sweat standing out in beads on his forehead and running down his face, down his chest, down his arms as they flattened trembling against the wall. The two native constables stood silent witnesses but Smith stopped a yard or so in front of the cowering boy. Two other prisoners sat against a wall, their heads bowed low, resting on their arms over raised knees, not watching what was going on.

'You were searched before you were brought in here from the charge office,' he said, pointing an accusing finger, 'And yet you managed to smuggle in dagga, matches and paper. Now if you know what's good for you, you are going to hand over what is left... Aren't you? And we don't have all fucking night.'

The boy nodded quickly, silently. He slipped his hand under and between his legs and after a moment's fumbling came out with a small brown paper packet, spilled at the ends, no bigger than an acid drop. Smith's eyes narrowed. He beckoned Tefu forward and the constable walked over to the boy and held out his hand into which was dropped the tiny packet. Tefu shuddered visibly. Smith lashed out with his boot, catching the boy square on the shin. He screamed and fell, rolling into a tight ball on the floor, trying to rub the pain from the bone. When he had quietened down Smith turned to Tefu and said softly, 'Get him dressed and back to the charge office. We've got a score to settle, haven't we?' He touched the boy with the tip of his boot then turned to Kumalo who had been patiently waiting all this while. 'What did you want?'

Kumalo held out the mortuary keys. 'Ambulance coming,' he said.

Smith turned back to Tefu as he took the ring of keys, and handed the cell keys over. 'Take these back to the office and give them to Meyer, and mind you do or you'll be on a charge. We'll collect this little shit later.' Then he nodded to Kumalo, 'Come with me.'

Kumalo hated the house of the dead with the primitive fear of the unknown. A smart Khaki uniform and shiny toecaps did not ease his fear. He did not join the police force to fool around with corpses. He joined because his uniform gave him a sense of security and a sense of power and superiority over his fellow Africans. White policemen can be vicious and cruel but never with the same sadistic brutality that a black constable can use against a black if he so feels like it. But what power can he have over a dead thing? What power can a dead thing have over him? Smith knew his fear and insisted against all Kumalo's protestations that he accompany him.

'I've got a prisoner in there,' Kumalo wailed, pointing to the lighted windows of the charge office.

'Your prisoner can wait,' Smith replied. 'He's not going to go anywhere.'

Reluctantly Kumalo followed the white man down the yard, their heels crunching steadily on the gravel. As they left the cells Kumalo glanced back at the lights of the double storied main building. He would much prefer to be going back there, to its noise and its clatter, its motley, bedlam, and its smell of moving, breathing, vocal, fearful flesh.

Across the yard, opposite the cells for Indian, African and coloured, stood two cells for whites: egg, sausage and bacon for breakfast there as opposed to bread and tea; and alongside these cells, the corrugated iron flat roofed windowless storeroom with its stock of rough dark blankets, two to each prisoner – that's the regulations – one for lying on the cold concrete floor, the other for cover. Each prisoner collects his two blankets and returns them before making the short journey under escort of knobkerrie and a white warder's rifle, to the courts. The white prisoners go separately, riding in a maria.

At the bottom of the yard, past the latrines and a square of darkness, a solitary pale yellow light in a protective cage lights up a small redbrick building with white frosted windows in steel frames. As they leave behind them the noises of the station and the street alongside, in the dark stillness of the night, Kumalo gradually becomes aware of a dull rhythmic throbbing, the mortuary refrigerators keeping their contents from premature decay, and he shudders.

Smith mounts the two concrete steps outside the door, finds the right key, unlocks the door and enters, switching on the light. The mortuary, like the main office, is divided into three. They are standing in what is no more than a small entrance hall, its only furnishing a sloping desk set in the wall and on top of which stands an inkwell and pen, labels, receipt books and forms for particulars. From there they pass into the post-mortem room and Kumalo gazes about him at this strange, terrifying place: the cabinets of surgical instruments, the coat hooks from which hang red rubber aprons, the shelves of bottles containing bits and pieces of human anatomy, specimens from autopsies; on a pedestal in the centre of the room, the table, shaped like a shallow bath only narrower with a raised rim and in the centre a large plug hole covered with a steel strainer. He looked at the sinks, the rows of gumboots and hanging from the ceiling above the table, the hoses for washing down. His nostrils dilate at the unfamiliar smell. No, Kumalo most definitely does not like being in this place. Through a wide square opening they move on into the next room with the refrigerators set against one wall in two tiers of three, their metal doors lined with wood on the outside and with metal handles.

Smith crosses the room to open the double doors that lead into the alley outside, wide enough for only a single lane of traffic, but in the road directly opposite the doors an ambulance is parked, waiting. The men are having a quiet smoke while they wait, and seeing Smith, the one walks towards him whilst the other flicks away his cigarette end, climbs into the cab and starts the engine. The ambulance is backed up to the doorway so that its own doors open inside those of the mortuary and so prevents curious passers by from witnessing the transference of the corpse.

'Take a look,' Smith told Kumalo, 'See where we're going to put it.' Smith was used to corpses, he had seen and handled a great many. Recruits who came into the mortuary for the first time sometimes turned green with an overworked imagination but he usually managed to put them at their ease with his advice. 'A stiff,' he would say, 'is not a human being, it's a thing. It's a piece of meat, a chair, a log, think of it as anything but a human being. You've seen a dead cat haven't you? That never worried you, did it? Well, if you think of a dead man as a thing you'll be all right. Think of it as a man, or feel sorry for it and you'll be sick as a dog. Just never feel sorry. That's all. Okay?' The recruit would nod, still very unsure, but usually his curiosity gained the upper hand until, like Smith, he became so blasé that a corpse, no matter how mutilated, did in fact become a thing: a thing accepted, for which he made out a receipt and label and left in the refrigerator for the surgeons.

Kumalo opened the first door to be greeted by three pairs of feet, each with a label tied to a big toe. 'Full up,' he grunted to himself and opened the second. The lower and middle trays were occupied, the middle one having already been examined and in the dim light Kumalo frowned at the long roughly stitched incision from neck to pubic hair. He could not see the top of the head, which would have been removed and loosely replaced. The top tray was empty. 'Up there,' he said, turning to Smith who was engaged in conversation with the ambulance men standing around the body which now on its stretcher beneath a white sheet stitched with a large red cross that had been placed on the concrete floor.

'Well get it out then,' Smith commanded.

Kumalo reached up for the tray. He was not tall enough to manage it with ease. He took hold of the rubber handle and the tray slid out fast and easy on its rollers. Kumalo was not watching what he was doing. He was looking at the new addition beneath its white sheet, but he could still see the refrigerators out of the corner of his eye. The far end of the tray dropped and hit the handle of the tray beneath. Kumalo did not exactly see this, nor did he hear it, the sound was deadened by the rubber encased handles. All he saw was a cold corpse suddenly jump on its tray. Kumalo let out a yell, the suddenness of which, shattering the quiet of the room, caused the other three to jump violently.

'What the bloody hell's the matter with you?' Smith bellowed at the trembling wide-eyed Kumalo.

'It moved, Baas!' Kumalo whispered.

They gazed in the direction of his pointing finger, all waiting. They knew it was impossible but somehow they waited, just in case. Then Smith laughed and the other two laughed with him.

'You stupid Kaffir!' Smith shook his head, 'Come on, get this one moving.' He bent down over the body and whipped back the sheet. Still suffering from his initial fright, Kumalo was not feeling up to it. The suicide, after falling three flights of stairs, was not a pretty sight. The skin was a baby sick yellow turning pale green over the abdomen. A leg was shattered just below the knee and lay grotesque, twisted the wrong way, and a collar bone protruded beneath the neck. One side of the face had been crushed but the other eye, open, was staring glassily at Kumalo. He gulped, feeling his knees wobbling. 'Stand still my trousers,' he murmured to himself, 'Your baas is not afraid.'

'Okay then,' the driver of the maria said to sergeant Nel, 'All done, we'll be off.'

'No, wait a minute,' he replied. 'Before you go off gallivanting again I want you to take Booysens to this address.' He searched for and found a piece of paper which he handed over.

'What's this for?' the driver asked.

'Oh, some damn fool kid! Showing off in a café, shot his foot half off with a stolen gun. Booysens has been down to the hospital but can't get a thing out of him except name and address. Anyway, we must inform the parents or they'll be getting worried about him so give Booysens a lift up there, hey? I think he's with the C.I.D. at the moment.' The driver nodded and went out, folding the paper into his tunic pocket. 'Oh, and Stevens!' Nel called after him. The driver stopped and turned around. 'Tell him to take constable Kumalo with him.' Stevens nodded, buttoned up his tunic pocket, patted it, and went out. Sergeant Nel wiped the tiredness from his eyes and went back to work.

They crunched back up the gravel yard and had almost reached the main building when Smith suddenly stopped and slapped his thigh in annoyance. 'Blast!' Kumalo looked at him enquiringly. 'I left the receipt.' Smith held out the keys, 'Go back and get it.' In the half light of the station yard, Kumalo's eyes gleamed white, large and round. 'It's all right,' Smith chuckled maliciously, 'They're all safely tucked up for the night. They're not going to move.' He slapped the keys into Kumalo's hand, turned, and went inside, leaving a stupefied

Kumalo staring after him. To go back there? Alone? In the pitch dark? With nobody around? After what he had just been through? He hated that man Smith! Oh how he hated him!

Booysens came out with the driver. 'Oh, Kumalo, I've been looking all over for you, come with me.'

'We going out Baas?'

'Don't ask damn fool questions! You think we're going to drive round and round the yard all night? Come on, get in.' He held the back door of the maria open. Kumalo heaved a delighted sigh of relief at this reprieve. 'Wait one moment Baas. I got to give these keys to Constable Smith.'

'Well be quick about it.' Booysens snapped, walking to the front of the van. Stevens was already seated behind the wheel as he climbed into the cab. 'Start her up if you like, but you know what these bloody munts are like.' Stevens pressed the starter, his foot on the accelerator and the engine turned over. 'Let them out of your sight for a second and you never know what nonsense the black sods get up to.'

Inside the office Kumalo placed the keys on the counter and said, 'Gotta go, Baasie, got a job on.'

'What?' Smith raised both eyebrows.

Nel looked down the counter. 'That's right,' he nodded, 'I'm sending him out with Booysens.' Smith muttered under his breath.

'Hey!' said Kumalo, suddenly remembering looking round the room, 'Where's my prisoner?' Meyer interrupted his work to answer, 'He's been booked and locked up. You can make out your statement when you get back.'

'Hokay!' Kumalo, in his enthusiasm and his eagerness to get going, rushed to the door, before anyone could stop him. He had no sooner disappeared than he reappeared, rushed up to the counter and, 'Where is my kerrie?' he asked. Meyer produced it from beneath the counter. 'And don't leave it in here again,' he said. Kumalo waltzed out of the room, out of the building, and into the back of the car, slamming the door after him. He peered through the wire grill between the cab and the back of the van, grinning broadly. 'Home James,' he said, 'and don't spare the horses!'

Stevens laughed. 'Any more of your lip you cheeky nigger and I won't spare your hide.' He slapped the wire with the flat of his hand so that it bounced against Kumalo's nose and Kumalo, in high spirits, fell over backwards, howling. The white men grinned at the antics of this monkey in his cage. Steven's car companion slipped in next to Booysens, the latter shifting up to make room for him, slammed the door, and Stevens, putting the van into gear, drove slowly out of the yard.

Chapter 11

Mama could not sleep. How long had she lain in bed now and she was still wide-awake lying next to her snoring mouth dropped open husband, staring into the dark, reliving the death of the snake. She remembered Guido's squeal of terror and how he tried to clamber up her frock, her lack of feeling as she brought the spade down across the creature's back. She could see every twist and turn of its dying body. She would go over to Madame Chang's first thing in the morning and tell her all about it. Well, maybe not first thing, she didn't like fruit cake first thing, maybe about eleven o'clock, time for morning tea. If she did not get to sleep in a minute she would get up and make herself a nice cup of tea just now. That would settle her nerves. How lucky it was she had warned Guido so often to be aware of snakes. What was that story Angelo told her? He read it in a magazine. That story about the child who had a choo-choo train in the back garden and when his father went out to see it, he found the child prodding a puff adder with a stick and making train noises Tcha! That was something. That child could have been bitten to death. That child could have been Guido had she not been so persistent with her warnings. Why had Angelo told her that story? Was it to frighten her? No… he would never do a thing like that! Not her Angelo, not her baby. Yes, he was still a baby for all his growing up; just a little boy who still needed his mother's affection; kind, gentle, with love in his heart. What was that Sarah said this afternoon? 'That boy… he holds your heart in his hands.' Sure he does, and why not? Was her heart not in the safest possible care in those hands? She smiled in the darkness, seeing before her her son's face, seeing his hands. He leaves school this year, only a few months time; what is he going to do, this son of hers? Huh! Pity they did not have the money to send him to a university. But what would he do there? Become a teacher maybe. No. He would make a fine doctor. She thought vaguely of hospital wards and Angelo in a white coat. A dentist maybe. Angelo, still in a white coat, was washing his hands in a basin. He took up a small towel and dried them as he approached the chair, smiling. Shoo! Don't think about that: poking around in other people's mouths all day? What a way to spend one's life. But then think of the money. Think of the pain! Mama turned her head to blot out the picture of Angelo in his white coat. Maybe... she tried to think of the word 'veterinary' but could not, so settled for... animal doctor, yes. Ah, but what was the use of dreaming? No doubt he would follow his father into the building trade. He would look nice in overalls. Tcha! They don't wear overalls any more, just filthy old work clothes. See him there... on that building site... stripped to the waist... his smooth brown chest gleaming with sweat in the hot sun. Every girl who passed by would turn her head and whisper, 'That's Angelo Lerici. Isn't he handsome? Isn't he marvellous?' Mama, in the excitement of her imagination would have clapped her hands, but remembered in time her sleeping husband. Hmph! He would have to bring them all home for her to approve, that's for sure. She wasn't going to allow any goodtime girl or worthless woman to lay hands on her lovely boy, oh no! No no no no! Mama shook her head very definitely and mentally put her foot down. She imagined herself standing in the kitchen, a cup of tea in her hand and looking across the table at the girl Angelo had brought home. She didn't like her. Angelo brought home another. 'Mama, this is...' Mama didn't like her either. A third, 'Mama, this is...' Mama shook her head. A fourth, 'Mama, I'd like you to meet...' Shoo! It was going to be very difficult.

'Angelo, why you never meet a nice girl, huh? Why you bring home all desa loose wimmins?'

'Mama, It's not that they're loose, it's just you refuse to like any girl I bring home.'

'Datsa not true. The wimmins you bring home I no lika! The wimmins I lika you no bring home! Whatsa matter wid you you no bring da nice girl home?'

'Mama, if you're going to be jealous of...'

'Jealous? Jealous! Me, jealous? What you saying? Jealous, huh!'

'Yes, Mama, you!'

Mama waved a hand at the darkness and decided she would never be jealous of her son's friends. No, she would be patient. She would try and like all the girls he brought home. But no loose woman was going to lay her hands on him that was for damn sure. She bit her lip. She hadn't meant to swear. She scratched her forehead with two fingers, closed her eyes and tried to sleep, but there was Angelo standing on his building site, and he would not let her sleep. Her eyes fluttered open and she yawned. She must be tired or she wouldn't yawn like that. Then why on earth could she not get to sleep? She saw his narrow-waisted stomach with its cobblestones, the end of the breastbone that protruded ever so slightly in a little round knob, the chest with its slightly rounded pectorals and the dark brown nipples, the black hair curling from under his arms. She could even remember how the veins stood out on his arms when he had been exerting them. She could even remember, she thought, the pores on his nose, at least she could picture them, and the tiny white cicatrise just below the hairline, a souvenir from when as a child he had fallen and smacked his head against a wall, the mole in the small of his back, even the shape of his beautiful slender feet and their long toes. She remembered, it seemed, every year of his growing up and the picture of him, as he had been, flashed in her imagination, one year, two years, three years; shedding his baby fat, shedding his chubbiness, the muscles hardening, the legs getting longer; and then suddenly the day when his hair was plastered down and he looked at himself often in the mirror. She watched his body change from babyhood until she lost it in the moment he became aware of himself. When was that moment? Could it be pinpointed to a particular day? A Month? A year maybe? She could not remember that. She could only remember that one day he was naked and unashamed before her and then suddenly, without warning, whenever she entered the bathroom he rolled over in the water or held a towel or flannel in front of him. Suddenly he was shy with her and wanted to hide from her. He had lost his innocence. Fancy a boy being shy in front of his own mother, ha! Was this what it was like in the Garden of Eden? The losing of innocence. Man suddenly becoming aware of his own nature and being embarrassed by it. Because why should children be so shy when they discover themselves? Not shy with everybody, but shy with their parents. Yes, would Adam have been shy before his mother? She wondered why this should be, it seemed so strange. Was this awareness the awareness of original sin maybe? And then when the physical shyness embraces an emotional one as well they make of everything the big big secret. Why should this be? It was not so much that words passed through Mama's mind, but ideas that came sliding in and then slipped away before she could really get a grip on them.

She saw the headlights flash across her window and heard the van draw up and stop outside the house. What would a car be doing parking outside the house at this time of night? She lay a moment, heard the door slam and someone get out; another door slam and then quiet voices, then the car drew away. Mama felt uneasy. She looked across at Ulrico still sleeping and gently pushing back the covers on her side, threw her legs over the side of the bed and felt with her toes for her mules. She stood up and crept across to a wicker chair to gather up her kimono, slipping it on as she crossed to the window. She held it with one hand in front of her while with the other she carefully pulled aside the curtain and peeped through. There was nothing to see now that the van had gone but she heard someone knocking on the door next door. She angled her cheek against the pane but it was no use, she could not see who it was. If she lifted the window the squeak would attract attention. The knocking was repeated and still went unheeded. Mama tiptoed back to the bed which seemed a little silly as she intended waking her unconscious husband, but then Mama always tiptoed in the dark. It was a habit now after always tiptoeing into children's bedrooms after they had gone to sleep.

'Ulrico!' She shook his shoulder. He grunted and stirred but did not wake up. 'Ulrico, wake up.'

'Huh? Huh? Wassa matter?' He was still more asleep then awake.

'Dere's a somtink 'appenin' next door.'

'Huh? What?'

'Somtink 'appenin'.'

'Where?'

'Next door.'

Ulrico tried to sit up but it was too much of an effort to shake off the sleep. He flopped back onto the pillows. Mama gave him another shake. With the second try he succeeded, pushing himself up with his arms, and leaning back against the tall slatted head of the bed, he closed his eyes again and yawned, sucked the taste out of his mouth and scratched his chin.

'Get up now, Ulrico,' Mama said, 'Dere's a someone come to call next door.'

'Well what of it?' he yawned again, wider and longer.

'At desa time of night? Esa nearly milnight now! I tink esa gone milnight. I tink ees early mornin'.' She took up an old double bell luminous alarm clock from the bedside table and held it to her ear. 'Ulrico,' she chided, 'you forgot to wine a da clock.' She shook the clock, wound it vigorously, and shook it again until its loud ticking filled the room, then she banged it back on the table. The ticking stopped. She listened for a moment to the silence of the room broken only by the steady rhythm of heavy breathing from the bed. Ulrico had fallen once more into a doze, sitting up. She gave him another shake and he started under her hand. 'It might help,' he mumbled, 'if you put on the light.'

'Are you awake?' she asked.

'No,' he replied. 'I'm talking in my sleep.'

'I'm a go through to da kitchen. Make a nice cuppa tea. I no can sleep.'

'Is that any reason to wake me up?' he slid down into a recumbent position and would have gone right off again had she not snapped on the light. He opened his eyes and immediately shut them again, screwing them up tight against the glare. Mama scowled at him.

'I wake you up because dere's a somtink 'appenin' next door so come outa da bed now an' don' forget to put on your slippers.'

She disappeared through the door and Ulrico, now wide awake, heard her switch on the kitchen light and a moment later the sound of the kettle being filled. Mama put the kettle on the stove to boil and went out on to the veranda, standing there arms folded across her chest, watching the house next door. There were lights on but obviously nothing to see. Ulrico still yawning came out and stood next to her. 'What is it?' he whispered.

Mama lifted her shoulders. 'I'm a not know. Can't see anytink.' She gave a little squeal of terror as they heard the latch on the yard door lifted, and her terror increased at the sight of Khaki uniforms. Terrifying visions of tragedy flashed through her mind until she remembered they had been knocking next door so it was all right. It must be all right! 'Angelo,' she whispered quickly to her husband as the policemen advanced down the yard, 'He has come home?' she threw a glance towards the darkened bedroom below.

'I don't know,' Ulrico hissed, 'See what they want first and then I'll go down and take a look.'

The two men were now standing by the bottom of the steps. Booysens saluted and removed his cap as he addressed Mama politely.

He's very young, she thought, Not more than eighteen, maybe nineteen. He could be Angelo but for his blonde hair. He has nice eyes.

'I'm sorry to trouble you, ma'am, but I'm looking for the Viljoen family.'

Mutely Mama pointed to the house next door.

'Yes,' the young policeman said, 'That's the address we have here,' he looked down at a piece of paper in his hand, 'But I can get no answer to my knock.'

Mama waved a hand, signalling to stay where he was, and walked over to the low partition that separated the two verandas. She clenched her fist and banged furiously with the side of her hand. The wood resounded in the night like some ancient drum. 'Only two women in dat 'ouse,' She turned to the policeman to explain, 'Dat's why no answer for your knocking. Too scared. Might be scallywags.'

Booysens could not help smiling at Mama's phraseology, though he had the courtesy to try and hide the smile behind his hand. Kumalo's teeth gleamed white beneath his helmet until Booysens saw it and frowned. The broad grin disappeared in a trice.

Mama was about to knock a second time when the kitchen window opened and a second latter Nina popped out her head. 'What's the matter?' She sounded irritable. 'What do you want?' and then she saw the policemen and gasped, her hand flying to her mouth.

'Mrs Viljoen?' Nina nodded speechlessly. 'I'm sorry to trouble you, ma'am but could I speak to you a moment, please?' What a polite young man, Mama thought, such good manners. Nina nodded and withdrew her head. 'Stay here,' Booysens commanded Kumalo. The black man nodded and leaned against the bathroom wall, his kerrie between his knees.

As Booysens walked down the yard they could hear Nina withdrawing the bolt on the kitchen door. The young policeman rattled up the stairs and disappeared into the house.

'Ulrico,' Mama urged, 'Go see if Angelo hesa come home yet.' But before Ulrico could move, Pepe appeared at the bedroom door. 'Pepe!' Mama leaned over the rails whispering urgently as though she wanted Pepe to hear but not Kumalo though as they were equidistant from her that was hardly possible. 'Has Angelo he's a come home yet?' Pepe looked at Kumalo who looked at Pepe. 'He's in bed?' Mama wanted Pepe to say yes but he shook his head. 'Tony neither,' he answered. They waited: Ulrico and Mama on the veranda, Pepe by the bedroom door and Kumalo leaning against the bathroom wall.

The silence settled heavily upon the house. Mama looked up at the sky brilliant with countless stars and they waited. Every now and again Mama turned her head in Kumalo's direction wondering whether or not she should speak to him, but Kumalo gazed straight ahead, ignoring them all. They heard Booysens come out of the house and all turned to watch his progress down the steps and up the yard until finally he reached the Lerici's again. He looked at Pepe who he had not seen before and then climbed up to where Mama and Ulrico were standing watching him. Booysens smiled, trying to put them at their ease but his smile only worsened Mama's fears.

'Lerici?' They nodded. 'Have either of you ever seen this before?' His hand came away from behind his cap and Mama stared fascinated at the gun in a plastic bag.

'A gun?'

Booysens thought it pretty obvious it was a gun but he repeated his question. 'Have you seen it before?' Mama shook her head. Booysens held the gun out to Ulrico. He shook his head.

'Papa!' Marina turned to her husband, 'What does this mean? What's a happen?'

The constable turned to Pepe still standing by the bedroom. 'You have seen this before?' Pepe shook his head. Booysens was growing used to this silent behaviour. It took time and patience before people relaxed sufficiently to find the use of their tongues. The uniform frightened them. He turned back to Mama who stepped back a pace transferring her attention from his hand to his face.

'Gun!' she yelped. 'No one in desa 'ouse got a gun!

What for we want a gun?'

'That is what I am trying to find out. We took this off Tony Viljoen tonight, he's your nephew I'm told?' Ulrico nodded. 'You have no idea where he could have got it.'

'He shoot someone?' Mama gasped, dreading the answer.

'He shot himself.'

Mama opened her mouth to scream, clapping her hands to her ears, but no sound came.

Booysens saw it and quickly continued. 'Oh, it's all right, ma'am, only in the foot, he shot himself in the foot. He's in the hospital right now.'

Ulrico threw his arm over Mama's shoulder and held her tight as she unwound. 'Madonna Mia!' she moaned, 'He's a gangster dat boy! I always say one day he do somtink terrible.'

Booysens tried harder. 'He's been taken to hospital and is being well looked after so there is no need to worry on that score. But we can't get a statement from him as yet you see.' He paused to think. 'However he will be charged with being in possession of an unlicensed firearm, and what is worse for him, this gun is stolen property.'

Having tried to reassure Mama, his last statement had completely undone his work. Constable Booysens had not been long in the force. He was a nice young man with an honest straightforward face and an honest straightforward mind to go with it though not over intelligent and, more often than not, lacking in tact. He had a genuine streak of kindliness in him towards physical suffering, but of mental suffering he knew nothing. Having no complexes himself worthy of mentioning he could not understand the sensitivity of others. He was not an educated young man and, like Nel and others before him, he chose the force as the only alternative to the railways. His leisure hours he spent on the beach, sunbathing or surf riding. Occasionally he visited the cinema but he thought crime films 'plain blerrie nonsense, man!' and he never seemed to see the joke in comedy unless it was of the slapstick variety. Romance either bored or embarrassed him, he was brought up in the strict reformed church, and horror films left him completely indifferent. Tales of the supernatural frightened him. 'Folk shouldn't mess around with things like that, man!' But he liked war films and westerns. He played snooker with the boys in the barracks clubroom and he was an ardent supporter of the police rugby team, the provincial side, and the Springboks. He thought that kaffirs, Cape coloureds, that is half-caste, and coolies should know and accept their rightful place in the world as explained in the Bible which was, after all the word of God Almighty, their father in heaven. He never questioned his superiors, and was a loving and devoted son. He once joined the police wrestling club but decided that wrestling was a sport to watch rather than participate in. Sometimes he would try to settle down with a paperback but invariably grew bored with it after a few chapters and gave the book away. The only ones he could read through to the end were tales of the Wild West, though even then he mostly liked those purported to be true, and at the end of his reading would fling the book down and say in disgust, 'Ach, man! These blerrie books, all the stories are the same!' This did not stop him from reading them. The exception was Zane Grey, the Shakespeare of the western.

The first statement he ever made, after investigating a traffic accident, read – 'The front bumper of the car hurt the rear right wheel of the rickshaw.' The station sergeant gazed at this for some time and then gently explained to the eager faced young man standing before him that as a rickshaw only had two wheels, none of them could be rear ones, and wheels being inanimate objects they could not suffer pain, would he please write it out again? Booysens was very hurt by this incident and never forgot it. The sergeant never forgot it either and wished he had kept his clever mouth shut. It now took Booysens three times longer than anyone else to make out a statement.

He did not like jokes directed against the force, feeling in his uniform a certain boyish pride, easily put out. A joker said to him once. 'You heard about the man down at the docks who badly wanted a piss? He saw a harbour policeman you see, so he went up to him and said, 'Excuse me, constable, but can you tell me where the urinal is please?' the constable looked around the docks for a while and then said, 'Has she got one or two funnels?' And the joker roared at his own joke until he noticed Booysens staring at him with a puzzled frown. 'What's a urinal?' he asked. The joker gave up. Later, when Booysens had discovered the nature of a urinal, he went back to the joker and in all seriousness said, 'Man, you shouldn't say things like that. You could get into trouble, hey?'

Now, noticing Mama's face, he averted his own, turning on his hips to peer over his shoulder at the bedroom below. 'He sleeps in there?' Pepe nodded and pushed his hand around the open door to switch on the lights. Booysens started down the steps, 'I would like to take a look through his things if you don't mind.' Pepe nodded again and followed the constable into the bedroom.

Mama shook her head and tut tutted in sympathy at this terrible thing that had happened. 'Tch, tch, tch, my poor Nina,' she murmured just as her sister-in-law came out of the house followed by a distraught, hand wringing, bosom thumping Sarah, overflowing in red flannel dressing gown.

Nina was now fully dressed, including hat and overcoat. She took her time going down the stairs as though reluctant to be moving or afraid that in her worry she might miss her footing and fall. Halfway down she stopped and looked around the yard, then at Mama and Ulrico. 'Has the policeman gone?' she asked. She could not see Kumalo who had crossed from the bathroom wall to sit on the dustbin beneath the veranda, having first made sure the lid was clean enough. In the gloom it looked as if it was.

'He's in there with Pepe,' Ulrico replied, pointing to the bedroom.

Nina looked at the lighted windows and turned back up the stairs, pulling herself up with her hand on the rail, climbing slowly, each step a tremendous effort. 'He's taking me to see Tony in the hospital.' She talked as she moved, 'The police car is coming back for us. Will you tell him I'm ready?' She shrugged off Sarah's sympathetic hands as she reached the top and went into the house. Sarah looked at the Lericis and shook her head sadly, crossed herself and disappeared inside.

Ulrico pulled Mama by the shoulder and said softly, 'Kettle's boiling, Marina.' But Mama was reluctant to move from her observation point while those two policemen were still about the place. 'I'll go down and take a look,' Ulrico offered, and set off down the stairs to follow the others into the bedroom.

Kumalo twisted his head to look up at Mama standing above him. He coughed to attract her attention, and then standing up where she could see him properly, said 'I'm thirsty, Missus, Can I get a drink of water please?'

Mama leaned over the rail and pointed to the far end of the yard. 'If you go 'roun' dat corner,' she directed, you see da tap, joost behine da shed.' Kumalo nodded and went down the yard followed by Mama's suspicious gaze. He found the tap and, turning it on, allowed the water to run for a second before cupping his hands beneath it and bending down to drink. Mama stood waiting for him to re-appear.

Suddenly the door in the wall was flung open and Angelo staggered into the yard, hurriedly slamming the gate behind. He leaned against it gasping for breath, gulping the air into his lungs like a man held too long under water and surfacing just as he thinks his lungs will burst. The boy hid his face against the wooden door and, from where he stood, mama heard his sobbing breath. Without warning her knees buckled so that she had to grip fast onto the veranda rail. Her heart was thumping against her ribs as she gazed in terror at her son. She could not think what caused the dreadful premonition of disaster but through her mind ran one phrase, that boy… he holds your heart in his hand… your heart in his hand… your heart in his hand...

Chapter 12

Ephraim hugs his brown paper tied up in string parcel closely to his chest and hurries towards home as fast as his old legs can carry him through the dark streets. It is not that he is afraid of the dark, or of skollies, thugs, but he is anxious about his pass, or rather, that he does not have it with him and does not know where it is. Now that was a truly stupid thing to do, to come out without his pass. What does he have in his head, cement? What in the world could have made him do such a stupid thing? He had never done anything like that before tonight so why tonight? He was getting old, his brain was slowing down. Like the elephant he should go back to his home to die peacefully in the sun. Not his city home, which is no more than a tin shack surrounded by hundreds of other tin shacks and the smell of sewage, but to his real home: his heart's home – the Kraal. To the long dry yellow grass and the sakabula bird with its long black tail sailing over a sea of copper headed mabela, kaffir corn, to the gentle cooing of doves in the early dawn: to the scent of wattle gum, and the soft lowing of cattle being driven in for the evening milk; that moment of the day which his people call, the time when the horns of the ox can be seen on the ridge. He should go back to the prickly pear and the tall bitter aloe where the earth, the red cracked earth, is as hard as concrete beneath the African sun. Ephraim rummages desperately through the drawers of his mind, turning over the day's events from the very beginning until this moment, but nowhere can he find the place, or the moment when he could have mislaid that precious document. If he did not find it soon he would have to inform his employer or the police. Is it sensible to put one's head in the lion's jaws? But then he could not hurry home like this every night, wondering each second whether he would make it, or whether an authoritative voice would suddenly bark an order for him to stop and produce his precious pass. He wiped the perspiration from his forehead just thinking about it. And what if he had to get another job? His pass was the first thing a prospective employer would demand to see. No… he shook his head and paused beneath a streetlight. No, he must find it! He must have it somewhere. How could he have lost it? It wasn't like losing a pencil or an exercise book, – Ephraim was learning to write – it was like losing one's memory, one's identity and, if one were not very careful, one's temporary liberty and, once convicted, you were forever after a marked man.

He peered up and down the street to ensure the absence of predatory patrol cars, before tucking his parcel tight between his knees, and searching once more through his pockets, just in case he had missed it the time before, or the time before, or the time before but, with the thought of the police ever present, he could not concentrate completely on his search. There were constant interruptions to pause and look, pause and listen. Could it have slipped down inside the lining of his jacket? He pulled the coat away from his body and squeezed the material through his fingers. Was there a pocket he had overlooked? He patted them all, mentally noting the contents, took out his wallet and carefully went through each piece of paper, unfolding those into which it could have slipped. That was where his pass should be, in the wallet, but there was still no sign of it. He stared hard at the plastic in his hands as though willing the document to appear and ease his fear. He had best be moving. All it needed was for a car to come cruising around the corner and he was in dead trouble. He slipped the wallet back into the inside pocket of his jacket and, taking the parcel from between his knees, set off once more.

As he walks he imagines the van's headlight's spotlighting him, isolating him in a circle of brilliance. It pulls in along side the kerb and a voice calls, out, 'Hey, you!' Ephraim stops and peers with a myopic eye into the dim interior of the cab. A Khaki clad arm emerges and waves him forward. Ephraim looks around the deserted street hoping against hope that the arm is beckoning someone else. 'Me, Baas?'

'Well who the bloody hell do you think? Come here you stupid Kaffir!'

Ephraim gingerly approaches the van. There is a silence and he knows that the occupants are watching him but can't see their faces, only the arm now dangling limply over the side of the door.

'What's your name?'

Ephraim stutters out his name. 'Ephraim, Baas.'

'Where are you going?'

'Home, Baas.'

'Where have you been?'

'My work, Baas.'

'At this time of night?'

'The missus she keep me late tonight, Baas.'

'You're lying.'

'Then I went to visit a friend.'

'You been drinking?'

'No, Baas!' When was that dreaded question coming? Maybe they would move on, tire of the little game, move on and leave him alone without asking it.

'What have you got in that parcel?'

Ephraim hesitated. 'Clothes, Baas.'

'Where did you pinch them?'

'How! Baas! I never did pinch them! The missus, she gave them to me, Baas.'

The arm disappears, the door swings open, and the policeman climbs out of the cab. This is it. He stares coldly at Ephraim, not with suspicion, but with active dislike. 'Open it up.'

'It's only old clothes, Baas.'

'Open it up!' The man shouts at him.

Hurriedly, with trembling fingers, Ephraim pulls at the string which holds together his parcel, talking as he does so. 'Clothes of my Baas, Baas, that the missus...'

Impatiently the man reaches out and grabs the parcel, ripping away the creased brown paper. Ephraim watches the desecration of his lovingly wrapped parcel and his heart is sore within him. His Missus was a good lady. She did not throw the clothes at him as one tosses a bone to a dog. She laid them on the table, folded them, and stroked them affectionately. They were her husband's and in a way they still seemed to be a part of him. 'Ephraim, here are some old clothes of my husband's, would you like them?'

'Thank you, Missus.' He admired the clothes, feeling the cloth, turning them over to inspect them, not in criticism but with pleasure. 'You'll find some brown paper and string behind the pantry door; you can make a parcel of them to take home.' And now his parcel, in the hands of this white man, was being torn to pieces, its contents spilling out onto the pavement: the sports jacket with the slightly torn sleeve, two frayed collar shirts, some socks in need of a little darning, an old crumpled tie, one by one the man drops them on the pavement, then hold out his hand, clicking his fingers, 'Pass!' The dreaded moment had come.

Ephraim cannot move, cannot speak, but for the thumping of his heart the world seems to have stopped moving at the sound of that fateful word.

'Come on come on come on! Are you deaf?' the man bellows, 'Pass!'

Why won't the words come? Why can't he open his mouth? Why does his tongue stick to the roof of his mouth, refusing to obey his bidding? Why does he stand there, staring at this white man as though his whole body were frozen into permanent immobility? The white man will not wait forever. He is getting angry, don't make him angry, that is the worst thing. Ephraim opens his mouth, his grizzled peppercorn beard trembling, and out it stumbles, 'Baas... Please, Baas... I...'

But the white man's limited patience is exhausted. He can't stand around here all night waiting for this blerrie Kaffir to make sense. He kicks the clothes lying at his feet, 'Pick 'em up,' he orders. Ephraim does so and stands up again to see the man has moved to the back of the van. Ephraim does not struggle but he drops the clothes, barks his shin against the floor not lifting his leg high enough, not given enough time; bangs his head on the edge of the roof, and a final shove sends him sprawling. The remains of his parcel are tossed in after him and the door slams shut. The cab door slams. The van moves off. Ephraim feels for his scattered belongings, gathers them up and hugs them to his chest. What now? He has heard tales of the white man's jail. The car lurches around a corner. Ephraim is thrown of balance. He picks himself up and looks out of the window in the door, at the street flashing by outside, the darkened houses, the alternate pools of light and shadow as they pass beneath the lamps. He hugs his present to his chest and silently weeps.

Ephraim, brought out of his day dreaming, was surprised to find that his eyes had filled with tears. He blinked them away and, spurred on by his imagination, tried to walk a little faster. What he had just imagined could indeed happen; but he was an old man and after a few yards his pace slowed down again. He could remember the time when it was no effort at all to lope mile after mile over the hot veld, jogging along, his whole body relaxed and easy. He sweated, sure, that was natural, but he did not breathe hard. The sweat was from the heat, not exertion. He saw his home, his mind dwelling fondly on all the remembered details, not just of the house, of his wife and his children, but seeing the trading store with it's cheap clothes and gaily coloured blankets hanging from the ceiling: the black three legged cooking pots, the billycans, the celluloid bangles and sacks of beans, stamp[1], and mielie-meal[2]: the ploughshares, hoes, picks, sickles and knives. He thought of the little railway siding with its corrugated iron shed-like waiting room and the full milk churns that always stood there every morning, were taken away and returned empty in the early evening.

He thought of his wife and his children. Every week he sent them a five-shilling postal order and he was saving up to go home for Christmas. He had already told them so in the very first letter he had ever written, in a large scrawling, shaking hand. What would they do if he were sent to jail? What would happen to them?

Ephraim walked on through the night, each step taking him a little closer to the safety of his own four walls. Perhaps when he got home he would find his pass. Maybe it had slipped from a pocket when he threw down his jacket the previous night and fallen between the bed and the wall. Maybe it was on top of the old chest of drawers or beneath the table. If it had fallen, there was no other furniture in the room that could be concealing it. Maybe he had dropped it when he left the house that morning. Then someone he knew could have picked it up and would be holding it for him. Or a skolly may have found it and want to make trouble for him. Ephraim hugged his brown paper tied up with string parcel closely to his chest and hurried home as fast as his old legs could carry him through the dark streets.

Steve, still furious, picked up his bike and dumped the wheels on the pavement, swung his leg over the cross bar and stood there, undecided which way to move. He would think twice tomorrow before tying himself down to this little lot. Kids! That's all they were, just a bunch of kids. He leaned back, lifting the front wheel by the handlebars, and then bounced the wheel on the pavement, wanting to go but not moving.

Ephraim came hurrying around the corner wrapped in his dreams. He walked towards the little group but it was

---

1 Broken maize and crushed maize for porridge
2 As above

not until he passed between the one on the cycle and the others by the gutter that he noticed them; but he was in too much of a hurry to throw more than a quick glance in the trio's direction as he moved on.

'Hey, you!'

Ephraim stopped and felt the prickle of fear up his spine. He turned quickly, already words spinning through his head as he thought what he was going to say, but it wasn't a cop, it was only the white kid on a cycle and Ephraim grinned in relief.

'What's so funny?' Steve said, 'You never seen a man sick before?'

Ephraim was apologetic at once and cast a sympathetic glance in Johnny's direction. He had not meant to be offensive and if he had done wrong it was only common decency for him to try to apologise. But he must not allow himself to be detained by these boys. He was sorry the one was sick but he must hurry home. If he lingered, they might make trouble for him, the police would come and want to see his pass.

Steve dropped the cycle, stepping away from it, and walked up to Ephraim. 'What's so funny, nigger? What're you laughing at?'

Ephraim frowned, perplexed by the boy's attitude. Could it be that he was deliberately trying to pick a fight? But why? For what reason? What had he done? He had not deliberately made fun of the boy's sickness. It was because it was not a policeman who had called to him that he laughed. Yet, although he knew he could explain this to himself, he also knew he would never be given the opportunity of explaining it to them. Was it something inside the white boy that made him so truculent? He was behaving in the manner of many white boys, but then he must not do the boy wrong by assuming motives that were false. There are boys who look upon every black skin as a threat. They hurl one-sided challenges in order to prove their superior status as white men, for if they feel, in any way, a sense of insecurity, they have to do something about it, usually in a gang, choosing a scapegoat on whom to vent their spleen. And there are black boys equally as vicious, who strut loudmouthed down the pavement in a long line, shoulder to shoulder so that no one can get by, and who viciously push into the gutter any white person who approaches them. What is this terrifying juxtaposition of peoples that attracts and, at the same time, repels? The white farm boy who like to drink Kaffir beer and who always addresses his friend in a Bantu tongue in preference to his own language: the black woman who tries to ape the fashions and habits of her white counterpart, even wearing lipstick that turns her black lips a hideous purple, and face powder that turns her beautiful skin an ash grey. Pathetic imitation – *Hair Straightened* – the sign says. *'Miss Priscilla Dhlamini,'* the advertisement runs, *'Fabulous star of stage and screen uses Punk's face cream to keep that soft lovely complexion'* Pathetic vulgarity, pathetic envy, pathetic aspirations. The white man who sleeps with black women even though it's against the law, and the black man who lusts after white women even though it can lead to a hangman's noose, and the black women who solicit white men and then hurl filthy abuse when repulsed, and the white women who secretly gaze at black bodies and whose eyes, beneath half-closed lids, wander down, as they imagine with shame the satisfaction that would be theirs if what they have heard rumoured proves to be true. All these people treading the same earth, breathing the same air, but living either side of a fence – EUROPEANS ONLY – NON-EUROPEANS ONLY a parallel existence, coming together only out of necessity or coming together only in violence and in moments of danger and high tragedy that override the tincture of the skin. The pathetic relationships, the pathetic misunderstandings, the pathetic blindness, the pathetic idealism, the pathetic mistrust, the pathetic fear, the pathetic revulsion, the pathetic aspirations, frustrations, limitations; the threnody of a great country forever at war with itself. When would it all come to an end? They stood facing each other on either side of the fence, the invisible barrier of misunderstanding and, because there existed this emotional barrier, with rare exceptions, physically there was nothing between them.

Steve grabbed the old man by the lapels of his jacket,

repeating his question, 'I said what are you laughing at?'

Johnny lifted a tear stained face. 'Was he laughing at me?'

'I'm not laughing Baas,' Ephraim answered softly, 'Let me go, please.' He lifted his free hand and tried to remove Steve's fingers from his lapel.

'Take your hands off me, nigger!' Steve hissed at him.

'You're holding me, Baas.'

'You don't like me holding you?' Steve stood a moment gripping the lapel, the black man's fingers around his wrist, then he let go and Ephraim let go. Elaborately Steve wiped his hands together in front of the other's face and then, without warning, his fist rammed into Ephraim's solar plexus. Winded and gasping, Ephraim dropped his parcel and staggered back, staring in puzzlement at the boy in front of him. Steve was suddenly afraid of what he had done. He did not know why he had done it. He wanted to go up to the old man and say he was sorry, he wanted to touch him, to shake him, to get through in some way and apologise but he stood staring back, uncertain and fearful. What would the man do, would he fight back? It was four to one. He did not want it to go any further. He wanted to pick up his bike and cycle out of there as fast as he could go, not looking back. He wanted to turn back the clock, erase these last few seconds and forget this ever happened. He wanted not to know of Ephraim's existence, not to see him, not to still feel the memory of his fist as it struck home. But his knuckles were tingling and he did see Ephraim and he could not wipe from his memory the thing he had done.

'Steve!' Angelo screamed at him, and, leaving Johnny's side, stepped quickly towards him. But Johnny and Carlos stepped forward too.

'Was he laughing at me?' Johnny cried, and Carlos backed him up with, 'Dirty nigger! What's he got to laugh at?'

Why don't they shut up? Steve thought. For God's sake why don't they realise I want it to finish? Why do they force me into something I don't want anymore?

Why do they call me, filthy nigger, Ephraim thought. What did I do that they should treat me like this? I am an old man who would not give offence. He bent down to pick up his parcel. Steve's leg moved. It moved as though he had lost control of it, as though it were a leg belonging to someone else, as though it had a life of its own separate from the rest of his body. He felt his knee jar against the lowered face, the teeth crunch against the bone. He saw the blood spurt from the shattered mouth. He saw the old man go down on his knees, trembling, unable to rise. He saw his other foot lash out and the old man fall forward on his face. He saw Johnny's boot, he heard the savage screaming, saw the menace in their faces. He saw the horror on Angelo's face; he saw his own mingled with terror. He saw the world he knew collapsing. He saw Carlos, his face distorted, join in next to Johnny. He saw the whirling bodies, the terrible eyes. He saw Angelo grab frantically at their arms, trying to pull them away. He saw the resistance. He saw mouths moving and shouting. He saw lights appearing in windows. He saw the shadow of people on verandas and in doorways. He saw the old man's hands desperately, instinctively, trying to ward off blows from his head. He saw the bruises and the cuts. He saw again and again his shoe hit the crumbling body. He heard the gasps and the groans. He saw it all, he saw it and he could not stop it. He saw Angelo suddenly running, then Johnny, then Carlos. He saw the two mount their bikes. He saw the brown paper parcel tied up with string lying where it had fallen. He saw the now still Ephraim and the blood staining the pavement and then, gradually, forcing its way through the trance he was in, he heard the whistle. Now he saw nothing. He heard only that whistle and in a flash was astride the saddle and racing into the night.

The telephone rang. Sergeant Nel picked it up without looking at it and sat listening to the voice on the other end. When he put the phone down he turned to Smith and said, 'Smith, go and open the mortuary, one of our vans has picked up another body.' Smith muttered a malediction against people who die at night, although that seems to be the time when most people die, yanked the key from the wall and lifted the flap in the counter. He let it drop with a loud bang behind him to show his disgust and stalked out of the office. Outside he paused to light a cigarette. The flaming match threw a brief orange glow over his face and hands, then he shook it out and blew a cloud of smoke towards the clear, starlit sky. The moon had risen and it was almost bright enough to be dawn. Constable Smith spat on the gravel and set off down the yard.

'Angelo!' Mama whispered his name urgently, coming down a few steps and leaning over the banister towards him.

At the sound of her voice Angelo swung around, knocking his bike leaning against the wall. The bike clattered to the ground.

'Angelo! Where you bin?' Mama gripped the banisters, her face almost ferocious with fear and the accusation of something not yet known. Angelo lurched away from the gate and across to the steps, gripped the uprights in front of Mama and looked at her, his head level with her knees. She moved down further until, reaching out, she could touch his face. The skin was wet and feverish, his eyes unnaturally bright. She touched his forehead and neck with the back of her hand. Angelo grabbed at her fingers and, turning the palm upwards, lowered his face and buried it. She stroked his hair with quick nervous movements. 'Angelo,' She whispered, 'What 'as happen?' She cast a quick glance in the direction of the bedroom and then looked back at the top of his head. 'Why you bin runnin'? You all hot.' He didn't answer, just kept her hand against his face and she could feel the trembling in his body. 'Where you bin?' Mama demanded, 'You know what time it is? We tol' you not to go out. Your father kill you when he fines you! Why you no listen to Mama? Now there's all sorts of trouble.' Angelo looked up quickly and his grip tightened about Mama's hand.

'What kind of trouble?'

She stared at him, aghast at his sudden ferocity. 'Angelo, let go please, you hurt my han'.' Mama tried to pull away but the boy clung on desperately.

'Mama! What kind of trouble?' He heard the faint

distant sound of a police whistle and glanced anxiously towards the door in the wall.

Mama did not hear the sound but she saw his look. 'Angelo? Whatsa wrong? What you bin doin'?' He looked up at the house, at the lighted kitchen window. 'Where's Papa?' He asked and Mama knew that whatever it was, it was terrible. Angelo did not ask for his father very often, only when he wanted something so badly he went to Ulrico first, instead of getting it though the agency of his mother. Ulrico was generally pleased and flattered that his son should come to him and in a weak moment the request, whatever it was and if not too outrageous, was complied with. Right now, Angelo needed help, and he needed it badly enough to ask for his papa, only papa would do. He heard the whistle again, closer now, and again his anxious glance flew towards the gate. Mama heard it too, and they both stood, staring towards the unseen. Why was his mother still up? Angelo thought. She should have been in bed hours ago. Why did she have to be here, standing in the night, when he could have slipped quietly into the bedroom and no one would have known what time he got in?

Booysens having finished his search and found nothing, came out of the bedroom, followed by Ulrico and Pepe, and Kumalo, having finished his drink and his snooping behind the shed, came walking slowly up the yard wiping his mouth and hands with his green handkerchief, his kerrie tucked under his arm.

'Angelo!' Ulrico barked, and Angelo with the sudden fright of the guilty, swung around to face his father... and saw Booysens, standing there, looking at him. Angelo's legs seemed to disappear. His body disappeared. He was one huge staring all seeing eye. In one ice cold moment the whole world stood out in stark relief, every detail of it, their faces, their clothes, the bathroom, the bedroom, the sky, the vegetation, the houses, Mama, the grapevine, the mortice, and above all, a vision of Ephraim, the memory of the boys and what they had done. For one brief moment, the world stood silent and waiting and then, the whistle... Angelo turned his head wildly in all directions. Where lay his escape?

'Here,' Booysens said, taking a step forward.

Angelo ran.

But Booysens was like a greyhound who sees a hare. What difference whether it be live or a dummy? He is trained to catch it. In two running strides he grabbed at Angelo's shirt as the boy crashed into his fallen bike and fell to his knees. He was pulled up, twisting, straining forward, and the shirt ripped in a long grinding tear. Angelo stumbled again with the sudden release against the strain and in a flash Booysens was on top of him, hauled him to his feet and held on. If the boy ran at the sight of his uniform it was through fear, and if he were afraid then he was also guilty of something.

'All right, All right!' Booysens yelled at the struggling Angelo and with the suddenness of his voice, Angelo collapsed like a sack of grain. There was no more fight, there was only a darkness in the world that a moment before had surrounded him with such intense clarity. 'What's all this about then?' Booysens said and with the question, Angelo found again the will to struggle.

'Let me go!' he screamed, 'Let me go! I didn't do it!'

Booysens shook him viciously, trying to calm him down but only making matters worse. The boy's head jerked on his neck and Mama hid her face in her hands. Ulrico and Pepe stepped forward. They wanted to protest, but they said nothing.

'Yes?' Booysens questioned, 'Didn't do what? Come on, what didn't you do?'

Mama, Ulrico and Pepe stared at Angelo in the grip of the policeman and waited for his reply. Attracted by the noise, Sarah and Nina had come out onto their veranda to add their silent witness to the scene, and Kumalo quietly walked over to the gate and stood there, blocking the way of escape. Angelo's guilty panic, caused by the unexpected sight of Booysens, had betrayed him, and now the words swirled like rapids over the rocks of his panic. He gibbered hysterically, trying to make his excuses. 'It wasn't me, it was the others... the others... I had nothing to do with it, I swear... You must believe me! Please believe me! It wasn't me!' the police whistle sounded again, practically outside the house. 'I tied to stop them! On my oath I tried to stop them! I told them to stop but they wouldn't! They wouldn't listen to me! I tried to pull them away but they kept on! Oh God!'

'I don't know what you're talking about,' Booysens said, 'but I'll soon find out.' He handed Angelo over to Ulrico with the command, 'Here, hold him,' and obediently Ulrico took hold of Angelo's arm and gripped it tight. Angelo did not feel the hard fingers bruise his flesh. He watched Booysens cross over to the gate, Kumalo stepped aside, Booysens opened the gate and looked out into the street, and then he turned to his father and pleaded.

'Dad, I didn't do it, please! listen to me!'

'Keep quiet!' Ulrico whispered, still looking towards the street. He saw Booysens go outside and talk to someone and then turn back into the yard followed by another man in khaki. Angelo collapsed against his father and clung to him. Ulrico put his arms over the boy and hugged him tight. 'Papa!' the boy sobbed, 'Papa, help me!'

Chapter 13

'According to a number of witnesses he got beaten up by a gang of young hooligans,' the ambulance man said. 'Two of your guys have been around there asking all the questions. It will probably end up murder by person or persons unknown hey?' He looked down at the corpse and shook his head. 'Pretty savage beating, huh? Why do people do these things? It's beyond me to tell you the truth. No identity by the way.' He waved a vague hand over the corpse and handed Smith the black plastic wallet. 'Nothing in it to tell you anything,' he said as Smith opened it.

'What's in there?' Smith asked, pointing. 'Oh, just some old clothes. There's a laundry mark but I doubt it will help, they're most probably stolen.'

'What about his pass?'

'Wasn't carrying one.'

Smith cursed loudly and stared with accusation at the body on its stretcher. 'Bloody stupid Kaffirs!' he said. 'They're given passes to carry and the law requires they carry one. How we supposed to tell one Kaffir from another? They're like baboons, they all look exactly the same. He looked down at the nameless, unidentified body and sucked his teeth with irritation, tapping the wallet against the palm of his hand and shook his head. 'If only they realised the trouble they give us, not carrying their passes,' he said.

Ephraim lay on his stretcher, gazing back with unseeing eyes at his accusers. They had folded his arms over his chest against which he hugged a brown paper parcel tied up with string, one torn sleeve of a sports jacket hanging from its ripped wrapping.

Sergeant Nel saw the dawn and glanced up at the charge office clock, checking it with his own gold wristwatch. Only another half hour and the long night would be over. Maybe on his way out he would call in on the boy, try and say a few words, it might help. He had told Meyer to give him three blankets. The dawns could be chilly, even in summer sometimes, and especially in a concrete box of a cell with its steel door and steel bars at the small high up window. By the time he came on duty again they would have got the other three, might even get them before he went off home. It had been a long hard night.

Angelo sat against the far wall of the cell, his three blankets folded neatly beneath him. They had never been unfolded. The young bicycle thief had long since cried himself to sleep. Angelo stared blankly at the steel door with its recessed peephole. Like an unblinking eye, it stared back, a small round black eye. A thin shaft of grey light penetrated the high window, turned pink, and the eye's blackness began to fade. Angelo's head dropped forward onto his folded arms and he slept. He did not have long. In two hours a stranger would peer through the spy hole and open the door ushering in a native constable with a tray covered with plates under stainless steel, dented, battered with much used warmers, and the egg, sausage and bacon would grow cold, hardening in its own congealed fat. But in the meantime an exhausted Angelo slept.

Chapter 14

Summer, another burning summer of dry days and hot winds, of crackling crumbling foliage, ready at a spark to spring instantly into a blaze, sweeping with the wind, leaving behind a trail of blackened earth. The civic authorities have rationed the water. Hose pipes are forbidden and the plants in the front garden wilt and die, stretched along the sun baked earth, turning brown, crumbling into dust. The city lies sticky and sweltering beneath the cloudless deep blue sky, the heat radiating from the burning pavements and the melted surface of the roads, the haze shimmering above the hot sand and the ocean, beyond the breakers an almost motionless blue and silver.

Madame Chang, unable any longer to bear the oven heat of her little shop, joins her husband on the veranda and the carved ivory fans never stop their tiny puffs of comfort. If only it would rain, but a few scattered drops that have fallen over parched country in the last seven weeks have hardly had time to hit the earth before evaporating and, beyond the limits of the city, only the cacti and the eucalyptus have not withered.

It is a Saturday afternoon. In the public gardens the crowds stroll so slowly, unable to exert themselves, their clothes clinging to their skins, not a jacket in sight, only loose shirts and sandals and flimsy cottons beneath wide brimmed hats. The sportsmen seem the only ones unaffected by the heat, bowlers on their greens, the cricketers at the pitch, the beaches, bright with deck chairs and gaudy striped umbrellas, swarming with people like so many ants. The sales of ice cream and cooling drinks have rocketed phenomenally, but if only it would rain.

Pepe dozes in his chair, replete after Mama's delicious as usual cooking; having this day given Nina's a miss. He ignores the bluebottle that buzzes insistently about his head and dreams of faraway places and incidents long ago. But added to his dreams now are tender thoughts of his beloved Angelo who was like his own son.

Each Sunday night he wrote a letter and took a stroll up the street to pop it into the red pillar box. The letter was not a masterpiece of literature, it was not over long, but it said all that he had to say, written in a rounded laborious hand without a single punctuation mark. *'Dear Angelo I hope you are well we are all well are they treating you all right we are always thinking of you and remain your ever loving uncle Pepe.'* Sometimes he would go on to mention the progress of the building site, or that he had seen in the street someone Angelo knew and who had been asking after the family by name, and occasionally he mentioned the weather. But as it was only bricks and mortar that separated them and not a great distance it seemed a little futile to tell the boy what he already knew.

Tony had started work, as an apprentice electrical engineer in the post office. He was exceptionally proud of his new status and had quietened down considerably since the accident, much to the gratification of his mother. He still slept in the bedroom with uncle Pepe, still read lurid comics, but he could afford now to buy his own cigarettes and he only called in at Nick's after night school twice a week.

Unbeknown to his mother, who would have died of

mortification had she known, he was having an affair with a married woman almost twice his age, the mother of two children, and with whom, on this hot Saturday afternoon, he was enjoying a mild flutter at the races. His mother thought he was at the cinema. In fairness to Tony, it was the woman herself who had opened the bidding and played all the cards. Tony merely laid down his hand and played dummy. He did not know why she liked him, he did not question it, merely accepted it.

The husband, a nondescript little man with a liking for beer, was a dealer in farming equipment and away from home for long periods selling his wares; sometimes a fortnight, sometimes a month, sometimes longer, travelling the Transvaal, traversing the great Karoo, one little dorp after another, centres of a farming community, too many of which were too poor to consider his implements but he never stopped trying, never gave up hope and was occasionally rewarded for his efforts by making a sale. He invariably gave his wife good notice of his intended return, perhaps because he had a shrewd suspicion of what was going on and did not want to catch the pair of them in the act.

The whole intrigue had come about through an accident – two accidents – one with a stolen gun and the other a man lying side by side with Tony in *Surgical 2.* After a couple of visits, the wife made sympathetic enquires about the boy in the next bed, and her husband in whispers related the whole story. Tony heard every word although he pretended to be engrossed in a magazine. He looked across to the next bed and smiled. The woman smiled back. On her next visit and from then on she always had a word or two for him, and even brought an extra little gift "for that poor boy in the next bed," some fruit, sweets maybe, a magazine, cigarettes, and much to Tony's surprise, after her husband's discharge, the visits and the gifts continued. The next step was to visit her home and from then on it worked itself out to a logical conclusion. He became uncle Tony to the kids and never put in an appearance when the husband was home. There wasn't much point. Tony's despairing virginity had ended with a bang, to coin a phrase. With quite a few bangs in fact.

Seraphina, wearing a discarded pair of high heel shoes and with an old shawl of her mother's wrapped around her shoulders and clutched to her chest, was swinging one of aunt Nina's worn out handbags. She and a friend were throwing a dolly's tea party with a tin tea set, mud pies and cold water tea in the back yard. The friend, also in a pair of high heels and a long dress of her mother's hitched high at her waist, had added to her ensemble a felt hat set at a rakish angle. They staggered about on wobbling legs and twisting ankles, the friend sometimes tripping over the dress, and both of them every now and again stepping out of their shoes and leaving them behind – the shoes protruded a good inch or more behind their heels. But both of them were utterly serious as children are at play, talking grown up talk, and Seraphina opening and snapping too her handbag every two minutes with all the sophistication of a woman in a powder room.

They have set the table for four, the guests being one doll with a paint peeling face belonging to Seraphina and three dolls belonging to her friend, one of which was a black piccaniny. More tea is being spilled, however, than served, it being very difficult to walk with bent knees, not lifting the feet from the ground but sliding them along, clutching a shawl and a hand bag, and trying to carry a tin cup of tea, and with the friend, the added hazard of tripping on a trailing skirt. There was constant coming and going, tut-tutting, and refilling of teacups.

Guido has found himself a nondescript piece of wood and from the workshop comes the monotonous steady sound of hammering. It drives Nina, who is playing patience on the green chenille covered dining room table, nearly frantic with nerves. She keeps losing track of the game and misplaying. 'If someone doesn't tell that child to stop that awful hammering,' she grumbles loudly to Sarah, 'I'll go out there and do it myself. Never any peace in this wretched house!'

'I think I'll go and have a rest,' Sarah notices the time on the Parthenon clock below the portrait of Garibaldi and between the two Chelsea poodles on the mantelpiece and pushes herself out of her chair. There is no funeral for her to enjoy today and, anyway, she has had a real ticking off from her sister for taking Seraphina to the cemetery for the last one. 'That is *no* place to take a child!'

'Fat lot of rest you'll get with that racket going on.' Nina slams down a card and gazes at the spread, willing it to be different and for the game to come out. Not one game in ten had come out for her and she was fast growing impatient with patience. Sarah slouched out of the room and in her bedroom closed the Venetian blind, preparing to get right into bed. She never could sleep on top of a bed, or under an eiderdown thrown loosely over. If she was going to sleep at all it had to be right inside, in her nightdress, in the dark. She felt under her pillow for her nightie and started to unbutton her blouse.

'Well Ulrico?' Father Joseph blinked almost owlishly across the veranda table at the couple sitting opposite him and wished he were wearing something looser than a dog collar and blue serge. He ran a finger around the inside of the collar trying to ease it away from the red wheals where it was chafing his skin. Father Joseph was beginning to put on a little weight, South African food and plenty of it obviously appealed to him and he was fast losing his good looks. He feels the heat more, sweats more, and does not move as nimbly as when he first arrived in the country. He shifts uncomfortably on his hard chair. 'What are you going to do? Are you going to help him?'

Ulrico gazed straight ahead.

'Ulrico...' Father Joseph leans forward across the table, his face intensely serious as he pleads against the opposition of Ulrico's stubbornness, his fingers interlaced in an attitude of prayer, the sides of his hands hitting the table to emphasise the urgency of what he is saying. 'Ulrico, no matter what he has done, he is still your son!'

For a brief second Ulrico's dark eyes flicker over Father Joseph's face and then he looks away again, and continues to stare out front. After a short silence he coughs to clear his throat and 'No!' he says, 'He is no longer my son.' His voice is quiet but determined. He stands up.

Why must these people be so obstinate? the priest thought. I am their spiritual father yet they do not listen to a word I say. He was becoming irritated by this mulish attitude and his voice lost its note of humility, its soft persuasiveness. 'He was given to you as your son by Almighty God, you cannot alter that! You wanted him, you got him, and you loved him.' He paused for effect, hoping his words were finally finding their mark. 'And he loved you, he still does. From you he expects help and encouragement and guidance. Bear in mind the parable of the prodigal.'

'We tried to give him that before but what happened? He killed a man. What for? For no reason he kills a man! For no reason, Father, he kills a stranger, someone who has done him no harm. That is not the doing of a son of mine. No. Never.'

Father Joseph opened his hands, palms upward in supplication. 'Ulrico, I know it's hard for you to see it in any way but that of a father who believes his son has done a terrible thing, but he was with three other boys! He swears he tried to stop them. And I believe him when he says he had nothing to do with it.'

Ulrico casts a glance in the priest's direction that says if he believes that then he is a bigger fool than I thought.

''Ow many times I tol' 'im?' Mama whispered, ''Ow many times?' She intertwined her trembling fingers. 'Dose boys, dose boys.' She shook her head. No longer able to find words, her voice faded.

These days Mama could not so easily control the tears. Her face was drawn and her eyes sunk deep behind pouches of violet blue. She tired easily and her unkempt hair had turned, overnight it seemed, a dull grey. She was ready to weep at the slightest provocation. It frightened the children who sometimes had to weep with her, not because they understood her sorrow, but because they wanted to show their sympathy and knew no other way. She wanted her son. She wanted to see his face, to touch his hand, but knowing how Ulrico felt, her boy was as good as dead to her. She prayed many times, long and hard for God to soften her husband's attitude, but

God's ears were deaf to her pleas and Ulrico would hear no mention of Angelo's name.

'So there were four of them,' Ulrico said bitterly, 'Four against one!' He sat down again with a thump as though his legs could no longer support him.

'I tol' 'im! I tol' 'im!' Mama moaned and felt for her husband's hand. She lifted the edge of her apron on which to blow her nose. Father Joseph was deeply sorry. He had not come here to upset them like this but the whole business had to be sorted out and he must do his duty as he saw it.

'They picked on a harmless old black minding his own business,' Ulrico went on, 'and they kill him. And my son is one of them, no matter what he says! He is a hooligan, a thug, a killer! And he is not my son!' The last was said with such emphasis Ulrico had to get up from the table once more and walk over to the veranda rail, leaning on it, his head hunched into his shoulders. Guido trotted up the yard carrying in one hand his piece of wood. 'Guido, what you doin'?' Ulrico said.

'Making a house for my guinea pig.'

'What guinea pig? You ain't got no guinea pig'

'I'm getting one.'

'That's what you think! And who says you can play with daddy's hammer?'

'I'm not playing, I'm building.' Guido looks appealingly at his father.

'You put that thing away now and it's no good looking at me like that. You should ask papa in the first place then it's okay. You must learn not to take things don't belong to you. Now go put it back.'

'What about my guinea pig? Guido said.

'No matter 'bout your guinea pig, go put back that hammer.'

Guido tightened his lips in disgust and thumped back down the yard to replace the hammer and throw down his piece of wood. His animals were becoming a household nuisance and the cause of much childish heartache when homeless dogs and stray kittens were refused admittance; but there was a succession of other creatures, silk worms that made Mama's flesh crawl until finally she could stand it no longer and threw the shoeboxes full of worms, eggs and moths, into the rubbish bin. Fortunately Guido had grown tired of them or all hell would have been let loose. He had fed some on beetroot leaves to produce red silk, others on cabbage to produce green, and others on mulberry to make yellow. The fatigue caused by collecting their food which they ravaged with enormous appetites, proved too much for him. Then followed goldfish but he forgot to feed them and they died. There was a tortoise that disappeared and a Belgian hare he exchanged for a chameleon but that also died. Ulrico said because the boy made it change its colour so often by transferring it to different backgrounds that the poor thing did not know whether it was coming or going and gave up the ghost in disgust. Ulrico watched Guido disappear around the corner and heard behind his back the priest's plaintive palliation.

'He has paid the penalty imposed,' he pleaded. 'He has been to prison. He has been whipped.'

Ulrico closed his eyes and slammed his palm down hard on the rail. In the workshop he heard Guido in childish temper hurl the hammer down on the bench. If he breaks that handle, Ulrico thought, I'll lambaste the hide off him. What he said was, 'Father, you're a priest, a man of the church and you can sit there and talk like that? Does a whipping pay for a life? He heard again the witness's voice, "He was lying there, on the pavement, and they were kicking him," and then the question, "All four of them?" and the answer, "Yes, all four of them. They kicked him even after he had stopped moving. They went on kicking, all four of them, until they heard the police whistle, then they left."

"You're quite sure of that? That is exactly what you saw, all four accused took part?" the witness nodded and looked across the courtroom at the four accused. "All four," he said. Angelo was shaking his head slowly, in disbelief, as the angry self-righteous whispers ran through the court so that they had to be silenced with a peremptory pounding of the gavel. Ulrico too saw his son's gesture but looked away.

Guido was hammering with something else now. He had found half a brick lying in the compost heap and was hammering great dents in his piece of wood.

'Nothing pays for a life!' Father Joseph persisted, 'Nothing! Who can be punished, except by God, for wantonly destroying life, no matter who he is? We cannot give life unless God wills it, and we cannot take it away, we have no right to take it away. "Verily I say unto you, inasmuch as you have done it unto one of the least of these my brethren, ye have done it to me." That is why I can sit here and talk the way I do. What has happened has happened and we must surely face up to it? A man has been killed; senselessly, stupidly, brutally. He died because four silly boys were bored, because four boys were feeling sour with life, and with nothing better to do found an outlet for their grievance in physical violence. They did not mean to kill him but he was an old man and they did not reckon on the final result. Are we to do more than hold up our hands in horror and say, "I told you so?" They pleaded drunkenness: they pleaded this; they pleaded that. But what do we plead? Answer me Ulrico?' His voice was trembling with anger that this man still refused to see the sense in what he was saying. 'Are they alone in their blame?'

But Ulrico does not answer. He grips the rail, his knuckles showing white, and stares straight ahead as though he would deliberately close his ears to the priest's impassioned words.

There is a silence and then Father Joseph's voice regains its tone of benevolence as he continues. 'Are they alone in their punishment?' He turns away and sighs, 'Manslaughter! If it had been a white man they attacked and killed it would have been a murder charge.' He turns back to Ulrico, 'So society has punished them as it sees fit, but do we know, Ulrico, when their punishment will end?' And, having left his seat, he lays a gentle hand on Ulrico's shoulder. Ulrico looked at the hand and Father Joseph took it away. Can you tell the fire not to burn? Or the ice not to freeze? Can you tell a tree to uproot itself or the desert to flower overnight? He stared into Ulrico's face and the man turned to look at him.

'And what about us?' He asked, 'His mother and father. Look...' And Ulrico looked over his shoulder and nodded towards the chair in which Mama sat, quietly weeping. He looked back at the priest. 'Have you thought of us?'

'Oh, Ulrico!'

'And what about the dead man's wife? And his children? Have you thought about them?'

'Of course I have, but that does not alter...'

'So they have been whipped, they have been sent to jail, and that must be enough for us?' Ulrico walked towards the partition and carefully examined it, running his hand down the wood, picking at the paint.

Father Joseph looked at his back and said, 'It is not the scars on the bodies, Ulrico, it is the scars on their minds. Angelo is no criminal. No murderer, I believe he is a good boy and he is still your son.' He turned away, back to the table, he did not wish to see the reaction but heard the voice: hard, unforgiving, obdurate.

'He is not my son! He will never enter my house, never again! Do you hear me?'

'Oh God!' Father Joseph closed his eyes. 'Oh God! Put words into my mouth that will touch this man's heart!' He turned on Ulrico and his voice now was harsh. 'Father I have sinned against heaven and in Thy sight and am no more worthy to be called Thy son.'

Ulrico's eyes blazed with anger. 'I know my Bible!' he shouted, the side of his fist hammering the partition, almost splintering the wood. Mama looked at him, pleading. This was no way to talk to a man like Father Joseph. 'I know my Bible, Father! Don't preach at me!'

But Father Joseph's anger flared too and his voice was every bit as loud as his adversary's, 'If you know it so well then you will know the rest of it too! "For this my son was dead, and is alive again; he was lost and is found," but where is your son, Ulrico? Where is yours?'

Ulrico was taken aback by this sudden fire and a little ashamed of his outburst though he still meant every word he had said. His voice softened in apology for the way in which he had spoken. 'Father, you are a good priest,' and hurried on before Father Joseph could interrupt as he was obviously going to. 'We appreciate your interest in us but this is not the church and this is no time or place for preaching.'

'Ulrico, Christ did not need a church as such in which to preach his teachings. And what are his sermons? His parables? They are words of wisdom, Ulrico, a way of life to follow. The church is not stone and brick and fine words! The church is people, Ulrico, flesh and blood people, and every one of these people matters!' He was trembling with exertion and the sweat was trickling down his back and down his chest, down his legs and arms and face. He wiped his face with his handkerchief.

'You are a priest,' Ulrico said, 'And something more than an ordinary man...'

'No!' It was a cry of despair as he averted his face.

'I am only a man. Go back to your church, stand in your pulpit and preach the ways of God. It is the way of our children that we do not understand.'

'Can you have the one without the other? Why do you ask for understanding and then turn your face from it? Why do you close your mind? Your eyes? Your heart? Will you live in ignorance all your life?'

'Father!' Ulrico felt the anger rising again.

'It was ignorance that killed that old man, and the weapon of ignorance was four foolish children!'

'They are not children!' Ulrico shouted.

In the next-door house, Nina had stopped playing and was staring dully at the table before her, listening to her brother, may God forgive him. The noise also woke Pepe who sat in his chair pretending to be asleep and wishing he could go away and not hear what his brother was saying.

Seraphina and her friend, frightened now, abandoned their dolls' tea party and, carrying their shoes so as not to make a clatter, slowly climbed the next-door stairs, going in search of Aunt Sarah and comfort.

'They are children,' Father Joseph said, 'As you are a child, and I tell you, that if you persist in this action, it is ignorance and will lead to violence and more violence; and violence will lead to more violence and so it will go on and on! You want understanding? Or would you prefer violence?' Father Joseph's eyes were alight with crusading fire, his voice thundered, and he hammered the table with his fist. How dare this man stand there and ignore his warnings? How dare he stand there sullenly refusing to believe in the rightness of what he was saying? How dare he stand there in stubborn pride, defending the vanity of his own hurt, nursing it, caressing it, holding it to him, refusing to relinquish one iota of shame he felt in his heart for the thing his son had done? They faced each other over the table, over Mama's lowered head, and then very quietly, Ulrico said, 'I think it would be best... I think you had better go now, Father.'

'Ulrico!'

'Please! No more. Go now.'

'Is it too much to ask you to think over what I have said?'

'Please! Go now.'

There was nothing more to say. Father Joseph bent down and picked up his black homburg where it had fallen from the table to the floor. He brushed the dust from the brim with his fingertips. Why did he have to get angry? Harsh words only lead to harsh words and are in themselves violence. A fine priest he was, preaching against violence, and using it himself, falling into the trap, slipping into a slanging match like any street hooligan. He was disgusted. He walked around the table and paused at Mama's chair to give her shoulder a little squeeze, then he turned back to Ulrico and said, although the words were meant primarily for Mama, 'If you want me, you know where I am.'

Ulrico nodded and Father Joseph walked through the kitchen door in the direction of Ulrico's motioning hand. Mama got up and, with Ulrico's arm around her shoulder, they followed Father Joseph to the front door to see him out. They shook hands, but there was no more to say. Father Joseph placed his hat on his head and, without looking back, set off up the road.

Guido came up the yard still carrying his much dented piece of wood and his half brick. He knelt beside the bottom step and started to hammer happily. Pepe raised an eyebrow and squinted in his direction. How the boy thought he was going to make anything with one solitary piece of wood and half a brick was more than he could imagine. Kids! He snuggled down in his chair again and brooded, not looking up when the latch on the yard door clicked up and the door swung open. Guido looked up from his hammering, paused, and then ran silently into the house.

Angelo stood at the gate, the same Angelo, outwardly untouched, and gazed around the yard in which nothing had changed. It was exactly as he remembered it; the whitewashed wall of the bathroom with the muddy stains, the bricks that bordered the flower beds, the junk beneath the veranda, the grapevine, the mortice machine, even uncle Pepe dozing in his chair; just as he pictured it every night, lying in his cot, gazing at the tiny barred window high in the brick wall of his cell. Slowly, silently, Angelo crossed over to where uncle Pepe sat, head bowed, in his chair. He would give him a surprise. The old man would wake up and, there Angelo would be, standing in front of him. His uncle's letters had assured him of his welcome in this direction at least, although there was a shyness, a hesitation in his movements. The situation was unnatural. It was strange to see someone after so long a time, when so much has happened that should never have been. He did not know that uncle Pepe was awake, gazing at the ground in front of his chair, and it was only when a pair of shoes and a pair of legs stepped into his line of vision that he frowned and looked up, staring in disbelief at the boy who stood there. Angelo smiled, a tentative smile, and then looked down in embarrassment at his feet, grinding the heel of his shoe into the earth, making little divots with short hard kicks of his toe. He carried a small cardboard suitcase that he placed beside him as Pepe continued to stare, saying nothing, as gradually his face puckered and his lips trembled.

Pepe could not remember when he had last cried. In fact he could not remember ever crying. He did not cry when his father died, or his mother. He did not cry as a youth when, after an absence of months from home, he yearned for a sight of the familiar with all the ache of the desperately homesick. He did not cry at physical pain or emotional distress. He was not a man given to tears. But now, with no warning, with no sound, the tears welled up and ran down his cheeks and into his white moustache with its yellow stain of nicotine. He took hold of the arms of his chair and struggled with his fat belly, turning slightly sideways to lever himself to his feet. 'Angelo!' He cried, 'Angelo!' and he held out his two enormous arms. 'My boy, my boy!' Laughing, crying, trembling with excitement, Pepe clutched the boy to him and squeezed the breath from his body with a tremendous bear hug, the pressure relieved only by the little pats of welcome on the back: and the tears of the one started off the tears of the other, tears of joy, of relief and the end of pain, tears of embarrassed affection as the old man in his ecstasy, smothered his face with kisses, stroked his hair, pushed him back to look at him, shook his head unbelievingly an then pulled him forward again, into another powerful hug that left Angelo weak kneed and limp.

Ulrico, informed by Guido of his son's return, came out of the kitchen and stood watching, his face hard and set. Pepe saw him and then Angelo too turned to see his father, following the direction of Pepe's glance. Gently he released himself from Pepe's embrace and, smiling up at his father, walked to the bottom of the steps. He had not noticed the look on Ulrico's face, the coldness, the hostility. He still felt Pepe's arms crushing him, the rough beard that had set his cheeks tingling hotly, the wet tears drying on his skin. But Pepe saw it and, without a word, turned and silently entered the bedroom, closing the door behind him. He knew what was about to take place, and there was nothing he could do. He could not plead with his brother, he could not explain to Angelo, not now. There is nothing he could do. In time it would pass, this bitterness, these accusations and counter accusations, this hurt, it would pass; but right now, what has to be between father and son has to be, and it is not in his power to interfere. He takes an old shoebox from a drawer, a box of papers, letters and mementoes, and seating himself on the edge of the bed, he tries to obliterate the present by burying himself in the past.

'Papa?' Angelo wanted his father to speak, to say something, anything that would lessen the distance between them, but the silence continued until he laughed in his apprehension and explained smiling, 'It's me, Papa. Angelo. I'm home!' But Ulrico said nothing. Angelo could feel his heart beating, Please, he thought, Dad, say something to me! Anything. Just say something. He looked away, about the yard, and the smile flickered across his face. No, nothing had changed. Maybe a new chicken or two in the hen house. He stared at the grapevine but he could not make out whether there were any bunches hanging there or whether, for once, they had matured passed their hard greenness, then he looked back at his father, still smiling hopefully. He wondered where Tony could be. No doubt lying on his fat arse in the bedroom reading a comic. No, if that were the case, he would have already been out to see him. He wondered whether Tony's foot was badly scarred, even deformed, after the accident. He thought of him sitting in court with his stick and his plastered leg, looking for all the world like some super hero instead of the ass he was. At least that's what someone had told him. Well, he would soon find out all the news about everybody. He could do with a cup of tea too, one of Mama's cups of tea. His mouth was as dry as the Kalahari. Where's Seraphina? And Aunt Sarah? At a funeral? No... Saturday... more likely to be weeping at a wedding. He pictured Millie, with pins in her mouth, moving slowly around the judy, practically squinting in her concentration as she worked on the wedding gown. What would Millie say to him? How would she...? Angelo pushed the thought from his mind. She would not see him at all, he knew that, and he did not want to think about it.

'What you want?' Only Ulrico's lips moved and then not much. His head, his eyes, his hands, his whole body apart from his lips, remained still. He seemed to be looking in the distance, over Angelo's head. 'What you want?'

The question in its coldness took Angelo's breath

away so that for a second his chest did not move either as he stared incredulously at his father. Then he gulped in air and whispered tremulously, 'I've... come home,' and then, not being able to stand the silence any longer, 'Where's Mama?'

'Aren't youse ashamed? What you want your mama for? Go away.' And Ulrico turned abruptly on his heel and went into the house, closing the door behind him. Angelo felt the hair rising on his scalp and, in the intense heat of the day, he shivered as though he had stepped suddenly from burning sunlight into deep shade. Never in his life could he remember the kitchen door being closed except last thing at night. No one ever closed it, it was forever open, "Come in and have a nice cup of tea. Come in and have some nice curried chicken. Come in and sit down a while. Come in and talk to us while we eat. Come in and listen to the wireless. Come in and keep company." And now his own father had slammed that door in his face. Was this the longed for homecoming he had dreamed about during the long tedious days and nights of his imprisonment? Was this all it was going to be? A door slammed in his face? The stricken, terrified boy stood at the bottom of the steps, staring up at the still silent house. It was macabre, in the middle of the afternoon when it was usually resounding with the sounds of life, to listen to its silence. It was as though someone in the house had died. They were all there gathered in the front bedroom with its blinds drawn and its double bed with the cotton bedspread, gathered around an imagined corpse that lay there, and the corpse wore the face of Angelo.

He threw back his head and howled. 'Mamaaaaa!' It was a sound that came not from his throat, from his lungs, from his mouth, but from his whole body. 'Mamaaaa!' He screamed it at the top of his voice, hurling it like a challenge at the house. In the street outside, passers by paused to listen to the sound, like an animal in pain. In the house next-door, Nina got up from her cards and went through the passage into the small seldom used front room, shutting the door behind her. Seraphina and her friend asked if they could creep into bed with Aunt Sarah and of course she agreed. From the yard, muffled now by the protective walls, Nina heard again the scream and, sitting on the swivelling piano stool, she looked at her hands and realised she had torn the jack of hearts clean in two.

Sarah wondered if she was hearing things. She thought she heard Angelo calling. She hoped he was all right and not in any trouble. In the darkness of her room she waited in case she heard the call again. It must have been a dream, a nightmare. She had eaten too much at lunch and gone to sleep too soon afterwards. She had only herself to blame if her digestion gave her nightmares. She snuggled comfortably beneath the eiderdown, a small girl holding her close on either side.

Angelo paused in his screaming; taking in another deep breath, just as the kitchen door was flung open and Ulrico reappeared. He carried a razor strop, an old black strop that once belonged to his father and with which he sharpened his cutthroat every morning before shaving. Once, when he was very young, Angelo had tried to sharpen the razor, and had sliced deeply into the black leather. It was a wonder he didn't lose a finger. He remembered the whole incident and how his father had given him a good hiding for playing with that which did not belong to him. The strop still showed the cut on the one side.

'I told you to go away!' Ulrico shouted. 'We don't want you here. You bring disgrace on our family. You been to prison. You break your Mama's heart with what you do. You kill her for sure! We don't want you here! No more, you hear? No More.'

Angelo glared sulkily at his father and his mouth now set in a hard thin line of bitterness. 'So I've been to prison,' he growled. He looked like a surly dog that had been kicked into a corner and, cowering there, was ready to turn, snapping and snarling, on his attacker. 'I've had my punishment.'

'Angelo, I'm warning you!' Ulrico advanced to the edge of the top step and brandished the strop.

Angelo knew his father. He knew what he was like when his temper was aroused. It took a great deal to make him angry, but once gone, he was implacable. He hesitated and then stepped back, shut his eyes, put his hands to his head, and yelled, 'Mamaaaa!'

Ulrico's feet clattered down the wooden steps. Angelo opened his eyes in time to see the strop descending and lifted his arms to protect his head. The leather hit his forearm, was lifted, came down again, delivered with all the force of Ulrico's body. Angelo stumbled backwards and, as the strop came down a third time, he fell. He rolled over onto his hands and knees and it came across his back, sending him sprawling once more with a scream of pain. He got to his feet and ran for the semi safety of the steps behind which he could dodge, tensing the muscles of his back to ease the pain there, writhing, rubbing his arm. He felt as though he had been in the blazing sun for a week and his skin was blistered so that even the light touch of a shirt was too much to bear. He held a step and peered through a couple of treads at eye level just as the strop came down again. He withdrew his fingers in time and dodged around the steps, away from the pursuing Ulrico. The strop hit the wood with a crack that echoed down the yard like a pistol shot. 'I've been in prison!' Angelo sobbed. Crack. 'I've been in prison!' He dodged around in the opposite direction. Crack. 'They whipped me too! Didn't you hear the judge when he said it?' Dodge. Crack. 'Six cuts with a medium cane, that's what he said!' He was trapped behind the steps. Whichever way he went, the strop would come down. He shouted at Ulrico through the treads, 'You heard it! You were there!' Ulrico stepped back and lowered the strop. Tentatively Angelo came out from behind the steps and said softly, 'Do you want me to show you where they whipped me? Do you want to see it?' He ripped open his flies and pushed down his trousers and his underpants in one swift movement, turning his back on Ulrico as he did so. The boy stood there, holding up his shirt with both hands, his trousers around his ankles, his body jerking occasionally with a sob, his head lowered. Ulrico looked at the round buttocks across which, quite discernable, he saw the white scars. And above, in the small of his back, a red and blue welt where his own leather had come down across his son's back. Without a word he walked away up the steps. Angelo heard his tread and looked up, bent hastily to pull up his trousers, and called in a whisper, 'Papa!' But Ulrico went on. Angelo, tucking in his shirt, backed over to the front of the steps and called urgently, 'Papa!' Ulrico strode across the veranda. He reached the door, he went into the kitchen and the door began to close behind him. Angelo's pleading changed into angry despair. 'You dirty, lousy, stinking, son of a bitch! You bastard! You dirty bastard! Who do you think you are?'

There was no stopping it now. In his intense rage, Ulrico threw himself down the steps, tossing aside his strop and going for Angelo with his bare fists. The boy staggered back under the impact but he held his ground in defiance of his father's fury.

'You call yourself a father? Go on! Beat me! I'm your son, Angelo! See if I care! Go on! Go on!'

Anything was preferable to complete exclusion, but it could not last. Suddenly he could take no more. He threw himself forward, fumbling for his father's arms to hold them, desperately trying to stop the blows that kept on coming. He felt no pain now, only a tiredness, a desire to fall, to stop thinking, stop seeing, stop breathing. The brightness of the day had given way to a dull grey, images were blurred, he could no longer see clearly his father's figure.

'Father…' His voice was no more than a whimper, forced out through his aching throat. 'Father...' They had swung around now and Ulrico had him against the side of the steps. The boy's head drooped, eyes closed. 'Kill me if you want. Kill me for something I didn't do. I was only there... I was only there.' His head lolled back against the wood as Mama, unable to control herself any longer, came quickly out of the house and down the stairs. She grabbed Ulrico, trying to pull him away. 'Ulrico!' she screamed, 'For the love of God, stop! Holy Mother of God, will you kill him?'

Ulrico breathing heavily, stepped back from Angelo, who leaned against the side of the steps, choking and exhausted. He removed his wife's fingers from his arm, shook his head, and stared in astonishment at his son's bleeding face. What had he done? If Mama's scream had not stopped him, what would he have done? He looked down at his quivering hands, the knuckles grazed, and then lifted them to his face, holding them either side of his nose as he looked again at Angelo. The boy had not moved, he stood against the steps with his eyes closed, his face turned away. I could have killed him! Ulrico thought. I could have killed him. My own son! I did this, to my own son, my own boy! The blood was his own, the bruises were his. Was Father Joseph right? That violence can only lead to violence? Was he no better than these kids he so roundly condemned? He could have killed his son, blindly, as senselessly as Angelo and his friends had set about the old man. He wanted to put out his hand and wipe away the blood that oozed from Angelo's mouth, dribbling over his chin: his blood; his very own. He wanted to say, Forgive me, Angelo, forgive me my son. In my anger I did not know what I did. He wanted to take the boy in his arms and hold him there, in comfort and protection, like a small child, but all he did was turn slowly away and, like a tired old man, climb slowly up the stairs and go into the house through the open door that remained open.

Mama watched him go, then she looked at Angelo, and her hands went out to him. If only, at that moment, he had moved his face towards her, she could have touched him, would have touched him, and it would have ended. But his eyes remained closed, his cheek against the wood. She dropped her hands and, like her husband before her, climbed slowly the wooden steps. Half way to the top she heard his quiet voice, like a small child in the night who has woken in the dark, and needs the company of its parent to brush away with gentle hands and calm voice, the fear, the loneliness. 'Mama...'

She stopped, but she did not look down at him, for she was afraid: afraid for her son, for her husband, for herself, for her whole family. She wanted only to protect them from the world, from each other, from themselves. 'Angelo,' she whispered, 'Go away.' But where would he go? She had not thought. What would he do? She had not thought. She only knew he must leave. And what about her? Inwardly she shrugged. She would get along. She closed her eyes and waited for him to go.

'Is that all? Is that all you have to say to me?'

'Your father,' she tried to explain her motives, 'He's a very angry man.' She turned to look down at him and he lifted his head, pleading with her to yield to him just one inch of charity. 'My chile… why you do such a dreadful ting?'

Angelo dropped his head and leaned against the hard wood. 'I don't know,' he whispered, 'I don't know.' He was no longer sure of his own innocence or his guilt.

'After all we have done for you, Angelo? After all we have given you?'

'Given me?' Angelo looked up at her and then around the little yard. He tried to think of something to say in reply to his question.

Mama heard the doubt in his voice. 'We tried,' she said, pleading with him now.

He ran his tongue over his cut lip. The blood was metallic to the taste. He wiped his chin with the back of his hand and looked at the scarlet smear, already turning a darker shade and drying in the heat, like an astringent on the skin. He wanted to say something that would give some small measure of comfort. He wanted to try and make amends, to say he was sorry for her grief of which he had been the cause although through no fault of his own. No fault of his own? Anyway, he wanted to tell her he loved her, but the gulf was too wide. 'Given me,' he murmured and looked up from his blood-smeared hand. 'What do you give me now, Mama? What?' he searched her face, her tired face, and he was filled with a longing so intense it was a physical ache in the pit of his stomach. He wanted to fly up the stairs to her, to kiss away the hurt, to caress the grey hair and murmur in her ear, Mama, I love you, I love you. It's me, Angelo, and I love you. When the mind cannot reach out toward another, when emotion overflows and can find no outlet in words sufficient to its purpose, what is there left but the touch of skin against skin, lip against lip, hand against hand, the warm comfort of the animal? He wanted her to know his own sorrow, the bitterness of false accusations and the lack of faith in those who should have stood by him, but in these few small feet that separated them, the gulf was immeasurable. 'What have you given me? Nothing, if you can't give now. Now is the time, Mama, now!' he waited 'What do you give me, Mama?' He waited. 'Nothing? Nothing.' He turned away so that she did not see his face. 'Nothing Mama, do you understand that? Nothing.' Behind him there was only silence. He moved away from the steps and walked towards the gate. When he looked back, Mama had carried her sorrow silently into the house. He was glad to see she had not closed the door. He went to the gate and lifted the latch. A voice called to him. He turned. It was Pepe. The old man picked up Angelo's forgotten case and hurried across the yard, casting a quick anxious glance at the house. Angelo reached out and took the case.

'Angelo,' Pepe whispered, 'You send me word, huh?' Angelo nodded. 'You tell your uncle where he can find you, okay? An' don't worry. Everything will work out okay. You'll see.' Angelo nodded again and tried to smile but the smile turned into a wince as it dragged at his cut lip.

'That's fine!' Pepe took the boy's hand and pressed it. 'You better go now,' he said and, turning away, went back towards the bedroom. Angelo watched him go and then looked down at his hand; in it lay two crumpled five pound notes. He looked swiftly at Pepe's departing back but before he found his voice, his uncle had once more disappeared into the bedroom.

'Thank you,' Angelo whispered and went out into the street.

He did not see her at first. He looked back into the yard, empty and silent, before pulling too the gate. He stared at the blistering green paint for a moment, his thumb lingering on the latch, and then he let it drop and turned. She had been leaning against the wall waiting for him, now she smiled. He stared at her softly, 'What are you doing here?'

'I waited for you at the...' she couldn't bring herself to

say it, '... but they told me you had left so I came here.'

'Why?'

'To see you,' and then hurriedly, 'I hope you don't mind.' She looked at him anxiously and raised her hand to her face

He took the long brown fingers and held them to his cheek. 'Does your mother know you're here?' He put his case down on the pavement.

She smiled, shaking her head, and lowering her eyes to his chest. He was still holding her hand and now, with the other, he touched her cheek. She looked up.

'I can't smile,' he said. 'It hurts.'

'What happened?'

'My father.' Angelo sniffed.

She pressed her cheek against his hand and tossed her head, smiling at him. He heaved a sigh and then chuckled softly, keeping his lips still. She laughed. It looked very funny. He laughed then, despite the hurt. 'Let's go,' he said.

'Where to?'

Angelo raised a shoulder and picked up his suitcase. 'I don't know. Let's... just go.' He looked at the green door. 'I'll come back one day.'

'Yes,' she said simply, believing him.

'One day,' he whispered. He felt the tears again, hot behind his lids, but he controlled them. He had closed the gate on his childhood; his boyhood. He was a man now with the whole world in front of him. If he stopped to think about it he might be afraid. They walked away: away from his childhood, from the memories, from the green gate; away from the long night when the careless puppeteer entangled the strings with which he moved his woodenheads, so that they jangled together and cracked heads, so that when he moved one limb, the others moved, jerkily, uncontrolled.

The yard lay silent and empty as they walked away from the green door, away from the long night.

www.ingramcontent.com/pod-product-compliance
Lightning Source LLC
Chambersburg PA
CBHW020551310726
48979CB00008B/1177/J

* 9 7 8 9 6 0 9 8 4 1 8 6 3 *